PLAY OR PAY

A September and Shadow Thriller, #8

by

AMY SHOJAI

Copyright

First Print Edition, November 2024
Furry Muse Publishing
Paperback ISBN **978-1-948366-62-5**
Graphics licensed via DepositPhotos.com
Cover Designed by & Licensed from FlintlockCovers.com

FURRY MUSE
PUBLICATIONS
P.O. Box 1904
Sherman TX 75091
(903)814-4319
amy@shojai.com

**September & Shadow Pet-centric Thrillers
By Amy Shojai**

LOST AND FOUND

HIDE AND SEEK

SHOW AND TELL

FIGHT OR FLIGHT
Introducing Lia, Tee, and Karma

HIT AND RUN

WIN OR LOSE

DARE OR DIE

PLAY OR PAY

Chapter One: Jared

Happy ever after stalked his nightmares.

Jared's alarm woke him with a start, his eyes snapping open. He groaned, and pressed both hands to his eyes, rubbing to relieve the sandy feeling. Three hours sleep, better than nothing, and only four hours yesterday. The intermittent nightmares, or worse—dreams of the good ol' days, when a nap led to horror—left him in a constant state of sleep deprivation. And remorse.

The clock on his phone blinked, and chimed again, the third snooze warning designed to get his butt moving. He canceled the alarm and rolled out of bed—no need to dress, he still wore the dingy tee-shirt and jeans from yesterday— then grabbed a potent energy drink from the mini-fridge. He couldn't stand coffee, so Red Bull kept him vertical.

These days, Jared juggled three jobs: construction during the day, call center at night, and odd jobs in between, all designed to keep him busy and away from the third-rate motel room he had generously called home for the past year.

When their world blew up over a year ago, Lannie blamed him. Hell, he blamed himself. She'd stayed three months after the tragedy, longer than he expected, before bailing, and he deserved every terrible thing she'd said when she left. Now, the only times he heard from her were the monthly reports she forwarded from the police: "No news."

His fault. He'd taken their nice life for granted. He'd made a fine living in construction while Lannie worked part time as a substitute teacher. She planned to go back full time once Alana got older.

He worked hard, deserved nights out with his friends, and he'd resented Lannie's insistence on "family time." To placate her, he planned a camping vacation on the mainland at a budget locale. He convinced Lannie they'd save money they could later put toward something more important. He, Jared, had done all that.

He'd even agreed to watch Alana when his wife needed a few extra minutes before joining them on the perfect vacation outing: fishing. Lannie wasn't a fan, but his daughter couldn't wait to drop a line into the cool green Colorado lake, so very different than the sapphire ocean at home. A good kid, she followed the simple rules he and Lannie established. She had even hugged him that morning, excited to go fishing with her papa. He wanted to rent a boat, but Lannie argued for shoreline safety, since Alana had yet to learn how to swim. They set up in a shady spot, Alana with her bandanna-wearing kangaroo toy holding its own fishing pole. She even baited her own hook without making a face. Alana caught a sunfish, too small to keep. But oh, was she excited. Called it a "sunny fish" and happily released it so the fish family could "live happy ever after..." Jared's throat ached at the memory.

Ever after...ever after...

He'd only dozed briefly—vacation time, you could do that, right?—mere moments asleep, couldn't have been longer than fifteen minutes tops. Jared woke to Lannie's strident voice calling for their missing daughter...gone, disappeared.

The toy kangaroo floated nearby.

Days, weeks, and months followed, filled with regrets and recriminations. The police dragged the lake but found no trace of his sweet Alana. God help him, he'd come to accept that Alana had drowned, probably never to be found.

But not Lannie. She quit her job, stayed here to hound the police, and him. He couldn't leave, either, stuck in his own personal *kehena*. He ached to find their daughter, and he'd tried, oh how he'd tried. And failed. Over and over.

Jared lived with that failure, knew he deserved every bit of the misery he'd earned. Once he saved enough, he'd go back where he belonged. To the islands. And try to forget the nightmare of losing his happy ever after.

The phone buzzed again. He'd shut off the alarm, at least he thought he had, but lack of sleep sometimes played tricks on his memory. Jared took another slug of the energy drink and checked the phone. A text.

>Have your daughter. Call me.

He set the drink down, brows lowered to thunderous levels, studying the number. This wasn't the first fraudulent claim they'd got. What kind of monsters preyed on the pain and suffering of families of missing kids? After the third extortion attempt, he'd blocked incoming unknown callers, and later changed his phone number.

Jared knew his daughter died that day at the lake. The finest, best parts of him died that day, too. After months of suffocating sadness, sudden black rage welled. He'd find a way to make the creature at the other end pay for this horrible pain.

He stabbed the numbers into his phone, grinding his teeth as he waited for the connection to go through. Jared didn't wait for an acknowledgment. He spewed venom into the phone, screaming so loudly his neighbor in the adjoining motel room banged on the wall. Finally, he stopped, panting, surprised the person hadn't disconnected.

"Feel better?" The husky voice, chuckling after the brief words, brought additional heat to Jared's cheeks. Before he could answer, the woman cut him off. "Oh, the offer's for real. I have your Alana, only a little the worse for wear. The real question, do you want her back? And at what price?" She laughed again. "How about $25,000. Say 'yes, please' or in thirty seconds the price goes up."

"My daughter died. Drowned. You'd know that. How'd you get my number? Don't waste my time." He started to disconnect. Why had he bothered? He had to catch the bus in twenty minutes.

"Paid search services spit out unlisted numbers for a nominal fee." She laughed. "Proof, you wanna talk to her? Price just doubled to $50K."

He hesitated. Nobody had gone this far before. Had this crank brought a kid into the ruse?

"Papa?" The small voice trembled.

He cleared his throat, calming himself. Might be an adult play-acting, but he wouldn't take the chance and shout at a kid. "Don't play tricks on people, kid, that hurts them."

"Papa?" The child's voice whimpered. "I miss you and Mama. Please come get me, I promise I'll be good. I wanna come home. Please, Papa…"

"Stop! My daughter drowned." He choked on the words, fist clenched so hard on the phone he heard it crack.

"I didn't! I followed the rules. Remember? You said stay

back, even when I caught the sunny fish and had to let it go. But then you fell asleep, and that *hammajang* man took me..."

His mouth dropped open, gulping silently mimicking the memory of the sunny fish itself. He whispered, "Alana?" Nobody knew about the sunny fish. "What messed up man?"

The woman's voice came back on the line. "That's your proof, but the price just doubled because you doubted me."

"You have her? You've had Alana all this time!" His legs shook, suddenly weak, and he collapsed onto the bed.

"You've got until the weekend to pull funds together. $100,000, cash. Small bills."

His head spun. He blinked hard to keep himself from passing out. He didn't have that kind of money. Had no way to raise it. "But how can I..."

"Now, $200K. Oh, and this phone number disappears as soon as I disconnect, so don't try to call me. I'll message you with where and how. I detect even a sniff of cops, the deal's off. You'll never see sweet lil' Alana again."

"There's no way I can get—"

"She's worth more, but I'm cutting you a deal. You'll find a way to get me $250K."

"I want my daughter! There's no way I can raise that kind of cash..."

Another low chuckle, then, with deliberation, she gave him what he didn't know he needed. "The Magpie will help you get her back. Look her up, she's in Texas. I'd say she owes you at least a half-mil for pain and suffering. But I'll give ya the friends and family discount. Wring her dry, get as much as you can from her, long as I get my $500K, you keep whatever extra. Won't take much for a fresh start with your little darling. And no cops, or you'll never see your kid again." She chuckled, clearly enjoying the torture her words conjured. "Her Family destroyed yours. Time to make Sorokin Glass pay."

Chapter Two: September

September Day watched the sun tipping over the eastern horizon as she took deep breaths, grasping her bo staff in one hand. September made it a habit to practice early mornings to avoid the worst of the weather—triple digits were forecast this first week of August.

The bottom of the garden, ground zero of the bomb blast, offered the most open place for the daily routine that kept her limber, focused, and in shape. Across the garden, Shadow and Kinsler barked as they chased and wrestled. Best for the dogs to keep their distance. She didn't want them encroaching too close at the wrong moment, and getting cracked with her wooden pole. Shadow knew better, but Kinsler—you never knew with that holy terrier.

She assumed the *ready* position, holding the long oak staff before her horizontally. September took a forward step with her right foot. Her left hand, fist clenched, rose to the side of her face while the right hand performed forward figure-eights with the staff. It made a whooshing sound whipping through the air. On the fifth figure-eight, she passed the staff behind her back to her left hand.

She looked over her left shoulder, turning the same direction in a full circle. Her right hand grabbed the staff directly above her left, and pulled the end down to briefly touch that shoulder. Left foot strode forward in a long stance as September performed a forward strike, disarming her imaginary sparring partner with the stick.

The dogs zoomed by. Kinsler carried a long stick, and Shadow pursued him to wrestle away the prize. She smiled when they played a brief game of tug. No contest, the German Shepherd won. Shadow proudly paraded the stick around the smaller dog, teasing him, whipping it around like his bear-toy. Or like one of the figure-eight forms.

"Are you trying to copy me, baby dog?" He woofed and pranced away as she continued to practice.

With a big day—weekend—ahead, she needed to finish quickly and get cleaned up. One more round should do it. She'd already packed, so a quick shower, and … no, she'd think about that later.

September continued the familiar exercises, rapidly performing complex combinations of spins, strikes, pokes, and defensive blocks. Not a master by any means, she made up for lack of expertise with raw determination. This skill must become so ingrained that she wouldn't need to think if called to defend herself, or others.

The six-foot oaken staff had saved her life before. And no doubt would again.

"William Stanley Combs, last warning." When she impatiently jingled her car keys, Shadow leaned hard against her knees, telling September to *chill*. Macy-cat meowed hopefully from the top of the fridge, wanting the key fob laser light to click on.

"Coming." The boy's high-pitched voice echoed down the stairs from the upper balcony.

September took three deep, calming breaths at the dog's pressure. Shadow always knew what to do. She stroked the dog's face, tracing the white scar on his black cheek. She silently promised Macy a game of laser tag after the eventful weekend.

"I can't find my shoes. The special ones. The choreographer says we have to start practicing in jazz shoes."

She met the dog's eyes. "Shadow, *find* Willie's shoes." She smiled when he woofed under his breath and dashed away, thundering up the stairs. To him, the command meant a game.

"In thirty seconds, we're leaving, barefoot or shod, your choice. And grab your breakfast from the kitchen island on your way out." As she spoke, September strode from the stairs to the rear kitchen door of the old Victorian. The stained glass in the kitchen had been repaired, and while the added safety bars looked out of place, they were necessary for security after the wedding debacle. It would take longer than six weeks to repair the emotional damage left behind.

Macy meerowed. He owned the kitchen but let them

timeshare. The Maine Coon stood, arching his back and waving his plume-like coffee-colored tail, adding a chirping reminder.

"Yes, I know, time for your second breakfast." September quickly grabbed a quarter handful of high-protein kibble from the cat's canister and dumped it into his high-rise bowl. Macy ate his meals on second-story territory to keep the dogs from snarfing everything. Although Shadow and Kinsler loved to tease the 18-pound cat, they acknowledged Macy as boss. With the cat's heart condition, though, she tried to keep high energy interactions to a minimum.

She winced as Willie pelted down the stairs, followed by Shadow with one of the shoes still clutched in his mouth. At eleven years old, the boy had two speeds: "zoom" and "sleep." *Sort of like a puppy.* Kinsler flew in his wake with the other shoe, wired to match the boy's attitude.

"Close the gates. Both of them. Double check the latch, Willie, I don't want Kinsler eating sofa cushions again." He scowled, but didn't complain. "You're responsible for cleanup if your dog gets out. Don't put that responsibility on Aunt Ethel. Your dad will take the funds out of your allowance for any damage."

"Why can't Kinsler come with me? It's a script about stray dogs and cats finding their new homes." Voice hopeful, eyebrows raised, as he grabbed his shoe from Shadow. But Kinsler tried to play keep away with his.

She rolled her eyes. "You're supposed to *act* like cats and dogs, not bring in a method actor."

Willie wrinkled his nose, not understanding the reference.

"Look it up, young thespian." Maybe the drama teacher would explain it.

She turned to the terrier. "Drop it." Kinsler released the

shoe and wriggled with delight. "Good boy. Hurry up, Willie." She had a long drive after dropping him off at his summer theater workshop. Aunt Ethel would pick him up and keep Willie over the weekend. "Remind Ethel y'all can stay here, if she doesn't want to risk Kinsler at her place. Remember to turn off the water to the roses at lunch time." Her poor roses needed a good drenching, so she'd turned on the drip irrigation system when she headed out to practice.

Usually, she'd ask Lia to babysit Willie and board his terrier. But the young woman finally jumped off her cliff-of-dreams and enrolled in the police academy in Dallas, temporarily shutting down Corazon Kennels. So when Ethel offered, September eagerly accepted. Ethel said she welcomed the distraction and fun of spending time with the boy.

Shadow nose-poked the white and tan dog. Kinsler answered, with an open-mouth invitation for their favorite bitey-face game.

They didn't have time for that. "Off, Shadow. Clock's ticking, we have lots to do today." The black shepherd immediately pranced to the door.

Kinsler raced to Willie, at the last minute raising up to paw-punch with both forelegs into the boy's chest. Willie grabbed at the counter to keep his balance. Even a small dog packed a wallop.

"What did I tell you about Kinsler jumping up?" *Everything's fun and games until someone falls and cracks their head.*

"Put the behavior on command. I did. See?" Willie turned to the terrier, held both palms toward the dog and waited until Kinsler backed away. Then he patted his chest and said, "*Ka-pow!*" The little dog leaped forward, bounding again paws-up into the boy. "Atta boy, home run, Kinsler!"

She couldn't help smiling. "Nice cue, Willie. But he can't go with us, so get him settled."

Shadow danced around, excited by the action. She sighed. At least the dogs had come to an understanding.

She pretended not to watch as Willie carefully secured the two pet gates that kept the small dog confined in the kitchen. Macy-cat could easily stay out of dog range by leaping counter-to-counter and hop over either gate. September forced herself not to double check the latches. He'd been warned.

"When's Dad getting home?" Willie skipped to join the dogs jittering at the door. "And Melinda."

He asked September the same thing every morning. "Your sister has another week in Dallas at her cheer-leading camp." Melinda and two girlfriends campaigned intensively before Combs finally agreed, in part to make up for the recent disruption and angst. And also take the pressure off September having to "stepmom" alone while he spent time in rehab.

Willie grimaced. "Melinda only wanted to go to make kissy face with that new guy at camp. All the girls are crushing on *Delaney*." He pronounced the name and blew a raspberry. Mostly, September knew, he missed his sister, whether he'd admit it or not.

He wasn't wrong. Melinda looked and acted older than her age, always in a hurry to grow up—while September felt like time sped by too fast. The girl had a history of sneaking out to meet her latest crush. Combs had employed all his detective skills to vet the camp, and especially the teachers and chaperons.

"Call your dad tonight for latest updates. But I don't think anything's changed from two days ago."

Combs needed extensive surgery to repair his damaged

leg after the bomb attack at the wedding. He might need more, depending on how the leg healed. Combs still suffered short-term memory issues, but they all felt encouraged with his breakthrough remembering her. For a while, their future together had been iffy.

After his first surgery, Combs qualified for rehab. Running him back and forth to the Dallas location meant hours enroute, which left no time to address the latest crises in her life—learning to live with a new identity, something she'd not yet fully divulged to Combs. He'd finally agreed to stay on site for the remainder of the intensive therapy. He'd come home the day after Melinda finished her camp, in about a week.

"C'mon, Willie, stop dragging your paws." She opened the back door, let Shadow out, then stuck out her leg to block the other dog's escape. "Grab a treat for Kinsler. Two or three tops. And don't forget your breakfast." She squeezed through the door after Shadow, and pulled it shut before the smaller dog could escape.

The heat sucked the breath from her lungs. August in Texas wasn't for weenies. September strode down the brick pathway, ducking between the several wind chimes, and paused at the stained glass window to watch inside.

Willie grabbed a couple of dog treats, and showed them to his dog. She couldn't hear him but saw him mouth the command to sit. Kinsler planted his tail on the slate floor, wriggling with excitement. Willie showed him the treats again, broke one in half—*who taught him that?*—and fed a piece to the happy dog. The boy signaled *wait* with his palm facing the dog's nose, and began to back toward the door. Halfway there, he snagged the paper bag with his breakfast, broke the second treat in half, and tossed all three pieces across the room. Kinsler didn't move, he just stared at

Willie, a spring ready to explode. The boy opened the door, shouted, "Find!" and exited, slamming the door.

September smiled. *Good job, Willie.* It took longer to teach the boy how to train than to do it herself, but he needed to know how to communicate with his own dog. Kinsler had the attention span of a gnat but worked more willingly for his boy than for her. She turned with Shadow and trotted across the drive to reach the carriage house garage, as Willie raced to catch up.

"Did you lock the door?"

"'Course I did. It still sticks. I had to slam it." He showed her his key, then stuck it into his pocket.

She handed him her car keys. "You do the honors."

"*Ka-pow!*" He grinned and raced ahead.

At the word, Shadow jumped up and gently pawed September's chest. She laughed out loud with surprise. "Who's been watching Kinsler's training, huh? Okay, baby dog. *Sit.*" She gave the closed fist hand signal, and when he followed the command, opened her hand to pat her chest. "*Ka-pow!*" He rose, thumped her in the chest with both paws, then paused to slurp her face thoroughly.

September smoothed his face, waited for him to drop to her side, then took her time reaching the garage. She scanned the surrounding area for anything out of the ordinary, knowing Shadow would alert to any danger. He'd saved her more times than she could count. And while her nemesis could no longer touch her, those loyal to Kaliko Wong had ambitions to reap the rewards of the changing landscape.

With Combs occupied with doctor visits and recovery, she'd dodged detailed explanation about her newly discovered family ties. She still hadn't figured out how to manage information that came with all kinds of potentially lethal strings attached. Combs had enough going on, hoping to get back to his career as a detective. That was another hard discussion they must face, sooner or later.

She reached the car and watched with amusement as Willie climbed from the driver's seat to the passenger side. He'd started the SUV for her. "Thanks. Once your dad gets better, I'll leave it to him to provide the driving lessons."

"Bootleg turn, oh yeah!" He pumped his fist, knocking into the bag that held his breakfast.

She laughed. "Careful you don't squish your sandwich." She opened the rear door and signaled for Shadow to take his place. She felt safe inside the retrofitted vehicle Combs had got for her prior to their non-wedding. With protective bullet proof glass, and an engine able to outrace most vehicles, it offered insurance she hoped they wouldn't need.

"You enjoying the theater workshop?" Combs had suggested baseball camp, something Willie had always loved, but he'd surprised them with his request. Combs worried Willie might get teased by other kids in his class. But so far, the boy seemed happy and excited by the experience. He told them people who bullied were *most heinous*. She wasn't sure what slang terms kids used these days but agreed with the sentiment.

"Acting's pretty neat. I like pretending to be other people, you know, like superheroes and stuff." He grinned. "I'm lucky because we're doing the *Strays* show and I already know how dogs and cats act. The director says I'm a natural." He whispered. "Some of the kids don't get it, about the dogs and cats, I mean." He opened the sack and pulled out the sandwich.

"PB and J, thanks, September." He munched. Just like a puppy, always ready for another meal. She pulled up to the big gate, thumbed the remote, and drove through. "You playing a superhero dog like Kinsler? Or a cat?"

"We're still practicing. There's music, too, and choreo. That means dance. We get to try out for our favorite parts on Monday. I wanna be the puppy character, but the chorus would be fun." He took another bite. "Even if he's not in the show, Kinsler's for sure a hero dog. And so's Shadow, of course."

Behind them in the back seat, Shadow's tail thumped at the mention of his name.

Willie hesitated, and added, shyly, "I like the theater. I fit in. Ya know that anything bad is just pretend, and you can pick stories with happy endings. Lots of the kids are like me, even the ones don't understand the pet stuff. We're all weirdos. But in a good way."

"You're not a weirdo, Willie." Had somebody picked on him? Gone *most heinous* on Willie? A surge of protective adrenaline increased her pulse. With all the media attention surrounding their lives, it wouldn't surprise her, but he hadn't complained. Or mentioned anything, until now.

He shrugged and looked away.

"Well, if you're a weirdo, then you're my kind of superhero weirdo." She reached over and cupped his cheek.

Willie allowed the touch for only a moment, leaned in briefly, then pulled away. He polished off the sandwich, then pulled out the banana. He spoke around a mouthful of the mush. "Hungry. And I'm a monkey." He made monkey sounds with his mouth open.

She grimaced. "Mouth closed, monkey boy." The kid was a bottomless pit.

Twenty minutes later, she stopped in front of the theater and waited while Willie climbed out. A couple of the kids waved through the glass door of the lobby, clearly eager to welcome him into their group. Good for him. Everybody needed to find their own special tribe. She'd struggled to find her own place for years.

And now she'd discovered her heritage, she had to reinvent herself. "Talk about learning a new role. Shadow, I should ask Willie's director for acting help."

Shadow leaned forward between the seats, and cold-nosed her neck.

September never imagined learning her true parentage would create even more stress and danger. As the eldest child of the founder of the Wong organization, Henry Wong's second wife Kaliko had tried to kill her—twice. First as an infant, and most recently at her wedding. The Family ran untold numbers of illegal but profitable enterprises. Now, all that belonged to September. All the wealth, power, and risk came to her.

She hadn't figured out how to navigate this news with Combs. He'd lost his partner, Gonzalez, his Uncle Stanley, and his mobility. She prayed his injury would heal so he didn't lose his career. She'd lost her sister, April, and the only family she'd ever known. Refusing the inheritance risked the lives of those who mattered most: Combs. Willie and Melinda. And her friends. She'd sworn to stop future atrocities, and reverse the horrible wrongs perpetuated by her family.

Her newfound Uncle Jack created a plausible explanation for her disappearance as an infant, and sudden reemergence as the heir. He'd pulled enough from reality to make it believable and supplemented with AI-generated pictures and video that recreated her into the image of her long-dead mother. He'd already seeded the revisionist history out into the ether-world, creating rumors and legends that she must incorporate into her new reality. September had to play the part or pay the price.

The principles of the organizations met tomorrow morning, in Dallas. They would arrive from all over the country, all over the world. Her overnight bag, with her laptop, rested in the back of the car, along with her bo staff and go bag.

While Combs labored with rehab, she struggled to learn her new history. First impressions mattered. She must avoid stepping on dangerous toes while asserting her position as the new head of the Family. Whether they liked it or not, job one meant removing the worst offenders who'd crossed the line, along with those loyal to the previous head of the family.

September shoved the car into gear. She drove away from the happy theater kids ready to play their cat and dog parts. She had her own part to play.

The Magpie. Sorokin Glass. She wished to God she'd never been cast in this crazy role.

Chapter Three: Jared

For three days, running on emotion and Red Bull, Jared did what he had to do. A quick search found the Magpie—she appeared all over the Internet in multiple searches—and where she lived: Heartland, Texas. He called, left messages, and even texted, all to no avail, so he emptied his account of its meager funds, caught a plane to DFW, and rented a car. And he worried, any delay meant losing his daughter again.

Jared drove slowly past the old Victorian house, then pulled into the empty field opposite, which had been used more than once as a parking lot. He sheltered his vehicle in a stand of evergreens.

Staying hidden, he stared at the closed green gate fronting the circle drive and worried how to get into the house proper. The cryptic message from the *tutua*—monster—left him no option. He must convince the Magpie to help him, and barring that, make her do the right thing. He must get Alana back.

He briefly wished he had his tools, not that the airlines would allow them, but Jared couldn't risk breaking into the expensive home, as nice as any he'd helped build. A security fence encircled the property. And probably an alarm system inside the house.

Jared focused the camera of his phone on the front of the house, using the zoom to look closer. Motion through the front windows indicated people at home, but he couldn't tell how many. She lived with a cop. After the *tutua's* warning, he didn't dare speak with anyone but Sorokin Glass—alone. She had all the power, all the money, the sole ability to pay the ransom and retrieve Alana from the snake's jaws.

Motion at one side of the house startled him, as a tall slim woman strode into view. Her long dark hair, complete with the white streak, was tied in a low ponytail, and she wore casual denim capris and a sleeveless pale green top. *Sorokin, the Magpie.*

A large black dog, maybe a shepherd, paced by her side. Everything Jared knew about dogs—fangs, claws, snarls— frightened him. Thank goodness he hadn't approached the house with that beast around.

Moments later, a boy a few years older than his Alana raced from the house and dashed into the garage. The woman and dog disappeared after him into the brick building.

Within moments, a large expensive-looking vehicle rolled onto the driveway and approached the gated entrance. Jared swiftly crossed the road, hugging the security fence, crouching in the scrubby overgrowth that sprouted everywhere.

The car paused, waiting for the gate to trundle open. When she turned halfway around in the driver seat, probably to address the boy, Jared sprinted closer to the gate. He took shelter in bushy saplings, and shiny three-leaf vines. As the woman's car passed through the gate, Jared squeezed his eyes shut like a little boy pretending no one could see him if he hid his eyes. He must get inside the fortress.

The car turned onto the road, spinning tires as if late to an appointment. The gate hung wide open for a brief time. He checked if she watched for it to close, but he couldn't tell from the distance.

Before it completely shut, he scurried through, heard it click-latch-lock closed. Jared tripped and rolled on the brick drive. He glanced over his shoulder, imagining the eyes of the big black dog staring with accusation at him through the rear window of the car, and fangs eager to rend his flesh.

Never mind don't think, run, for Alana, my baby girl, only Alana matters… He ran, racing to reach the shelter of the buildings.

He searched for a good hiding spot. Jared followed a brick pathway between the garage and the house itself. On one side, a decorative iron gate led into an elaborate rose garden at the back of the house.

On the other side of the path, a door into the house teased Jared with possibilities. He wasn't above breaking a window, but it could alert the cops. The heat of the August morning had already drenched his work shirt with sweat. He smelled like fear, and loss, anger and anguish…and hope. He'd do anything to leverage this woman's help. He didn't need to be inside the house.

The Magpie would return to roost sooner or later. He'd wait.

Chapter Four: Noah

T he dog sniffed carefully. Cat food still clung to the bowl on the stranger's back porch. Noah cautiously paced forward, one white paw after the other, checking out the back yard for other animals. Sometimes, places that fed cats also kept dogs.

Sized just right to snuggle on a lap, almost all outside dogs outweighed him. They wouldn't want him trespassing. Quickly, he cleaned out the bowl then slunk away in the moonlight. The glow shined his white fur into a halo.

He'd been on his own for almost a month, ever since those big bright BOOM sounds filled the sky. After the third BOOM, he'd flung himself at the fence, again and again, until the gate sprang open. Then he ran until he could run no more and shivered under a stranger's car until morning.

Nobody came for him. And he didn't remember the way

back. That night when BOOM lights again lit the sky, he ran some more. The third night, the sky stayed quiet. So he just found a spot to shiver and worry.

He stayed out of sight. If people caught a glimpse, they yelled or called to him, and some threw things. A few tossed food. But he worried the BOOM lights might happen again. Or that people could throw hurtful things instead of food. Noah had to be ready to run.

Finding enough food to ease the empty ache in his middle meant constant scrounging, not like when he had his own bowl. A girl—she didn't live with him but visited sometimes—used to put nice things in his bowl. Special yummies. She didn't have her own dog friend, and he didn't have a girl to pat him and tickle his tummy. That's just the way things were.

After many days spent on his own, more days than a dog had paws, he'd learned a routine and rhythm to the new life. He haunted backyards where careless cats and dogs left behind kibble. Garbage containers tempted him once or twice. Nighttime gave cover. Daytime meant baking sun, burnt paw pads, and thirst that hurt. Rare rain offered cool water, but too often brought back the terrifying BOOM lights. A dog couldn't escape from the sky that yelled and flashed all around.

Finally, Noah sniffed out a massive place filled with water. He spent most days there, lapping the treasured wet as needed and sometimes lounging in the shallows. His long white fur turned red brown from the mud. Noah didn't care. It helped keep off the sun. Once, he caught a fish!

Daylight streaked the sky. Houselights flickered on as the new day began. Time to retreat.

Noah padded quickly down the sidewalk. As he ran, lights lining the car path flickered off. The sun chased them away at this time every morning. By the time cars began traveling past all the houses, Noah must disappear for the day.

He dashed across the last road to reach the grassy expanse where no houses stood. How odd… fields usually empty now housed rows of cars. Rope strung up like fences kept cars inside from straying. Did cars run away like dogs? Noah paused to sniff one of the big cars that lined up on the pavement to enter the grassy area.

Nearby, people bustled to and fro. They carried boxes, and rolled carts, setting up odd tiny tent houses with open sides and canvas roofs. Tables stood underneath with mysterious items displayed. So many people…so much noise, and turmoil. Nowhere for a shy dog to hide…

"Hey! Hey dog, where's your owner? You can't run loose around here. Somebody catch that dirty little guy. He'll get trampled! Besides, the festival rules say even little dogs stay on leash."

Noah tucked his tail, whining, and worried. He licked his lips, turned his head away. Maybe they'd understand and leave him alone.

Or would they chase him away from his favorite spot? Had someone else claimed his lake?

Scurrying into a stand of trees, Noah stayed close to the ground. He scampered from bushy clump to tree trunk, squeezing through tiny spots to stay hidden from prying people-eyes, to get to his secret hideaway and reclaim it— before the world turned even more upside down.

Chapter Five: Ethel

E thel Combs stood at the front door of the cozy ranch-style house. She waved as her niece backed the car out of the drive, honked a cheerful goodbye, and drove away. Her hand fell to her pocket, where the lone, single sock spilled out. Ethel's smile slipped. She'd found Stan's sock that morning.

She caught herself against the door and folded into herself onto the top steps. Arms crossed and tightened. *Look at anything, don't think about the sock, focus on anything else...*

Look there...How had the garden fallen into such a state? Orangey-red blanketflowers covered everything. Poking bright faces through, yellow black-eyed Susan, purple asters, and blue balloon flowers vied for recognition in the crowded beds. Creeping phlox in white, pink, and purple carpeted the edge of each flowerbed bordering the house, a fancy apron playing dress up for guests. But thistle, creeping Charlie, henbit, and spurge, along with pernicious dandelions, ruined the beds. At least the yard looked tidy thanks to hot August weather keeping Bermuda grass in check. Stan mowed right before the wedding—

Oh God. The wedding. Stan. She buried her face in her hands.

Finally alone. No need to mask the pain, or act brave for company. The endless visitors, many of them officers Stan served alongside for years, never stopped. Everyone wanted to bring food, talk, help her do this-and-that, keep her busy, so she didn't have to think, *don't think about Stanley...* and how to go on, despite her shattered world. She smiled, thanked them, while inside the emptiness echoed in a vast black abyss. A space devoid of color. Nothing mattered. Not anymore.

Her niece, Naomi, lived an hour away, and she meant well. Without kids of their own, Ethel and Stan acted as second parents to Naomi and Jeff, and Godparents to Jeff's kids, Willie and Melinda. She didn't say so, but Ethel guessed Naomi lived with guilt that she'd been spared the wedding debacle when unable to attend because of the last-minute changes.

Thank God, Jeff survived. His rehab and handling the kids took all of September and Jeff's time, with little to spare. So Ethel appreciated Naomi's help.

But over a month of constant being *looked after* set Ethel's teeth on edge. She'd always done for herself and Stan. Ethel worked as an attorney and had her own hobbies, until Stan retired, and she followed suit. These days, cast in an unfamiliar role, she had to play the expected part of brave police officer's widow, a duty and honor Stan deserved.

They had planned for years how to spend retirement together. Instead...well, she wasn't the only one paying the ultimate price too many police families endured.

Each new day, Ethel faced an empty chair at breakfast. Their cozy tidy home now felt cavernous, with dark shadows in every corner. She didn't want to get up. But she couldn't sleep, spent hours counting cracks in the ceiling Stan promised to get fixed. She wanted to doze and wake up like the silly Groundhog Day movie Stan loved and get a frigging do-over!

Ethel didn't want to act brave anymore. Not for Naomi, or anyone else.

She didn't have to pretend for Willie. Jeff's son loved and missed Stan, too. He'd been a bright spot over the weeks since her loss. He had spent nearly every afternoon with her. Sometimes, kids accepted honesty more easily than adults.

She missed Stan with a deep, abiding ache. And she hated him, too, for playing the damn hero, and leaving her. She missed his bluster, his speaking too loud, his stubborn determination to always do the right thing. Missed his drinking too much beer, forgetting to take his pills, and losing his stupid socks.

Her hand clenched on the single white sock. The hole in the toe spoke to the sharp nails he hated to trim and let poke through.

A sob caught her throat. She yearned to hear his heavy tread on the hallway. Wanted those irksome multiple bathroom visits in the middle of the night, the too-loud toilet flush, and his soft apology as he slipped back in bed. Missed his horrible, awful too-strong coffee. Missed his snoring—go figure, he'd laugh at that one! And, oh God in heaven, she missed his scent—not aftershave or cologne, just clean Stanley man-smell.

She snugged his abandoned pillow to her at night to muffle her sobs and breathe in that scent. Dreamed of his rough warm hand dwarfing hers. Wanted to laugh again at his white hair sticking every-which-way after doffing his signature cowboy hat. Wanted to feel, just one more time, his strong arm around her waist as they danced to a favorite tune in the kitchen (but only when nobody was looking). He'd promised to dance with her in front of God and everyone, at the wedding reception…and he'd even *kind of* agreed to wear his MacThomas tartan at the Celtic Festival this weekend. She'd teased him about showing his knees, and he'd rolled his eyes at first, then said, "You know I'm a sucker for my Irish honey."

But now… No more dancing. Or spooning. No growing older together.

Not that either of 'em were spring chicks, him in his mid-sixties and she in her early fifties. He called her his trophy wife. She snorted at the thought, and glanced at her mosquito-bit swollen ankles, chubby waist, and red hair with snowy strands streaking through. He'd been forced to retire early with his bum heart. They still had years to live. Plans made.

Promises blasted away in an eye blink.

Her cell phone rang. Ethel hiccupped, sat up, and knuckled away the tears. She cleared her throat and answered with a cheery lilt. "September, on your way?"

"Yep. Just dropped Willie at the theater, and heading out now. You sure about this? I could call Teddy Williams to watch him if you'd rather…"

Ethel shook her head, and stood, dusting the back of her fresh jeans. A hummingbird buzzed near, hovered to check out the red flowers blooming on her yellow tee-shirt, and then zoomed away. "Naomi just left. I'm fixing a pot of tea and plan a couple of hours on my garden before the temps go higher. I need that." She repeated the words and straightened her shoulders. "I need some alone-time, just like you do."

September deserved her own vacation from real life, if only for a long weekend. "Enjoy your down time, get a massage, relax, and don't worry about us. Willie is just the medicine I need. I'll put him to work weeding my flowers."

"He's a handful. Oh, and about Kinsler. I told Willie, but he'll probably forget. He won't mean to, but that terrier's likely to dig up your carpet, or your garden. Why not stay at the house? That way you don't have to run back and forth to deal with him and Macy-cat. Melinda's bed has fresh sheets." She didn't say it, but clearly meant the change of scene might also help. "Also, I left the water running for the roses, and Willie won't remember to shut it off at noon."

Smiling, Ethel looked around. Not a bad idea. Maybe a couple of days away would help reset her emotions. At least she wouldn't find any more sock reminders. "Thank you, September, we may do that. Now go on, you and Shadow have a good trip." She suspected the young woman planned a surprise visit to Jeff. That'd be lovely.

She disconnected the phone, and startled when the hummingbird returned, chittering at her. "Yes, I know, you want fresh nectar." She'd let the several feeders around the garden run dry. Drained. Like her.

Easy enough to refill the dry feeders. Not so much her heart.

Chapter Six: Shadow

Shadow pressed forward between the front seats of the car to cold-nose September's bare arm again. He whined as she finished her phone call. He recognized the older woman's voice that came out of the phone, but this wasn't the way to her house. Maybe they'd go visit Teddy? September mentioned him, too. The man drove his house all over, so Shadow never knew for sure where to find Teddy.

Thankfully, they'd left Willie's dog at home. Shadow wagged at the thought. It had taken him a while to get used to the smaller dog's frenetic energy. He didn't like Kinsler sneaking food from Shadow's bowl. He had to constantly remind Kinsler that Shadow owned the house, the yard, the garden, and everything and everyone that lived there.

At least Kinsler didn't presume to steal September's attention. She belonged to Shadow, and Shadow belonged to her. Once Kinsler understood about September, Shadow relaxed and enjoyed the other dog's company. Sometimes. When he wasn't a jerky pest.

In the same way, Shadow accepted Combs. He knew the man cared deeply about September, too, and wanted to keep her safe. That made Combs okay. More than that, Combs and the kids mattered to September. That made them matter to Shadow, too. He wanted to please her above all.

Even though Shadow and September lived together, and went everywhere together, lately Shadow felt lonely. He didn't know why. The feeling lasted more days than a good dog could count.

For a while they spent alone-time at the lake-house place. He loved having her to himself, and roaming the new area to learn all the best sniffy spots, wading in the water, and barking at all the critters that lived there. One time, he caught a fish! September took it from him, and tossed it back into the water, though.

Too soon, they always returned to their place, where Combs and the kids crowded around. Never alone. September always paid attention to someone else. Shadow had to ride in the back of the car while September ferried the kids and Combs to different places. She worried so much over Combs, Melinda, and Willie, September had no time for him.

Well, they snuggled at night, because Combs couldn't climb stairs and slept on the downstairs bed. But September hardly ever played anymore. Shadow missed search games, and Frisbee-fetch, and even lap snuggles. It was a good dog's job to help people play and be happy. Instead, September always said, "Later, baby dog."

But "later" never came.

When Combs and Melinda left and didn't come back

right away, Shadow's tail wagged a bunch thinking he'd get more time with her. But after she dropped Willie off each day, they'd go home, and September would stare at her computer for hours muttering to herself.

What had he done wrong that September shut herself away from him? Didn't she want him anymore? Or need him? Oh, how he needed her!

Everything had changed after the garden party and the horrible noise and destruction. He'd tried to warn her, tried to warn everyone. But he'd failed. And now...now everything had changed. His tummy hurt at the thought.

Deep lines furrowed her forehead, speaking of stress and fear and worry. It was a good dog's job to keep his person calm, happy. He chased away dangers that sneaked up on September in her dreams. But now, she acted haunted even while awake. How could he chase away waking nightmares?

His own brow furrowed at the thought. Shadow whined deep in his throat and cold-nosed her arm again. He had to try something different, something new. Shadow had to prove to September he still loved her and could do a good dog's work. He wouldn't fail, not again.

"Hey baby dog, we've got a job. An important job." She reached her hand back through the gap in the seats to stroke his cheek. "I'm fine. As long as you're with me, I'm fine. Okay?"

He whined again, thumped his tail, and licked her hand. Maybe she really did want him with her. Bliss!

All that could change in a heartbeat, though. Noisy explosions gave no warning. Danger lurked just a paw step away. No matter what words she spoke, September couldn't fool him. She was scared. Terrified. And he couldn't understand why. He didn't know how to defend from this invisible monster, however much he tried.

No matter what, he'd keep her safe. Never leave her side. He must make her happy again. That was his job. And if he failed, oh…then he'd get what a bad dog deserved.

Chapter Seven: September

S eptember kept the car just under the speed limit for the next ninety minutes. She planned to meet Jack—she couldn't bring herself to call him "uncle"— for a late breakfast. Blood relative or no, she didn't trust him. While he'd helped take down Kaliko, she'd seen his ruthless side, and knew he'd used her without remorse. For most of his life, Jack had focused on vengeance for the loss of his parents and sister. Instead of accepting September as a unique individual, he conflated her with the memory of his beloved older sister.

But she wasn't her mother, and she had no desire to step into that yawning hole in the man's heart. She'd conceded by answering to her birth name, and that seemed to mollify him. "*Sorokin,* what a mouthful. Right, Shadow?" She met the dog's eyes in the mirror, and grinned when he woofed an answer. "Well, I've answered to *September* for nearly thirty years." She'd gotten a boatload of grief over that name, as well.

September had never been to the Grand Chisholm Hotel, one of the most expensive in the Metroplex, so paid attention to her phone instructions. She belatedly wished she'd clued Combs in and delayed long enough for him to attend with her. Jack would've objected; besides, she had to prove to her new board of directors—lordy, that felt crazy!—her worthiness to take the reins. She'd call Combs tonight and let him know she was in Dallas to regroup, like she'd told Ethel. *Close enough.*

"The Family," she whispered. That's how Jack referred to Wong Enterprises, and it made her think of the Godfather movies. She shivered. That might not be far from the mark. She needed Jack to help her remember who did what, and the hierarchy of the organization.

A series of meetings were planned over the weekend, beginning early tomorrow morning with the current principles of the organization. She had prepared an introduction of herself and her life, trying to explain how and why Sorokin Glass, aka September Day, suddenly resurfaced after remaining hidden for decades. Jack had scripted most of that, and she let him. Some parts of her life remained too raw and hidden for even a newfound uncle to know.

Then she must attend an introduction cocktail party. "Cinderella at the ball," she said, voice raw with emotion. Shadow's whine turned into a yelp. "Sorry, baby dog. I hate dress up but have to go through the motions." She'd packed a simple outfit for what she thought of as the unveiling— missing heiress takes her throne. Jack said close to 500 would attend. Of those, some might have had her in their crosshairs while working for Kaliko.

"You're the only one I trust, Shadow. I need you by my side." She hadn't had a panic attack in months, despite every reason in the world for a PTSD episode. Shadow had suffered so much trauma lately, she feared he'd develop his own PTSD symptoms.

She'd found stress relief in the daily training drills. But Shadow hadn't had a fun day in a long time. She needed to remedy that.

"Love you, baby dog." Aside from training, much of her emotional stability had to do with Shadow's steady presence. She'd taken him for granted lately, been distracted with everything going on. "We'll try to find some fun time this weekend for us to just play and snuggle. Would you like that?" He knew the words, of course.

His happy bark—three in a row—and thumping tail made her laugh out loud. "Okay, that's a deal. Now get ready, we need to put on our professional faces." She pulled into the front of the hotel, and a valet hurried to open her door.

Shadow barked a low warning. The man leaped away, with a startled curse.

Shocked, September half turned in her seat. "Shadow, *chill*. Go on, good dog." His hackles continued to stand erect and bristled the back of his shoulders. "*Chill*, Shadow, he's okay."

She apologized and eyed the gentleman's outfit. The formal attire looked like what some of the guests wore to the wedding-that-wasn't. Maybe that triggered Shadow? "He's my service dog. Let me get him out and settled, then you can take the car."

The man nodded, stepping well away from the vehicle. She got her go bag and small overnight bag from the back, then opened the rear door for Shadow. September grabbed the leash she'd already attached to his harness. With a silent hand signal, Shadow walked closely beside her. Whenever in public, she kept him on leash, as both a protection for him and to signal his on-duty status to the public.

When another valet would have taken her bags, she declined, not wanting to increase Shadow's arousal. He fed into her own emotions, making him hyper-vigilant.

Shadow's nails clicked on the polished marble lobby floor. The overhead chandelier dripped crystals creating rainbow prisms against the walls and marble entryway. September's sandals shu-shushed, and her plain denim capris and sleeveless silk shirt, chosen with such care, felt woefully off target. Nothing in her carryall could compete with the tailored outfits worn by the desk staff.

"May I help you?" The model-thin glamorous woman at the check-in eyed her, and one corner of her lip curled. Her training kicked in and she didn't blink at Shadow, even when September signaled him to paws-up on the counter, a trick that usually gained smiles and good will.

"Checking in for two and possibly three nights. My name's Sept… That is, you have me listed as Sorokin Glass." She pulled out her wallet with the new ID and credit card Jack got for her.

"Oh my goodness! Ms. Glass, I'm so very sorry, I didn't recognize you!" She pushed a hidden buzzer, and a swarm of staff appeared. "We have the presidential suite prepared. Take her bags, and escort Ms. Glass to her room." She smiled, the white brilliance evidence of a high-dollar dentist.

Shadow jumped down from the counter, backing away from the shiny smile as though from a dangerous snarl. September put a hand on Shadow's neck. "Uhm, that's okay, we can find our way, just give us the key and point us to the elevators." *Presidential suite? Had Jack arranged this?*

"Not at all, Ms. Glass, we've been expecting you. Call me personally for anything. Anything at all. We want your visit to meet...no, to go above and beyond expectations." She handed September an embossed card with a phone number, her hand trembling.

"Wow, that's very kind. I don't think I've ever had this kind of reception before." She took the card and tucked it into the top of her bag. Of course, she'd never checked into a $750 a night hotel, either.

"Our pleasure, and our honor, to welcome you. And your beautiful pet."

"Pet? Oh, he's my service dog, Shadow."

The girl wilted, lower lip trembled, despite efforts to keep the smile pasted on. "I beg your pardon. Of course, not a pet. Service dog, I should have realized that. My apologies. I'll send up a steak for it. Him. Shadow...it's Shadow? Unless he wants something else? Please, I'm sorry, we weren't told about the dog...I mean Shadow."

September would have laughed if the woman hadn't seemed so distraught. "Really, it's fine. And no steak, I've brought some of his regular food."

"Please, let me make it up to you." She took a big breath, calming her nerves, but clearly terrified. "We want your stay with us to be perfect. Just tell us what to do. Please." A single tear rolled down one cheek. "It's not every day we get to meet the new owner of the Grand Chisholm Hotel."

Chapter Eight: Ethel

E thel packed a small bag, tucking in the few essentials she'd need over the long weekend to stay at September's house. Gardening or other outdoor pastimes meant she and Willie would need several changes to stay fresh. Oh, to have youth again like Willie, with nonstop energy and excitement, no achy knees, and the belief in happily ever after dreams. What kind of dreams could she find now?

Ethel resolutely set aside that train of thought. No, she'd concentrate on Willie this weekend and keep her promise to help her friend at the Celtic Festival set up her booth. Willie had enjoyed attending with her in the past. But kids these days changed their minds and fads more often than dirty socks…*oh dang, not socks again*! Plan ahead, not a year in advance or months, but a day here and there. That would serve her best.

As she backed out of the garage, she waved at the neighbor watering thirsty flowers. Ethel rolled down her window and called to the woman. "I'm spending the next few days at my nephew's house."

The neighbor nodded and waved.

She rolled up the window. She cranked the AC to high, appreciating how the coolness dried the damp from her face. She'd always worn minimal makeup, and the heat would melt off any attempt to use it. Willie wouldn't notice, or care.

"Melinda would, though." She smiled. Before the girl headed out to her summer cheer camp, she'd spent time with Ethel and coached her on the latest in hairstyles and makeup, "For ladies of a certain age. Saw it online," the girl had said.

A certain age. Several of her friends, also of that *certain age*, either lived alone after divorces or were widows. Only a few still had partners. She'd always felt like the odd woman out, and had often made excuses to duck invitations because, well, she preferred sitting home with Stan. Most of those invitations had dried up. Life moved on. Reinvention happens at every age.

She pressed harder on the gas and sped down the narrow lane. Ethel liked Heartland, small enough to get around quickly but within only an hour or so of the Metroplex. Within fifteen minutes she pulled up outside of the small building that housed the community theater. Ethel hesitated, then swung out the car and headed into the lobby.

Two other adults waited. They briefly looked up from phones, nodded, and went back to peering at their phones. Ethel took a seat as far away as possible, relieved she didn't have to navigate small talk. She could hear a chorus of young voices in the next room, singing in sweet harmony.

She only recently realized Willie liked musicals. Maybe living with September rubbed off on him.

The voices stilled, and a single adult spoke quietly, then more than a dozen kids—a laughing, talking, squealing cacophony—spilled out of the room.

Willie ran to her as Ethel rose from her seat. She welcomed his hug, and the smell of his freshly shampooed hair. *Still young enough to hug in public, thank goodness.* "You need a haircut, boyo." She smiled when he pulled away and tossed the long locks out of his eyes.

"Nope, not until after the show. I'm a sheepdog puppy. Well, I hope that's my part. We can't cut our hair or make changes until then. That's what the director says." He turned to give fist-bumps and other complicated hand-greetings to friends as they departed. "See you Monday. Ready or not!" His bright laughter lightened Ethel's dark mood.

"What's Monday?" She let him tug her to the door and followed in his wake when he skipped ahead to reach her waiting car.

"Try outs. For the play." He waited for the tweep-burp sound that unlocked the car, then jumped into the back seat. Willie knew better than to argue for a front seat; she and Stan never fudged on safety. "We've been practicing and practicing. I don't *have* to get a solo. If I don't get the puppy part, there's some fudgy parts in the chorus me and my friends are gonna try for."

"Sounds like a plan. If you want, I can help you practice this weekend." She watched him in the mirror.

"That's okay. I got my own method." He slammed the door. "Found out today about method acting." He raised an eyebrow, daring her to ask.

She started the car. "What got you interested in plays all of a sudden?" Neither of his parents ever attended the theater, as far as she knew. She met his eyes in the mirror.

He shrugged, and the sunny expression faded.

Huh. Touched a nerve there.

She pretended not to notice and pulled out of the parking place. "Thought we'd stop for early lunch at a drive through, then head over to your house. Or would you rather have breakfast?"

"My house?"

"Yep. I packed a bag and everything. That way, we don't have to run back and forth to take care of your dog, or Macy-cat. Oh, September said to remember to shut off the water out back."

"Can we get chicken nuggets? Kinsler loves those."

She rolled her eyes. "I'm not getting takeout for your dog. He's got his own food. What do you like to eat? Don't get crazy about it, though, or your dad will write me a ticket." Grinned at him in the mirror.

He pursed his lips.

Again, something going on there. "How about KFC? Figure out what sides you want before we hit the drive through." She hadn't had breakfast, so it'd serve double duty for her.

In another twenty minutes, they pulled up to the green gate in front of the historic house. Ethel had kept the warm food in the passenger front seat to keep the boy from eating along the way. For the first time in weeks, her stomach growled. Must be the company. That, and the mac and cheese.

Willie gave her the code that changed each week, and Ethel punched it in. When the gate swung wide, she quickly pulled around the circle drive, noting the roses in the center needed weeding. Clearly, September had way more on her mind than tending the garden. They all did. But Ethel considered gardening her meditation.

Almost before she stopped, Willie jumped out and grabbed one of the bags of food. "I'll open the door." He had his keys out and raced around to the rear kitchen entrance.

She took her time, grabbing her overnight bag and the other bag of food. He'd taken the one with the chicken. She smiled, figuring he already had some of his portion designated for his dog. She rounded the corner and walked briskly to catch up and stop Willie from feeding any bones. He should know better, but he had a kid brain, and that didn't always mean good sense.

He'd left the kitchen door ajar. "Proves my point," she muttered. She called loudly, "You left the door open." She sighed, shoved through into the kitchen, slamming the door closed to make sure it latched.

When she turned around, the bag of chicken sat on the kitchen floor, Kinsler's head buried in the sack. "Oh for heaven's sake…"

Across the room, she saw Willie, held in muscular arms, his eyes wide, mouth muzzled by the hard hand of a burly stranger.

Chapter Nine: Jared

Jared hardened his grasp on the boy and stared at the petite woman. "You're not her. Who're you, and where is she?" Despite his massive size, Jared's shaky voice betrayed him.

"Let Willie go. Then we'll talk." Her voice remained steady and calm, but the woman's eyes sparked with lightning. She eyed the nearby kitchen island with its array of sharp knives.

He stepped forward to block access to the knives. Jared kept the boy between himself and the graying redhead. They'd surprised him, but when the boy opened the door, Jared jumped at the opportunity. Now his head thrummed a counter beat rhythm to his panting breath.

When the boy struggled, and pried at the hand covering his mouth, Jared loosened his grip. A soft gasp brought the white and tan dog to attention.

His eyes filled, and he let go of the boy, backing away, blinking furiously. "Sorry. Sorry. Please, I need to talk to her." The smell of fried chicken made his mouth water and stomach roil simultaneously. When did he last eat? And the dog made the hairs stand up on his arms.

The boy ran to the woman and buried his face against her shoulder. Her arms enfolded him. "You okay, Willie?" The dog abandoned the food to run to the boy, jumping high to nose his face.

The kid nodded and peered out at Jared. "He didn't hurt me, and I wasn't scared. Not really. Kinsler, good boy. Down." Willie pulled away, crossing his arms hard against his narrow chest. He did his best to stand tall and look brave beside the woman. "September's not here. And you broke into our house. My dad's a cop, and he'll—"

"Hush." The woman's soft voice silenced the boy. "Get a hand on your dog, Willie. He won't bite, mister…but I just might." Her eyes, still on fire, nailed Jared in place. With one hand on her phone, she added: "I'll give you thirty seconds to vacate the premises. He's right, we have the Heartland Police on speed dial."

"You don't understand. I don't wanna hurt nobody. Just need help. For my little girl…she's alive! Thought she was dead all this time but she's alive. Please help me get her back before it's too late. Please!" His legs wobbled, and then the floor rushed up to punch him in the face.

Jared didn't know how much time had passed before he came to, but they'd tied his hands. The woman, "Call me Ethel," now had one arm around his waist and Willie supported his other side as they guided him into the next room. They plopped him onto a sofa that cost more than two months of his current wages.

"Are the cops coming?" He didn't blame them. But what choice did he have? He'd convince Sorokin, if they could just meet face to face. He had figured she lived in some high-end apartment, seeing as how she ran a huge international company. But people with money did things to get around laws and such, like having her house in somebody else's weird name. What kind of name was September Day? "I only need five minutes with her."

"With who? And where'd you come from? My dad and September got all kinds of security set up." Willie fairly sizzled with excitement, now that the initial scare had worn off. "Didn't see a car anywhere."

Ethel tsk-tsked. "The police will arrive by and by."

He winced. Why did the kid keep talking about his dad and this September person? "Parked across the road." He took a breath, rubbing his face with rough hands. "You got the right to press charges. Then I lose my daughter for good. I just want five minutes with the owner of this place. People say she's worth millions and got all kinds of influence and wants to help with restitution." Unless that horrible kidnapper lied to him. "The one who has my girl wants cash. I can't ever touch that kind of money. They said the Magpie, the new head of the Family, would help. Please let me talk to her, convince her."

"They? They said? Who told you she..." Ethel's brow furrowed; angry tone modulated.

"They. THEY! Everyone says. Doncha watch the news? I looked it up, she's all over the Internet." He struggled to grab his phone from his pocket. The bindings on his wrists left his fingers free. Jared thumbed the bookmarked site and held it up to her. "Sorokin Glass, the new owner of Wong Enterprises."

"Wong?" Voice trembling, Ethel took the phone from him and stared. She reached unsteadily for the arm of a chair and sank slowly onto the seat. "Sorokin Glass?"

Willie hurried to her side and peered over Ethel's shoulder. He shook his head. "Nope, somebody told you a whopper. That's September."

The older woman's lip trembled. "She runs Wong Enterprises?" Ethel thrust the phone back like it had become a snake. "They killed my Stanley."

Chapter Ten: Shadow

Shadow disliked elevators. The small space smelled of too many people, with no place to run should danger threaten. He leaned hard against September's thigh, hackles raised, pushing her back against the mirrored wall to gain distance from the strange man leading the way. She dropped one hand to smooth his cheek, and he whined softly under his breath.

She didn't say a word when the doors magically swooshed open. He followed September, still keeping his body between her and the stranger who led the way. The man waved a card at large double doors at the end of the short hallway, then stepped back.

Shadow waited for September's command. She made a sweeping gesture with one hand, *check-it-out,* and he sprang forward. He relished his work keeping her safe. He heard her murmur words to the man as they waited on the threshold. Shadow quickly swept through the room.

He detected lots of strange smells but nothing that screamed danger. The room held no hidden strangers eager to point guns at September or send long-distance hurts at good dogs. He sniffed the treats on the table in passing— apples, bananas (yum!), and chocolates (even better!). He never got chocolate, unless he stole some. Shadow turned from the temptation and focused on potential hiding spots.

Even when you couldn't see bad people, sometimes they left behind nasty surprises that could hurt September. It was a good dog's job to find danger, report it to his person, and keep her safe. And he could tell she still felt nervous, anxious, filled with worry. More than the lines that mapped her forehead, he could smell her disquiet. So Shadow took extra care to *check-it-out*, sweeping the room thoroughly from top to bottom.

Shadow bounded back to the open doorway, and skidded into a sit, *all clear*. When she smiled, his heart swelled. He couldn't stop his tail from sweeping the carpet; his ears slicked back.

"Good boy, baby dog." She turned to the man beside her. "I'll take it from here."

"Does he bite?" The man in the uniform quickly retreated, shoulders hunched. He stared at Shadow.

"All dogs bite. So do people." She shut the door in his face.

Shadow cocked his head at her tone and licked his lips.

"Was I rude, Shadow? Kind of a clueless question, don't you think? That's part of how to *guard*, right?"

He barked once, a sharp exclamation, at the command, and bounded to his feet. He'd always protected her, and that meant many things. Recently she had given it a name.

Guard. That meant to stand strong between September

and any threat, to keep danger away. Sometimes that meant showing his teeth and warning with loud growls and snarls. Sometimes it meant to bite hard, and not let go. His hackles bristled again at the thought, and his tail wagged hard and fast with excitement. Maybe somebody threatened her, and he missed it? Shadow decided to again sweep the room, this time at twice the speed.

Shadow zoomed around the perimeter, checking under furniture, paws-up to peer through windows. He nudged another door wider open and sniffed the bathroom thoroughly. Then he ran to the last double door, and raced into the bedroom, leaping onto the bouncy bed then off, to race back to September's side. Again, he sat before her, declaring an *all clear.*

She grabbed up her bag, crossed the room quickly and dumped it on one of the sofas. "What a place, big as our living room and kitchen combined. That's not even counting the bedroom."

He chased after, and hopped up beside the bag. She shook her head, pointed, and he hopped off obediently, but couldn't help voicing gurgling whines of excitement. New place, new smells, strangers, surprises all around… A third time, he planted his tail right in front of her. *All clear!*

She smiled. *"Chill,* Shadow."

But he still couldn't calm down. So much going on. And he had September to himself! She talked to him, like before. Nobody demanded her attention. They could snuggle, or play a game, or…

She took a deep breath and blew it out slowly, a trick he recognized she used to help calm herself. So he knew she felt as excited as he did. "Guy rubbed me the wrong way. Maybe you won't bite, but I do."

He stood up, woofed softly, and paw-danced before her

as she crossed the room. She'd said the *bite* word again. Would they play the game? Where she put on poofy arms, and he got to chomp her wrists and arms? He loved games!

She groaned but grinned. "I did say it. Created a monster, didn't I? After you saw Lia training with her dog, you just had to play the game, too. I know, baby dog, you live for games. Wanna play?"

He sat, cocked his head, and smiled. His tail sped up, sweeping the carpet.

"I didn't bring the sleeves." She looked around the large three-room suite, and finally strode to the distant bathroom. "Holy cats, it's as big as our kitchen. Jacuzzi, shower, double sink, toilet—I don't even want to know what that is."

Shadow followed, not understanding the words, but his tummy relaxed with her happy emotions. His hackles finally smoothed. Shadow always felt better when she relaxed.

September grabbed one of the fluffy towels stacked on the counter. "Since I own the place, they can't complain." She twisted it between her hands, and then moved out into the open room again. "This'll have to do. Okay, Shadow, wanna play *bite*?"

As she twirled the towel over her head, he growled and danced, focusing on the white fabric. When it swooped within range, Shadow leaped high, grabbed the thick material, and bit hard and deep. He held on when September pulled, digging in his paws and claws for purchase. Shaking his head with the cloth held firmly, he growled and tugged, and bit.

"Good boy, *bite* it, Shadow, *bite*!" She finally let go so he could dance around the room shaking and "killing" the offending fabric. "Shadow, *bring*. Good boy. *Drop it*."

He released the wadded towel at her feet, and backed away, tail waving faster in anticipation of the next part of the game. Shadow watched as she picked up the towel and wrapped it around and around her forearm. She held it tight to her skin.

"Shadow, *bite*." She held the arm out.

He lunged, grabbing hard on the towel.

"Ouch! *Drop it*, Shadow, *out!*" As he released, she let the fabric unroll off her arm and rubbed the bruised spot. "Okay, dumb move, September. Not you, Shadow, never you." She picked up the towel and tossed it onto a chair. "Better to play the *show-me* game. Wanna play *show-me?*"

He woofed in what she called *sotto voce*, using his inside voice. Sometimes he got so excited and loud it hurt people ears, so she'd taught him what to do. And he really enjoyed the *show-me* game. He'd play any game she wanted. As long as he could be with her.

She looked around the room, and he followed her gaze. He knew the names of almost everything he saw. There, where she'd tossed the towel, he knew the name for *pillow*. And beside it on the table, sat a *bowl* with *treats*. Maybe she'd give him part of a *banana*. He'd like that. A lot!

Reaching into her pocket, September took out a jangling bundle. His mouth closed with a snap, watching her every move. He knew that word. Then she picked up a knife that sat beside the bowl of treats.

"This is *knife*." She held out the item for him to sniff, taking care the sharp end pointed away. "And this is *keys*." September held out the jingling bundle in the other hand. "*Show-me keys*."

He didn't hesitate. Shadow leaped forward and nose-punched the hand holding the jingling keys. They flew out of her hand and sailed across the room.

She laughed. "Don't know your own strength, do you? Shadow, *bring keys*."

He bounded after the keys and struggled a bit to get a good grip. What fun! Shadow proudly delivered the keys to her hand.

September crossed to the far wall and grabbed a *bottle* out of a bucket. He knew that word, too. Then she reached into the bucket with her other hand and showed him. "This is *ice*. And this is *bottle*. Shadow, *show-me ice.*"

He leaped forward to nose-punch the hand holding the ice. Shiny rattling cold clear cubes that felt like *snow*—he knew that word, too!—scattered across the room.

"Good dog!"

He ran after the skittering crystals, grabbed up one to taste and crunched it with his teeth. Oh, how he'd missed these fun times! *Show-me,* with *bite!* He liked this game.

A knock sounded at the door, and September's mood shifted like a frightened cat. Shadow raced to the door, tail stiff and flagged high. He waited for her to decide what to do, as he sniffed to detect the interloper.

He didn't recognize that scent. Potent. A man. A low growl bubbled deep in his throat.

After checking the peephole, September swung open the door. "I didn't order room service. Did Jack Glass—"

The man pushed the cart into the room and stood blocking the exit. "I wanted a chance to talk with you before that master manipulator continued pulling your strings."

Chapter Eleven: Combs

Jeff Combs ignored the young woman pushing his wheelchair down the corridor but winced when she turned a corner too quickly. The PT specialist had put him through the ringer. Again. And he had more sessions this afternoon. But no way would he complain. He had put himself on a fast track to recover from his injuries. Nothing would stop Combs from reclaiming his position as a detective with the Heartland Police Department.

That meant he and September must spend time away from each other, time they could ill afford. The weeks following their wedding nearly destroyed their relationship. Rebuilding required one-on-one time. With him all stove-up and September riding herd on the kids, it wasn't happening.

He could have remained at home, and had the PT done there, not as efficient but… Anyway, he'd quashed his disappointment when September readily agreed to time apart. Maybe they both needed time alone to digest what happened and figure out where they could go from here.

September blamed herself. But there was plenty of guilt to go around. On top of his own injury, Combs couldn't get over losing Gonzalez and Uncle Stan. They'd died protecting others—himself included. That made Combs even more determined to figure out the root cause.

Oh, he knew Kaliko Wong orchestrated the bombing, and September's long-lost uncle stepped in to shield her. And now according to Uncle Jack she'd inherited lake property from another long-lost relative? His lips twitched with distaste.

He suggested she sell the property. She'd almost died there, why would she want such a reminder? Instead, she'd asked Teddy to make some kind of renovations. And how convenient Jack appeared out of nowhere… too many questions! And nobody to ask.

He loved September with all his heart. But ever since they'd met, something evil had followed her, no matter what she did to evade it.

Captain Gregory refused to loop him in on the investigation into Kaliko Wong and the organization she'd run. He'd reached out to Teddy Williams, a longtime friend and sophisticated Internet professional for help, but Gregory got to Teddy first, and the cone of silence surrounding Combs echoed with his own frustration.

Why had the head of Wong Enterprises fed a years' long bloody trail tracking September? His own research showed many legit businesses around the world, along with myriad shady dealings. Now the company attributed those questionable businesses to Kaliko. The mysterious sharpshooter who took Kali out had never been found, either. All that had happened while he lay in a hospital bed half out of his mind thinking he'd lose his leg. A spotty, slow to return memory didn't help.

Everyone told him to concentrate on healing. If he healed. One operation down, and who-knows-how-many to go. The specialists said he'd have a "hitch in his git along," as Uncle Stan liked to say.

Unacceptable. A detective needed both legs. He couldn't have a bum leg dragging him down. His memory improved, and he could still puzzle out cases, never mind the leg. How was he to come to terms with his new reality, and help September, if nobody would share information?

The young woman reached his room, pushed him through the door, then stepped away and pointedly gestured at the chair beside the bed. Combs nodded tersely. No more help, and no way he'd complain. He must get himself in and out of the wheelchair, to the bed or another chair, whichever he preferred.

And, he'd do it. But not while she watched. He crossed his arms, lips tightening, as he shook his head and turned away.

The familiar exchange repeated every day. He didn't want or need her help, but he sure didn't appreciate her judgy eyes. Or anyone else judging him, for that matter.

She smiled and looked pretty for a minute—despite her sadistic nature. Nodding, she gave him the win, and slowly closed the door behind her. Combs breathed with relief. His muscles ached from the workout, but that meant progress. Right?

While talking to Aunt Ethel last night, she'd let slip September had a weekend planned in Dallas. A hopeless romantic, Ethel thought September meant to surprise him with a visit. He smiled. He missed September, and planned to practice his surprised face when she showed up. Lately, he felt awkward talking to his aunt. She and Uncle Stan had been married for decades. How do you come to terms with such a loss?

His phone rang. His eyebrows shot up at the caller ID. He hadn't heard from officer Pilikia "Tee" Teves in close to a year. "Long time no talk. How's Chicago treating you?"

"Same old same old." Her lilting Hawaiian accent tickled him, and despite his frustration with the world at large, he smiled. "Got a favor, Combs. Help me with a case?"

"From Chicago, or a local case?" Maybe she didn't know about his injury. Surprising. He thought her sister—half-sister, he corrected himself—would share the gossip. He guessed Lia Corazon didn't want to revisit the wedding debacle any more than he did.

"Off the books. A personal project of mine. Ya know?"

He groaned and rubbed his eyes. Tee and Lia, one dark and small and the other blond and tall, had more in common than a daddy in prison. "A personal project?" These new cops loved to play the hero, and overeagerness got them in trouble.

Tee spoke quickly. "It's connected to that trafficking case I worked last summer."

That's where they'd met. She'd gone off protocol then, too, and nearly got herself and Lia killed. "I'm listening." Despite himself, Combs felt curious. If the captain wouldn't loop him in on the Wong investigation, Tee's side project could keep him distracted.

"You remember we caught Tony Kanoa. Still awaiting trial, and probably will go away for life. But his accomplice got away clean. A few months back, I got a tip that Robin D'Andri took over the girls in Kanoa's stable. Now she's liquidating her assets. At least, some of her customers are. Caught one bad guy who led us to three girls. All dead."

He shuddered at the terms she used. "I don't know that name." His brow furrowed. "She's in Texas?"

"That's the tip I got."

"So why off the books, Tee?" He waited. And waited some more. "You still there?"

"You know why Wayne Teves went to prison." He heard her swallow hard.

Combs flinched. Her father murdered Henry Wong. Everything led back to that name. Tee and Lia never knew their father, or about each other until last summer when they discovered that nugget. "Didn't know you two spoke."

She laughed, the sound dry and bitter. "My sister gets pretty insistent. Thing is, Wayne denies it. Like all felons." He noted she didn't honor him with the word *dad*. "My tipster also claims Robin D'Andri had a hand in Wong's murder, and framed Wayne."

Wait. "Took out Kaliko? We never found the sharpshooter…"

"No! Killed the old man, Kaliko's husband, Henry Wong. Kali had him killed to take over the organization. And the informant says—"

"Oh for the love of… Do you hear yourself, Tee? What informant? What tipster?" Geez Louise, didn't newbie cops have enough to do with real cases without listening to pot-stirring trolls?

"It's credible, Combs. Swear or I wouldn't call. Since September had run-ins with the organization, thought you might see your way to… Guess I just needed someone to listen. Never mind."

His jaw clenched. "Stop. I'm listening." Hell, stuck here in purgatory, he had nothing better to do. "What do you need?"

"D'Andri leaves bodies in her wake. If she's in Texas,

probably using a different name, there's a reason. Kaliko Wong ran the whole trafficking show, with handlers like Tony Kanoa and D'Andri handling the merchandise. With Kaliko gone, one of them must pull the strings." She hesitated, then spoke quickly as though the words burned. "I know Heartland investigation takes primary with all that's happened. But if you or September could share any insight about the new Wong leader, I'd owe you big time."

He took a big breath. "Guess you haven't heard. Our wedding didn't turn out the way we planned."

A beat. "Sorry. Lia mentioned something. She acted reluctant to share details, and I figured something went sideways." She hesitated, adding, "I couldn't get away to attend. But it seemed like a pretty closed down affair."

"I'm in rehab. Got my leg all bunged up, now working my butt off to get back to work. But the truth? The department has shut me out. Says they're protecting me emotionally so I can recover." He laughed without humor. "For any insider intel, I'm not your guy."

"Geez, sorry to hear that. I thought you'd have lots to say about the crazy long-lost daughter story Wong Enterprise keeps pimping. It's all over the Internet. Calling her the Magpie."

"Whose daughter? You lost me." Magpie?

"Henry Wong's missing daughter resurfaced after Kaliko got killed. Funny, I thought you and September would have a chuckle over that, since she looks so much like your wife."

He didn't bother to correct her. He and September weren't legally married. Yet.

"Combs, just do an Internet search. Type in the name Sorokin Glass."

Chapter Twelve: September

H e stood over a head taller than September, and wore a three-piece suit, pale yellow shirt with French cuffs, and cobalt tie knotted tight at his throat. The slate blue linen matched his eyes. When he turned to shut the door, September saw the fabric stretched taut over broad shoulders, nearly bursting the seams. The outline of a holster stood in stark relief. Curly dark hair crowned his head, shaved close on each side to show off the glittering pierced diamond earrings.

"You work for Wong Enterprises? In what capacity?" She rested one hand on Shadow's brow, and the other on the hidden gun beneath her own shirt. She felt more than heard the low growl of Shadow's concern.

"Oh, a little of this, a little of that." His voice rumbled; a tone so low it might vibrate her cello strings. He raised his eyebrows as if asking permission, and at her nod, stepped farther into the room. "I'm here at the Family's request. They thought it helpful to offer you guidance in these early days. Help you navigate any potential missteps."

Mr. Thomas had sent him. The attorney, a creepy man who had visited her at the lake house and spun the crazy fairytale that blew up her life. With Mr. Thomas, and she suspected this man, a misstep could prove lethal. "That doesn't give me any comfort. You said your name is…"

"Gabriel Pierce." He gestured toward the sofa and chair ensemble.

September took a seat and invited Shadow onto the cushions beside her. She owned the hotel, so who'd complain about a little dog fur? Besides, she needed contact with him. Her heart raced, waiting for the next awful revelation.

Pierce shot his cuffs, and jewels glinted in golden cuff links. On his left wrist, he wore a massive watch. Probably a Rolex.

"What questions do you have, Sorokin?" At her stricken look, he backtracked, and gestured a courtly apology with his right hand as though doffing a courtier's cap. A signet ring on the middle finger of his right hand shined blue, sapphire bright. "My apologies. I overstepped. You can call me Mr. Pierce, and I'll call you Ms. Glass. Or would you prefer September Day?" He crossed his legs, and the trousers rode up, revealing bare ankles.

She'd wager his loafers cost more than her last year's income. That is, before inheriting this hotel. She felt even more under-dressed, outclassed, and off balance. That may have been the intent. September hadn't prepared mentally or emotionally for this giant *basso profundo* visitor and didn't quite know how to react.

"I'll reserve my questions for my uncle. I'm having

breakfast with him—that's Jackson Glass—shortly. Very nice to meet you Mr. Pierce, but we can continue this conversation tomorrow morning, at the meeting with Wong Enterprises principles. I'm not a fan of ambushes." *Especially not from a wannabe graphic novel hero.*

She didn't say that last out loud, but still felt a bit vindicated by his expression. Sometimes her face said rude things all by itself. She quickly stood to walk him to the door. Shadow pressed close to her side. She reached for the doorknob—

Pierce sprang to his feet, reached the door in three long strides, and pressed one rough hand flat against the door to hold it closed. The sapphire glittered. He smelled of peppermint. And something more earthy.

September caught her breath, and quickly stepped away. Shadow growled, taking his threat up a notch. He planted himself between her and the stranger, hackles raised, assuming the *guard* behavior without waiting for her command. "*Chill* Shadow."

"Your dog doesn't know what to think of me, either." Pierce dropped his hand from the door, but didn't offer it to the dog, or make eye contact. The calluses and scars on that hand, the clearer view of his gun beneath the swanky suit, and a glimpse of an intricate feather tattoo climbing upward from the back of his hand belied her first impression. He wasn't some rich guy sent to intimidate her before the meeting. Or maybe he was that—but something more.

"I know you don't trust me, or this whole situation. Good. That's smart." His voice, a dark chocolate melody, filled the room with persuasion. "You have no idea how many wheels within wheels run this organization. Easy to manipulate someone inexperienced, easy to get crushed by the machine's cogs, or worse. And it is a machine that requires fuel to run. You don't want to know the kind of fuel…" He leaned closer, sparks igniting in the depths of his blue eyes. "Believe no one. Trust nobody. Especially be wary of Jackson Glass."

"You need to leave. Now." She refused to move away. With the past months of training for all kinds of situations, September felt confident she could protect herself, especially from a bore who wouldn't expect her to have any skills. Besides, Shadow was here, and the man didn't know what training he possessed. "Don't make me send the dog. Or call security."

A half-smile worked the corners of his lips. "Ms. Glass, I am security. Assigned to you by the Family." He pulled back one side of his suit jacket, to belatedly pull out identification. He handed it to her. "I expected someone of your experience to ask for credentials before letting me in."

She gave a cursory look, and shoved it back at him, flinching when his hand briefly touched her own. "You bullied your way in here. If you work for the Family, then you work for me."

"Then act like it."

She recoiled as if slapped.

"This is serious business. Act like an uncertain fish outta water, and you'll get bulldozed sooner rather than later. Act like the boss, or nobody will treat you like one. Command respect, demand they follow your orders."

"That how the old boss ran things? You respected Kaliko Wong?" He flinched, and she pressed on, each word a dagger aimed with precision. "She left a bloodbath in her wake. Destroyed innocents. Relished debauchery. And repaid disloyalty with death." September breathed heavily, and beside her, Shadow whined and pawed her leg. "She came after me, and my family—*my chosen family*! And she nearly destroyed us all. I found out about my birth parents"—she made air quotes—"a month ago. I don't remember them and have no loyalty to them or the horrific dynasty they created. So don't you *dare* lecture me."

"Ms. Glass…"

She talked over him. "I don't know if you're here to protect me, to spy on me, to coerce and manipulate me, or something else. And frankly, I don't care. I had no choice in my parents, but that legacy of terror ends with me."

"Sorokin…September!"

"Fair warning, Gabriel Pierce. Come that meeting tomorrow, Sorokin Glass cleans house. You can either help me, or take severance pay and get out."

He whistled. "You're really that naïve." He held up both hands as if warding off any further argument. "I admire your passion. I've always been a sucker for tilting at windmills. And if it matters at all, I never worked for Kaliko Wong. Jackson Glass hired me. And that, my dear, is why I know you shouldn't trust him."

Chapter Thirteen: Ethel

E thel stared. Stared at her hands, stared at the wall, looked at Willie and away, and anywhere but at this person who dared slander September. It couldn't be true. They said everyone in the world had an identical twin. Maybe more than one. There had to be another explanation.

Willie took the phone from her and steadied it for her to see. "Look, Aunt Ethel. That video? It looks kinda like September, but it's different. too."

"Willie, stay away from that man." She'd tied Jared's hands. But she had no illusions that he'd escape if he wanted to.

He was a big man, dark, with wavy chin-length hair, wearing worn frayed jeans, tee-shirt, and sandals. If he spoke the truth, a man would say and do anything to save his child.

"You must be mistaken." She licked her lips, staring

around the room. Macy dozed atop the dining room table, while Willie's dog nosed about the intruder's feet.

The man's face, streaked with tears, turned away from the dog. "Could ya keep him away from me. Dogs don't like me."

"Willie, go take care of Kinsler." She spoke, not taking her eyes off the images on the phone's screen. "Those pictures, that video, you say it's someone who now runs the Wong organization?"

"The kidnapper told me, yeah. Says she runs the company. Has money, and I'm spozed to ask her to help. I'm just following directions. I just want my little girl back." His voice cracked. "Please tell me where to find her. If I can just talk to her, explain about Alana. I'll do anything, pay her back forever. Don't you understand? She's my little girl!"

Willie still had the man's phone. He continued scrolling, a scowl starting to bloom across his young face. "She has a dog that looks like Shadow." Deep worry lines pinched his face. "Do ya think this has something to do with her meeting in Dallas, at that fancy-schmancy Grand Chisholm Hotel? September acted awful nervous this morning."

Meeting? September said—implied at least—she booked the trip to surprise Combs. The two needed some time together. Now, Ethel didn't know what to think.

"Honey, why don't you take Kinsler for a walk in the garden. Go shut off the water. Let me and Mister…" She raised her eyebrows in a questioning look.

"Jared, just Jared." His expression shuttered, as though suddenly realizing his position.

She nodded. "We're going to have a talk."

"No fair. Just when stuff gets interesting?" But Willie didn't argue further. He handed Ethel Jared's phone then clomped to the kitchen, escorting Kinsler into the back garden.

"Lady, I don't mean you or the boy no harm. Like I said, just need to talk with Sorokin, or September, whatever she calls herself."

"This family has been through enough rough times. I don't believe you, Jared, or whoever you are." She crossed her arms, hurried toward the kitchen area, and peered through the stained glass to be sure Willie was out of sight and hearing. "That boy out there nearly lost his daddy. And I lost my husband, all because of that horrible Wong family." She whirled and strode back into the living room to face Jared. "You want me to believe that September, my nephew's fiancé and future stepmom to Willie, runs that organization? How dare you!"

"I don't like it either. I didn't make nothing up. And I don't got no choice, and only one chance to get my little girl." He scooted forward on the sofa, already working his hands free from the ties. "Call her. Just put her on the phone with me, five minutes, that's all I ask. Please."

She tossed his phone back at him, and he fumbled to catch it before it fell. A sour taste filled her mouth. Nobody would make up such a wild story. Not and have the pictures and video to prove it. "I'm calling the police." She hunted for her own phone.

"No, please. They said no cops. They stole my daughter last year. She's so little, I just want her back. My wife blamed me, hell, I blame me. I thought she was dead, but now I got hope. I talked to her! Alana told me about the sunny fish!" He sobbed. "What would you do to save your child?"

I'd do anything to have a child.

Jeff Combs and his sister Naomi were the closest she and Stanley ever got. And God help them, Jeff loved September. It would kill him to learn her connection to that crime family, her complicity in all their family had suffered.

She couldn't tell Jeff, not until she knew something more concrete, had more evidence. Or some kind of explanation for what seemed to be the ultimate betrayal.

Jared scooted forward on the sofa, flexing his neck and shoulders. "Look, I came to talk, to beg for help, that's all. And she's not here so I'll just go away." He stood and sidled toward the kitchen and the back door, holding his phone in loosely bound hands before him to keep her at bay. "You don't have to help me. Just don't stop me. Or call the cops. I'll leave, you won't see me no more."

Ethel stepped aside, recognizing he offered no threat. She could still report him, but didn't want to prolong this encounter. Ethel wanted him gone. "Go on then. But don't come back here, and don't threaten my family ever again."

She followed him at a distance, watched as he clumsily opened the rear kitchen door, and stumbled out onto the brick pathway. She heard Willie and his dog playing noisily in the rose garden. Ethel moved quietly so they wouldn't notice Jared's departure.

Once outside, Jared broke into dogtrot, hurried around the brick walkway and sped down the circular drive. He raced through the gate she left wide open in her haste to reach the house. He dashed across Rabbit Run Road, and within forty seconds she heard the roar of an engine.

Ethel walked slowly down the driveway to the gate, clutching the cold green bars as she watched Jared's car speed away. September rebuilt this house, complete with iron bars and multiple locks, to keep out the evil stalking her young life. She brought happiness to Jeff when he'd all but given up on love.

Had September Day played them all for fools? Ethel took solace that Stan's sacrifice protected those they loved.

September's lies tarnished his heroic memory.

Grief surged, churning the pit of her stomach, grabbing her by the throat. She slid halfway down before catching herself. Deep guttural sobs wracked her body. Ethel pressed her face against the ornate metal, hoping the bruising pressure would help ground her, let her regain composure.

"Hey, Aunt Ethel? Where are you? Me and Kinsler are hungry."

She squared her shoulders, slowly pulling herself upright. Ethel scrubbed the wet from her face. The child was always hungry. "Coming Willie."

No, she wouldn't burden Jeff with this. And Captain Gregory had enough on his plate. Time to do research on her own—she had a couple of hours before meeting her friend at the festival. Like Willie said, the pictures and video she'd seen had something off about them, something a computer expert might be able to figure out.

They'd eat their KFC. Then she'd called Teddy Williams.

Chapter Fourteen: September

September changed clothes for the meeting with Jack, donning loose-fitting linen trousers and a turquoise and green silk blouse that fell to thigh length. September rarely carried a purse but added a small over-the-shoulder clutch. She'd swapped sandals for soft calfskin lace ups, dabbed on some makeup, and brushed out her long hair.

"Shadow, what do you want to eat? Since I own this dump, you get to enjoy the bounty as well. Beats kibble, right? Hungry?" She pulled one of the prepackaged baggies of food from her overnight bag and stuffed it in her go bag.

Shadow wagged his whole body at the word. Other than during their short play session, he'd stayed on high alert since entering the ornate hotel. He didn't trust Pierce, but neither had he reacted with overt aggression. Pierce acted appropriately around Shadow, too, not forcing eye contact or sticking out his hand to insist on a rushed meeting the way too many people did.

"He also knew my real name." Pierce had done his research. And, if he told the truth and Jack had hired him, he'd probably gotten more than an earful about her private business. "Two against one, not great odds. Unless they really are both on my side. What you think, Shadow?"

He licked his lips, telling her he still focused on the word *hungry*. He stared at the baggie she carried as they left the room.

The restaurant was a short ride up the escalator from her penthouse suite. She didn't like to think who roomed in the suite before her. The idea of spending time in the same space as Kaliko creeped her out. From what she'd learned, though, the woman spent most of her time in New York.

At the head of the escalator, she hesitated only a moment before striding down the long corridor toward the rooftop restaurant entrance, where Jack waited, carrying a narrow leather folder. Like Pierce, he wore a three-piece suit, the pale tan of it making his white skin and hair look even more washed out. A suit seemed out of character after seeing him in lethal action.

Jack motioned her to precede him into the restaurant proper. Other than staff the entire place echoed with emptiness. At her quizzical look, Jack shrugged. "Slow time of day, but I reserved the whole place. We needed private time to plan. And the waitstaff has been vetted. No worries there."

Her eyes widened. She hadn't thought about that. In the Family, anyone could work as a spy, threat, or suspect. *What a way to live.*

The waitstaff didn't blink as Shadow followed them to a table halfway down one wall. "Please bring me a bowl of water for my dog. And a dinner plate." She turned to Jack. "What's good? I brought a baggie of food for Shadow, but he wouldn't mind some grilled chicken as a topper." She hooked the purse strap over her chair and settled the go bag on the floor beside Shadow.

Jack grinned. "Haven't eaten here before. But the reviews are great. They'll fix the boss anything you want."

She wrinkled her nose, not sure she liked the "boss" moniker. But as Pierce pointed out, she had to own it and act the part. While they waited for his breakfast steak, and her everything-but-onions omelet, they talked quietly. "Tell me about Gabriel Pierce."

"You already met him? He moves fast." He played with his napkin, clearly stalling. "He hired me several years ago for…well, you'd have to ask him. Found him trustworthy, competent—actually more than competent—and thoughtful. The man actually has a conscience." He put out a hand, waggling it back and forth. "That's good, but can also get in the way of some things. Never mind. Bottom line, I can't always bird-dog you…" He again put up hands as though to ward off any argument. "I brought him aboard for this weekend. We'll see what you need moving forward."

They had discussed her. Her eyes narrowed, and jaw tightened. Beneath the table, she clenched her hands into fists. She would not be handled. Both men professed to have her best interest in mind and warned her about each other—and the often-stated Family's hidden agenda—but neither hesitated to manipulate her for their own ends.

Okay, message received. She just needed to figure out what each wanted out of this deal. If it didn't align with her goals, they could hit the road. She smiled at the thought.

Jack pushed cutlery away, brought up the folder and opened it. On a single sheet of paper, a double column of names lined the page. "Lists on the left in caps worked closely with Kali. Some headed up important operations that may still continue. Those on the right-hand list worked only as foot soldiers, part of teams. They may or may not be willing to switch allegiance."

She took the page and did a quick count. "That's nearly thirty names. I don't want anyone left that's dirty, whether they directed operations or did Kali's bidding."

"Nobody's squeaky clean. Haven't you and your dog had your share of dirty dealings?"

"That's not fair, and you know it. We only defended ourselves, or the people around us, when Kali and her minions came after us." She started to rub her eyes, but remembered she'd applied makeup to look a bit more professional. September forced her hands back into her lap, squinting with the heavy feeling of mascara. Beneath the table, Shadow nosed her fingers, and she stroked his muzzle. "I said we wanted to clean house, but how many of them will ride into the sunset without arguing?"

He shrugged. "They have no choice. New sheriff in town." He grinned. "We sound like an old cowboy picture. But bottom line, you'll give them their walking papers, a nice hefty severance, and they know better than to look back. Kali had them well-trained to never question orders. They'll be grateful to walk away with heads still on their shoulders. That's a whole sight better than getting wasted and left in a ditch somewhere."

She shuddered. "So they get away Scott free? No justice for what they've done?"

"Don't be naïve." He echoed Pierce. "That's not your job. Leave retribution up to the police. The bad actors will re-offend sooner or later and get caught when they do." He drained half his glass of water, and dabbed lips with the cloth. "You'll have enough to deal with handling your stockholders and board of directors."

She finished her coffee and poured more into the stingy-size cup. Caffeine helped her think. "Did any of the bigwigs have a hand in the mayhem? Or do you know?"

He shrugged. "They kept their distance, but who knows if they've dipped a toe into directing operations here and there. That'll have to be clarified as we move forward."

"What about the operations I flagged? The illegal ones to shut down immediately." When he would've interrupted her, she bulldozed on. "I don't want excuses, I want action."

"Sure, I agree. But it takes time, Sorokin."

She blinked, still not used to the new name. "If need be, I'll bring in the police to identify associated enterprises. One by one, I'll shut them down. And make restitution." She took a breath. "Before we release the people on that list, I want to know which ones potentially headed up the most horrific operations. We need their insight." She ignored his quizzical look, knowing what she asked might not be possible. But she had to try, she had to start somewhere. "Take me through what you've got."

Chapter Fifteen: Shadow

Shadow finished his chicken strips in three gulps. He licked his lips, took a few laps from the water bowl, and lay down beneath the table, ignoring the few pieces of dry kibble that remained. It didn't compare to chicken. He licked his lips again.

His chin rested across September's shoe, the smell of her a comforting constant that helped keep his emotions level. When she raised her voice in urgent conversation, he lifted his head and whined softly.

"Tomorrow will be a long day, Sorokin. First a breakfast meeting with the board, just to introduce you. And later that afternoon, a presentation giving you an overview of Wong Enterprises business." The man shifted in his chair. "The legit side of the business, that is."

Shadow heard September clack her fork on the plate, and shove it aside, signaling she'd finished. He stood and shook himself to shrug off negative emotions. At home, when the clink of forks hit plates, people got up from the table. And sometimes good dogs got to lick clean the dishes before they got stacked inside the dishwasher.

"I've got thinking to do. By myself, in the room." She shoved back her chair then stood, and Shadow panted happily, eager to get away from Jack. Chicken made him drool, but the man's presence left a bad taste. Also, no plates to lick clean on the floor. No joy for the dog.

Jack stood as well. "I'll hang on to the info for now. Unless you want the files…"

"No, that's fine. Soon enough in the morning. Oh, and Jack? Pierce said he's my protection. Will he be lurking around?" Shadow felt her slight shiver where he pressed against her thigh.

Jack laughed. "Oh, he's around, but don't expect to see him."

"Come on, baby dog. Let's go." September's hurried strides said she wanted to escape the restaurant. Shadow matched her pace, eager to have September to himself once again.

What a busy day. First, the early morning Willie car ride, and then the long drive together, just him and September. Shadow loved car rides. The wind in his face when September rolled down one of the magic windows gave his nose a vacation into a world of scent. Wonderful and sometimes mysterious sniffs rode on the breeze.

He also liked to watch cars whiz past on the car path. They made strange humming noises. Oh, and when he spied big animals behind fences sometimes he caught their musky smell. Long horns set on their heads like funny broom handles looked dangerous, but exciting. Sometimes, smaller animals with light-colored thick fur September called sheep flocked together and moved in waves, swimming over grassy fields. He'd like it better to meet one close up for a more detailed investigation. Shadow yearned to leg lift against the big fence posts, just to leave his mark on the world.

At the thought, Shadow nose-poked September's thigh, and whined. The long car ride, the big meal, and the day's excitement translated into a more pressing need.

September glanced down, pursed her lips, and nodded. As they passed one of the waitstaff on their way out, she stopped. "Where do I find the doggy relief station?"

Shadow ignored the murmuring voices, more interested in tracking the movement of someone lurking at the end of the hall. Peppermint smell meant Pierce. The big man hadn't even shared the minty candy, a big disappointment.

Shadow's ears came forward, and his tail stiffened as he stayed on high alert in case Pierce made a threatening move. It was a good dog's job to *guard* his person. This stranger must prove trustworthy before Shadow felt safe. Sharing peppermint would help.

"Come on Shadow, the *fast stairs* first. Then down the elevator." She waved at the big doors at the opposite end of the hallway.

He didn't like stairs that moved by themselves but knew September wouldn't put him in danger. *Fast stairs* going up weren't nearly as concerning as going down. So he watched what she did and copied her careful steps to ride down the steps. *Fast stairs.* New words to learn. At the bottom, he bounded off and turned to look back at them as the steps disappeared into the floor. How odd!

Shadow had visited many places and learned many words. He was smart that way. At least the *fast stairs* moved them away from the peppermint man.

When they reached the smooth doors of the elevator, he

looked for his next cue. September grinned. "What the heck. *Ka-pow*, Shadow!" She pointed at the button.

He jumped up to paw-thump the wall. When nothing happened, Shadow nose-poked the button.

"Good dog, Shadow. You remembered. Sometimes a job gets done in more than one way." The doors slid open, and they entered. He wasn't sure how the magic box worked, but knew whenever the doors opened again, they'd be in a new place. With new sniffs to explore.

Sure enough, when the door opened, they traded the cool air inside the elevator for a superheated stinky atmosphere. Shadow saw lots of cars waiting in long lines. Oil, exhaust, and cement dust made Shadow sneeze.

"I know you need to *take-a-break*. They said there's a grassy spot right outside the garage. Pretty inconvenient. We're going to fix that." She kept a firm hand on his leash as they trotted through the open-air parking garage to the patch of light on the far corner.

The sun hit him full force as he stepped out. After spending the past few hours in air conditioning, the heat made it hard to breathe. Shadow panted, trying to stay cool. He dipped his head, sniffing the lush grass and wanting to roam, to investigate the nearby flower bed that decorated the front of the fancy building.

September stepped into the sun only briefly, before ducking back into the shade of the garage. "*Take-a-break*, baby dog. Dang, that sunshine's bright." She pulled a plastic baggie from her go bag ready to clean up his creativity.

Shadow found a likely spot, quickly finished, and kicked up sod with his rear legs as an afterthought. Hardly any good sniffs here. The sun scalded everything away, traffic zoomed by, and no critter scent pooled amid the decorative vegetation. Not like at home, where bunnies and squirrels left their mark for inquisitive dogs to explore and relish.

As September moved forward to collect his gift to the grass, a car approached. The driver called out to them. "Nice dog."

September turned around, squinting from the sun and shading her eyes to see into the car's darkness. "Thanks." One hand still held the leash, and the other clutched the full baggie.

"You're Sorokin Glass." It wasn't a question.

September stiffened. Shadow watched, alert for any suspect movement. All of the car's windows stood open in deference to the sweltering temperatures. Shadow wondered why the driver didn't turn on his cold air. Shadow put his face near the icy breeze sometimes if September left the windows closed. Shadow pushed himself between September and the car. He told himself, *Guard.*

She dropped his leash and put a hand on her hidden gun. "Yes, I'm Sorokin Glass. Better to wait for a more formal introduction tomorrow. You'll excuse me —"

"Get in the car. Now. Drop the bag. No, not the dog." His voice rose, stress making it shake with strident emotion. "I got a gun pointed at you. Don't make me hurt you."

"Shadow *wait.*" Still squinting, September dropped her go bag on the cement and climbed into the passenger side as directed.

Shadow yelped but stayed in place as commanded. Of all the words he knew, he disliked *wait* the most. Why would she leave him? People did odd things sometimes. But September knew things a good dog didn't understood. So he'd *wait* until she explained.

The car started to roll, picking up speed, driving September away. Shadow yelped again, paw-dancing in place until he could bear it no longer.

He launched himself after the car, silent in pursuit, paws and claws clacking and scrabbling on the hard cement surface. If the car left the garage, drove off on the car path, he'd never catch up.

With a final burst of speed, Shadow drew level with the rear of the car, gathered his haunches, and sprang. Up and up he went, paws reaching, and neatly leaping through the open rear window. He landed with a snarl on the backseat.

At the same moment, September punched the man in the face with the open baggie of Shadow's poop.

Chapter Sixteen: Robin

Once you worked for Kaliko Wong, you said yes to all future jobs. Failure, or any show of reluctance, meant more than loss of reputation, it led to reprisals nobody wanted to earn. So Robin couldn't refuse to clean up Tony Kanoa's mess.

In lieu of payment, the Family graciously agreed Robin could keep any profit from the dispersal of freshies. The going rate for prime contraband could cha-ching up to five figures; you took the cash, handed 'em over—and never looked back. That should have set Robin up for a retirement paradise.

But because Kanoa sampled his own merchandise, none could claim "prime" anything. The bottom feeders with an ear on dark markets knew Kanoa's reputation. Robin's bank account mirrored that affront, and the Family knew they had her over a barrel.

In the back of the RV, the last kid wouldn't stop sniveling. "Shut up. Or I'll give ya a better reason to cry." It had taken months, but Robin had unloaded all but this last one, Kanoa's favorite, or so she'd been told. So far, three potential purchasers had taken one look and backed out.

They wanted prime freshies with at least a semblance of innocence, and after a year with Kanoa, none of his stable qualified. She shuddered and fingered the hilt of her favorite blade nested at her waist. She knew the reality, having experienced similar at that age. That was four identities ago. She no longer resembled that girl-child.

Robin had had to share and scrabble for everything, trading with "uncles" and other strangers for a full belly and safety. By age twelve, Robin got angry enough, and skilled enough, to demand what she needed without the nasty trades. Those unable or unwilling to fight didn't survive. She'd pulled herself out of the dregs and had no sympathy for those wallowing in misery often of their own making.

For more than fifteen years, the Family gave her a reason to hone her skills and make a decent if illegal living out of the hand she'd been dealt. Her dedication came to the attention of Kaliko and garnered her an incredible opportunity. The "favor" should have set Robin up for life.

But instead she'd lost everything. With Kaliko Wong dead, and the Family leadership in tatters, all contacts and resources had blown away like embers in a fire. Sure, she'd banked a sizable amount. But not enough. She needed more funds, to reinvent herself and keep the new Family snake-head—the Magpie—from going phoenix on her and taking her out.

They called her the Magpie, a nickname given to her by a long-dead mother, because she talked too much. That hadn't changed. People didn't like her chatter about *cleaning up* the

Family business. Robin snorted. Who'd throw away such power and easy cash, just to salve their conscience? She didn't believe the rumors. Nobody did that. No, this changing of the guard couldn't scrub away the bloodied history. Magpie would repay death with death—unless destroyed first. The vague warning she received, also sent to who-knows-how-many-others, needed no clarification.

She could run with the money, but Sorokin would stalk her ever after, ready to destroy. Or Robin could preserve Kali's legacy and impress the true power behind the throne. More danger there, but greater reward. She'd not only earn the cash, but also leverage. She'd done it before. The Magpie hadn't a clue she lived and breathed only so long as she *made nice* with the true power brokers. Even Kaliko understood that.

Kali died and took the blame for every outrageous horrific excess. But the true machine of the Family's business barely skipped a beat. A fresh face at the helm, oblivious and inexperienced, offered the cover they'd long needed.

Robin had a one-time shot, plus the opportunity for a life-changing bonus. Time to get what she deserved, enough to retire in anonymity if she wished and never want for a single luxury again. Cancun maybe. Or Switzerland...no, too cold. Somewhere with warm sandy beaches, and no extradition.

And no brats. Never again would she deal with them, no matter how high the markup.

"I said close your trap, Alana!" She turned sideways in the driver's seat. The large panel RV kept things nice and private with no windows in the back, and only small portals near the front on each side. It had a big open space in the back separated by a rickety fold-out paper screen when needed for privacy. She snorted at the thought. Like those bottom feeders needed privacy for what they did. "You don't want me to come back there." She picked up the roll of gaffer's tape and brandished it. The girl had red chaffing marks from previous experiences with muzzling.

The sound immediately dropped to half volume, and she smiled, turning back in the seat. Easier to train dogs than kids. She'd had plenty of experience in that field during her dogfighting days. She preferred dogs to people anyway. You knew where you stood with them—dogs never lied, if you know how to read 'em. You knew if they'd bite you or they'd grovel. Rarely any in between.

But with these kids—they'd swear love and sweetness in one breath, and scratch like hellcats the next. Robin didn't blame the girl. She'd been no different. That's how she'd learned what the big boys paid high dollar for. The sugar and spice and everything nasty…this last girl had only nasty left. She might have built up to enough hate to actually survive, if Kali's death hadn't upended things.

Robin had to focus on her own survival, though. Former clients no longer took her calls. Word had gone out. Robin had no safe houses, no favors to spend, no backup plans. The only "deal" available, killing the Magpie, could get herself killed, too. So she wanted out. Wanted a divorce from the Family. There couldn't be a better time.

To get top dollar for this used-up contraband, only one option remained: Alana's parents would pay or die trying. And along the way, she'd do her best to permanently clip the Magpie's wings.

Robin pulled into a gas station, choosing a stall as far away from traffic as possible. She needed the ransom. The kid in the back, when she was gone, would remove the last stain on this chapter of Robin's life. She couldn't wait to reinvent herself and start anew. She just had to deliver the kid to her dad, and collect the payday provided by Sorokin.

Before she got out of the RV, Robin peered over one shoulder to where the little girl slept. Or pretended to sleep. The girl had grown canny, and half the time Robin slept with one eye open, in case Alana decided to act on the venom that spilled from her expression. If the kid just played her cards right, she'd be back home and could forget all about this nightmare. If she acted out and threw a wrench in the works, Robin would happily disappear the girl, and her dad.

She counted on September living up to her bleeding-heart rep to cough up the cash. The Family might tie her hands, but surely the woman must have access to discretionary funds. Maybe Robin could disappear with the cash. More likely, though, she'd have to deal with Sorokin once and for all.

The squeal of the vehicle's door set her teeth on edge when she swung out of the vehicle. She locked it to keep the kid confined, and trotted to the front of the massive truck stop to pay in advance, with cash—plastic could be tracked—and to relieve herself. She washed her face in the huge shiny bathroom, so different from the usual places she frequented, that smelled of piss, mold, and despair.

Exiting the building, Robin saw a much newer and larger motor home parked at the gas pump next to hers. A woman in a broomstick skirt laced with silver threads, and wearing dangling earrings with tiny bells, stood outside the vehicle. She wore a sparkly scarf binding her head. Her hair, matching the silver threads, fell well past her waist in a pair of twin braids tied with bells. She looked like a refugee from Woodstock. And, she stared with keen interest into the window of Robin's vehicle.

Robin cursed under her breath. Had the kid tried to draw the woman's attention? She'd take that out of the girl's hide later. But right now, she must play damage control.

"That's some rig you got there. Always wanted something like that. Me, I have to make do with this old rattletrap. It's seen better days." Robin pushed between the woman's inquisitive gaze and the driver side door. She couldn't see the girl, must've ducked back into hiding.

"Doesn't matter so much what it looks like, long as it gets you where you're going." The hippie smiled and turned back to her own rig. "Just traded my old one for this beauty. It's used, got a lot of miles on her, but a whole sight better when you're on the road so much."

Might be someone inside. "Traveling with family, are you?" Robin grabbed the pump to fill her tank, keeping one eye on the stranger. Maybe the woman would shut up and go away.

"Not together, no. I'm meeting up with my cousin up the road. He got a head start on me. I'm a solo nomad, but he travels with Lord Byron, his 22-pound trained cat."

Robin squinted. She had no use for cats, or the wimpy-assed people who coddled them.

"We travel the circuit, festivals and fairs and the like." Hippie chick checked the nozzle of the pump as it filled the huge tank. "Before I retired, I played slave to the calendar, punching a clock for years on end. Now I've got nobody and nothing to claim my time or expect me anywhere except where I want to land. Freedom." She put both hands above her head and waggled them as though praising the sky for the gift of breath. "That cute little girl hiding away inside your rig might enjoy stopping by the fair. Kids her age shouldn't be sad."

Robin's eyes narrowed and her nostrils flared. Just as she

thought, the kid had stirred up trouble. "She's had kind of a tough year." She finished pumping, replace the nozzle, screwed the cap back on. "What did she tell you?"

"Nothing in words, something in her eyes." Hippie chick topped off her own tank, removed the nozzle and holstered it back in its cradle. "I couldn't hear her through the glass, but she sure seemed to want to tell me something. Is everything okay? I'm happy to lend a hand." She grinned, and Robin could see a gap of missing teeth on one side of her mouth. "I could tell her fortune, and maybe pick up her spirits. I always dress up as a fortuneteller. Just call me Magical Maeve." She gave a courtly bow.

Not a hippie. A frigging fortuneteller. Robin wondered if busybody Maeve knew what her own future held...

"This Sunday is Lughnasa, the Celtic Festival of first fruits and future harvests. It's always on the Sunday closest to August first, but the Heartland Celtic Festival runs all weekend. I hadda get up early this morning, cuz set up starts at noon."

Small world. "I know where Heartland is." She'd briefly worked at a vet clinic there. She grinned, thinking of the kid's dad trying to weasel into September's fortress to make his plea. *Oh, to be a fly on the wall...* Soon enough she'd confront the enemy, but not on September's home ground. Better on neutral territory, where Robin could plan her advantage. Robin returned to her vehicle.

Maeve caught her arm and squeezed hard. Her eyes glinted with a steely expression Robin had failed to notice. "Let me talk to the girl, now, before I call the cops."

Giving her own courtly bow to mock the woman, Robin motioned her to the door. She waited until Maeve had climbed into the vehicle, then followed.

"Hey sweet cheeks, this nice lady wants to make sure

you're okay. So tell her quick that you're all fine and dandy, before I do something you won't like at all."

Maeve twisted around, a scowl darkening her face at the sarcasm. Before she could speak, Robin's favorite knife drew a new smile beneath her double chins. A crimson tide spilled down the woman's peasant blouse. Robin held her until struggles and bleeding stopped. It didn't take long.

She spoke sharply to the child. "Look what you made me do. That's your fault. You just killed her. If you don't do exactly what I tell you I will do the same thing to you. Then I'll do it to your daddy. Do you believe me?"

Eyes saucer-wide, the child nodded solemnly. Only her trembling lower lip betrayed any emotion.

"Don't touch anything. You understand me?" Without awaiting acknowledgment, Robin took the driver's seat, started the old van, and drove to a parking space in the far corner of the Buc-cee's lot. She didn't need this vehicle any longer. She had Maeve's new upgrade.

Come to think of it, the Celtic Festival served as the perfect meet for the ransom exchange. Lots of crowds, nobody expecting her. She'd tell fortunes. And make sure her own came true.

"Gather your things, quickly. I don't want a peep out of you."

Before she left, Robin wiped her bloodied blade on Maeve's peasant blouse. It took a while to find a clean spot. She eyed the broomstick skirt, and grinning, skinned it off the woman and wrapped it into a bundle to carry. Robin sliced off both of the woman's long braids and grabbed the sparkly scarf for good measure.

"Magical Maeve. I like it." She took additional trophies to hide the victim's identity, then left to claim her new throne in the fortuneteller's vehicle.

Chapter Seventeen: September

The car plowed into one of the pillars lining the parking garage. September's head thumped against the side of the car door. Airbags deployed, leaving behind talcum and a smokey scent.

Shadow's snarls filled the car, hurting her ears, as she struggled upright. The smell of his waste smeared across the driver's face seemed a poetic end to the attempted... kidnapping? Robbery? Whatever the heck he intended.

The man armed the filth off and half-gagged with revulsion. The poop stained his shirt, and still clung to his hair. His voice squeaked. "Keep that dog off me."

"You should've thought of that before accosting me." Without changing her position, September gave a hand signal to Shadow and his barks switched off. With her other hand, she retrieved the gun from beneath her shirt.

Once he blinked his eyes clear enough to see the weapon,

he froze in the driver seat. The middle of his forehead boasted a sudden swelling from the airbag. Smacking the steering wheel would have caused worse damage.

"I didn't mean no harm."

She barked a short laugh. "You have a hell of a way of showing it." With the gun in one hand and twisted awkwardly in her seat, she couldn't reach her cell phone in her purse to call the police. Instead, she unlatched the door and climbed out, quickly putting distance between them. "Hand me the keys. Toss them."

He did so. As an afterthought, he used the hem of his shirt to wipe clean the rest of his face.

"Shadow, out." She waited for him to hop through the window. "Now you're gonna sit quietly while we wait for the police."

"No-no-please-no!" His demeanor shifted to near hysteria. He spoke so quickly, she had trouble understanding. "You'll get her killed, my little girl killed. I came to you for help, that's all. Just wanted to talk, beg you…see, I thought she was dead. Then that monster says will trade for money. More money than I would ever seen in a thousand lifetimes. I don't care, I'd pay it, but I don't got it. She says you got lotsa money, say you'll pay re-tri-bution." He carefully pronounced the word. "She said just ask and you'll pay, you'll save my Alana. I called, left phone messages, but got no answer. I had to come beg you for help."

September's shoulders hunched. She'd been inundated with requests, pleadings, and outright demands: investment, loans, gifts, and more. He may well have been one of the throng. But nobody ever acted this desperate. She'd need to hire a secretary or something. "Look, Mr. —"

"Jared. Just call me Jared. Please, just listen, five

minutes—wait, wait THREE minutes, please listen! My little girl…" His face reddened as tears poured over his filthy cheeks. "I just wanted to talk to you alone, without your danger-dog. Convince you. I tried at your house. The boy said you're visiting Grand Chisholm, I came here. Just to talk, got no gun, just wanted to make you listen. Please? They said you'd help."

She glanced around the parking garage. Her so-called bodyguard Pierce had yet to show up, not that she needed his help in this case. "They? Who has your daughter?" At his look she clarified. "You keep saying *they* said I would pay, what? A ransom?"

"Don't know who. They called me, let my daughter talk. It was really her! Said I must get money from Sorokin Glass, you'd fix things with all the money you got. S'pozed to swap cash for my Alana."

"Where? When?"

"Don't know. I'm s'pozed to get a text. I can't tell cops. Please…help me get my daughter back?" He hiccupped a sob.

She glanced in the backseat and saw a crumpled role of paper towels on the floor. Wrinkling her nose, she nodded at them. "If we're to continue this conversation, get cleaned up. I'm still calling the police but will hear you out first." She watched as he retrieved the paper towels, and scrubbed away the worst of the offense clinging to his clothing.

Shadow alerted, shifted beside her. He turned, staring over his shoulder and whining. She followed his gaze, and recognized Pierce's imposing form running toward them. "Listen Jared, spill it quick. I can't predict what happens when that fella gets here."

His eyes widened, probably thinking Pierce represented the police.

"My girl got taken a year ago. The cops gave up looking, said she drowned. Cops say a bunch of island girls disappeared that summer, only a couple were ever found." A big shuddering breath as Pierce drew within hearing.

Without speaking, September raised one hand toward the bodyguard, demanding he wait. She nodded at Jared to continue and holstered her gun. He posed no threat, especially with Pierce and Shadow closely watching his every move.

"I thought the phone call was just a mean trick, or faker out to make money from my misery. But then I heard Alana. It's really her!" He tore off a clean paper towel and wiped fresh tears from his face. "It's a miracle. But I gotta pay for this miracle, with money I don't got. Kidnapper said Sorokin Glass got plenty of cash and will help me get Alana back. That true? Or is that another lie?"

Pierce had trained his gun on Jared. "Sorokin, you said you were going to your room. Not smart, to come out here alone. I'll take care of this." He made a face. "Smells like an outhouse."

Poop defense probably wasn't in Pierce's tool chest. "Put away the gun. This is Jared. He's petitioning for my help." She remembered Combs worked a trafficking case involving island girls last summer. Lia had been up to her eyebrows in that one, and Shadow barely escaped wildfires during the adventure. Jared's story hit the right notes.

Combs would have the details, if his memory wasn't so shaky. But he didn't need the worry and had no access to the Heartland PD info from rehab. Besides, that would mean explaining the real reason for her Dallas trip. She could call Lia instead.

"Sad story, if true. Why come to you? You're not a charity for bad luck stories." Pierce crossed his arms, standing well away from the aromatic car.

Jared yelled, voice echoing in the vast cement underbelly of the hotel. "A monster has my girl. Said Sorokin will help 'cuz she's responsible." His pointing finger punched the air, accusation piercing her soul. "Said your Family did this. Stole my Alana. You run this evil thing. So you'll make it right. Please. Help me get back my girl." He panted.

Her mouth dropped open. That scanned, too—Kaliko Wong put together the trafficking scheme. He was right. She must help. Somehow.

"I do have funds." She held up her hands toward Jared, when he would've shouted his thanks. "Still no excuse for accosting me. For now, hold off on the police." She looked sharply at Pierce and stood taller with hands on hips to *act like a boss* and dictate the rules. Besides, a face full of poop offered enough punishment. Losing his daughter trumped pretty much any bad behavior.

"You can't just pick up every stray panhandler and believe their sob story."

She ignored Pierce. "Jared, I just found out about my, shall we say, windfall. Still figuring out how to navigate these new responsibilities. But believe me when I say amends will be made."

September turned to make direct hard eye contact with Pierce. It worked with dogs, and also with people. "I am the head of the Family. I decide what to do with the organization, and with the funds I control." She sharpened her voice. "Put away your gun!"

Pierce reluctantly holstered his weapon. His jaw tightened, clearly opposed to her decision.

"And no, I'm not some silly pushover believing every fairytale. But if there's a chance for a happy ending, I can't ignore it." *Heaven knows I've needed my own happy endings...*

"We'll conduct due diligence." She'd bet her inheritance the kidnapper had a home on one of Jack's bad guy lists.

"You can pick his brain, get more details, and corroborate to your satisfaction. Jack can help us identify likely suspects. We'll bring in the police for help—"

Jared shook his head, as that seemed to scare him as much as the *monster*.

"If we can do without police help, we will. But first we identify Alana's kidnapper. Then we figure out how to get her back."

Chapter Eighteen: Ethel

Ethel hunched over the wheel of her small car as they bumped over a narrow overgrown drive. Teddy was house sitting for somebody up here at the lake.

"I haven't been here in years. Stan and I used to rent a boat and go fishing." She smiled sadly. Fishing hadn't been the point, the company and memories were priceless.

Willie glued his nose to the windows, a human puppy eager to explore. "Remember, we gotta be home by five. Kinsler gets his dinner at six."

She didn't answer. Between now and dinner, they had to help her friend set up at the Celtic Festival. So she couldn't dawdle talking with Teddy.

"Wow. Looks like a haunted house. Oh, and there's the lake. Can I go swimming?"

"You didn't bring your trunks." He stuck out his lower

lip, ready to argue. "We're not here that long, Willie. Maybe another time—if Mr. Williams says it's okay." She parked beside Teddy's RV, which filled half of the space in front of the double garage.

She didn't know much about Teddy, other than he lost his wife a couple of years ago. As one of September's friends, Teddy had helped Jeff on some of his cases, using his computer expertise. She hoped he'd have explanations for this weird issue of September's look-alike.

The sliding glass patio door slid open, revealing a man barely a head taller than Ethel, with snow-white hair, wire-rimmed glasses, a splashy aloha shirt featuring parrots, frayed denim cutoffs, and green flip-flops.

"Welcome to Cat's Cradle! Hiya, Willie." His grin shed twenty years from his age, making him look like a summertime Santa. He modulated his expression and offered a hand to Ethel. "Mrs. Combs, come in. Happy to help if I can."

"Ethel please."

"Call me Teddy."

Her shoulders unclenched when he made no reference to her recent loss. It seemed Teddy understood: the loss never left. Nobody needed to underline the fact. "Thanks for taking the time. It's probably silly, but it really bothered me."

He led the way into the tidy house and waved them to a group of chairs facing a bay window overlooking the lake. "You just stumbled across this Sorokin Glass person on the Internet?"

"No this man told us about it, when he broke into the house."

"Hush Willie." That's all she needed, to have Mr. Williams—Teddy—read her the riot act about how she'd

handled the situation. "He's exaggerating." She changed the
subject to give her nerves time to calm. "You call this the
Cat's Cradle?" She looked around. "It's a pretty place. Three
stories?"

"Used to be a bed-and-breakfast, with a cat that came
with every room. I met a couple of them, quite the
characters." His eyes twinkled, and she guessed a lot more
came with that story. "They didn't care for all the
construction going on. Renovation, upgrading the electrical,
plumbing, you name it. One of September's clients lost a
bonded pair last year and ended up adopting the two cats.
Happy ever after for Nebulae and Sunset."

Ethel sighed. She used to believe in happy ever after…

Ethel startled when a very large cat with a majestic air
and extravagant orange and white fur flicked his tail, blinked
once, then went back to sleep. "Oh, I thought that was a
stuffed animal. He didn't come with the house?"

"That one's mine. Usually hangs out in Nellie Nova, my
RV. But it got too warm out there, and Meriwether prefers
AC. And treats." At the word, the cat blinked and stood,
arching his back, and yawning with a loud meow. Teddy
grinned. "Willie, why don't you take Meri to the kitchen,
that way"—he pointed—"and give him a treat from the
canister on the counter."

Willie leaped forward, scratched the big cat on the back
of his neck, and trotted to the kitchen with the feline loping
behind. Ethel smiled her thanks.

Teddy leaned forward in his chair, resting his elbows on
knobby pale knees. "Tell me about this intruder who alerted
you to that deepfake." He kept his voice soft.

Deepfake? Oh my, that's what she'd hoped! She quickly
explained the situation. "I don't know if it's true, or Jared
just wanted to shake September down. But the online stuff

about Sorokin Glass looks off. Kind of fake, as you said. The story reads like a graphic novel. All she needs is a cape. Some of it tracks as her history, just glorified. But with her face. And with a black German Shepherd also named Shadow."

"My computers are in Nellie. But I have a runabout laptop here and can do some initial snooping. Let me see what we've got." He retrieved the laptop then sat beside her on the sofa. Teddy balanced the computer so they both could see.

Ethel laced her fingers together, praying he wouldn't find anything bad. September had always kept secrets. But she'd never imagined they rose to the level of betrayal.

Teddy's fingers flew over the keyboard. He tried a couple spellings of the name, and finally settled on one that delivered the most information. "Glass? Jackson Glass served as part of the security detail I hired for the wedding. He came highly recommended. I vetted him myself."

He didn't have to specify who's wedding.

"You think he has something to do with this?"

Teddy shrugged. He tapped more keys. "Here we go." He read silently for a moment, then sucked in a breath. "That explains a lot. September told me a long-lost relative left her Cat's Cradle in their will."

This house belongs to September?

"It also opens a worm bed of questions. Or a rat's nest." He pointed to a press release.

Ethel read the title aloud: "Henry Wong's Missing Daughter, Sorokin Glass, Found After 28 Years, Inherits All."

She bit her lip, reading the rest silently. The release lauded her exploits, raising her to hero status. Ethel read the last line silently, and then again out loud. "Ms. Glass has the experience and skills to make her father proud as she continues the Family tradition and runs the organization."

The Wong family. She shook her head, sick at her stomach. "How long has she known?"

Teddy took off his glasses, polished them on the hem of his parrot shirt, clearly trying to gather his thoughts before answering. "Let's not borrow trouble, at least not yet. Criminal enterprises use sleight of hand to confuse the authorities. The images and the videos look real, but I know better than anyone how convincing a deepfake can be."

"So it's not real?"

He sighed. "I don't know. It'll take a while. Whoever created the videos has talent. They've used real footage, which makes it more difficult to suss out what's real and what's not. You and I both know the kinds of trouble September's dodged for years. This might explain some of that."

She took a deep trembling breath. "Please let me know as soon as you find out. If it's true, it'll just about kill Jeff. If she hurts him I don't think I could ever forgive September."

Chapter Nineteen: September

J ared, do you have anything that belongs to your little
girl?" September ran one hand through her hair,
wishing she'd left it tied up in the messy ponytail. The
long chestnut strands stuck to her damp neck and trailed
down her back.

The man nodded vigorously, then made an odd sound of
pain and put his hands to his head. "I don't feel so good."
He opened the car door, and climbed out, grabbing the roof
of the car to steady himself. "I got some of Alana's stuff in
the trunk. Maybe her stuffed kangaroo? She slept with that,
before…" His voice turned rough. "She never would leave
that behind if she had a choice. I saved it for her."

Pierce rolled his eyes. "Really? What you gonna do with a
stuffed toy?"

"You'd be surprised." September smiled softly, and
stroked Shadow's brow, smoothing the worry wrinkles from

his forehead. "Baby dog, you're going to help this man get his daughter back." Shadow wagged.

This was her opportunity to show the Family exactly who Sorokin Glass was.

Jared suddenly sat down hard on the pavement.

"Pierce, get this car parked in a legal spot, then find someone to check out Jared's head injury. Take care of him. I'm going after his daughter."

Sighing, Pierce took out his phone and dialed someone. He spoke softly, disconnected, and turned to help the man up. "Security's on the way. They'll get him checked out at the hospital."

"But I need to be there. I gotta go with you." Jared straightened himself, doing his best to remain upright without wobbling. "Kidnapper's s'pozed to text me where to go."

"Just hang tight, brother." Pierce swiveled and raised his hand as a pair of security personnel appeared from the hotel. "Go. Get yourself checked out, so you'll be there for your daughter when we retrieve her. We're gonna do this right." His glare at September said: *You're the boss.*

Her lips tightened. *Damn straight.* But she said nothing. "Pop the trunk. Give me the toy. I promise we'll do everything we can to bring Alana back to you."

One of the security guys released the trunk. The other slipped one arm around Jared's waist and helped the injured man to a waiting company car.

"You have my number. When you get the location and instructions, text me." She didn't feel comfortable speaking freely in front of hotel staff. Where did their allegiance rest? Were they employed by the Family? Or simply contract workers unaware of the inner workings?

September rummaged in the open trunk of the car,

opening the zipper on a large shabby suitcase. Inside was clean but worn clothing belonging to Jared, and a small pink backpack with a princess crown on the cover. She hadn't ask how old Alana was, assuming a trafficking case meant a teen or early twenties-something.

She flagged one of the security guys. "Jared will need a change of clothes." She indicated the suitcase, then opened the backpack, and her throat tightened. Petite clothing, child size. Sparkly sandals. And a kangaroo with a pink bandanna, a tiny Joey peeking out of its pouch.

September closed the backpack, leaving the stuffed toy inside. The whole thing was small enough to carry. The toy and her clothes in the tiny backpack would have condensed and held Alana's scent. She wasn't sure yet how to find the girl. But once they had a starting point, Shadow could narrow the search by her scent.

She understood Jared's reluctance to enlist the police. But she had made that mistake, when she should have asked for help. She'd reach out as soon as they confirmed Jared's story. Also, selfishly, she didn't want anyone to share this with Combs before she could explain.

God, she was tired of the secrets, especially secrets that could get him and the kids hurt. Yet, until she firmly established complete control, she refused to risk sharing too much. She'd protect Combs and his kids—and her chosen family—to the death. They'd do the same for her.

In the meantime, she'd get the dirt on this mysterious monster, and the horrific trafficking. Reaching out to Lia and picking her brain about last summer's case would be the first step.

Crappiocca happens. If Lia couldn't help, she'd hit up Teddy. He'd always been like a grandfather to her, ready to help, and always had her back. Teddy wouldn't ask too many questions. They trusted each other. That's what chosen family did.

Chapter Twenty: Combs

C ombs slouched in his chair. He couldn't get comfortable, not with his leg stuck out straight in a cast. The food had gone cold on the plate, so he pushed it aside. His eyes felt gritty from staring at the small screen on his phone. So much to read, watch, digest— and none of it good.

Sorokin Glass. The Magpie. Wong's long-lost daughter magically resurrected to take the reins of the organization at just at the right time. Not just a look-alike to laugh about, as Officer Teves suggested. After all his years working as a beat cop, undercover, and as a detective, Combs no longer believed in coincidence.

"Does she think I'm stupid?" He set down the phone and rubbed his face.

He'd heard of innocuous "sleeper agents," inserted into American society decades in advance, then activated and put into play when the need arose. While not a conspiracy nut, Combs couldn't help but speculate. Trusting his gut had saved him more than once, and this revelation lit the fuse on suspicion, doubt, and betrayal. The flames gnawed him from the inside out.

September Day, the love of his life—they'd been through so much—he wanted to save her. And God knows, she'd saved him in many ways. Had it all been a fabrication? A way to coldly manipulate his feelings?

No! She must have a reason, an explanation. He just had to ask.

Combs grabbed up the phone and called her before he could second guess himself. It rang until it finally went to voice mail. He bit his lip. Probably for the best. If they spoke now, he'd say things better left unsaid.

Calm down. Think. She wouldn't ignore his call for long, not if truly playing him.

Stop it! He couldn't read anything into a missed call. September had to ride herd on Willie while Combs stayed out of commission, plus handle her own pet behavior consults. Not to mention the renovations at the lake property she'd recently inherited.

Wait… September said it came from an unknown relative. What relative? Could that mean—

<Call me asap. We need to talk.

He sent the text before he could talk himself out of it, and again set down the phone.

When they first met, during a blizzard no less, he'd been struck by her despair, her hurt, and her brokenness. He'd only wanted to protect her, help her heal. With his own brokenness fueling his bruised heart, he'd fallen hard.

Had she lied to him from the beginning? Played him for a fool like a puppet master? And to what end? Yes, the

Family ran several legit operations, but the crime side tainted the whole. As the new head of one of the largest and most powerful crime families, how could he condone such behavior, consort with someone whose profession he abhorred, and an organization he'd sworn to bring to justice?

Combs groaned, resting his face in his hands. *Crazy thinking.* She'd kept secrets from him before, but always relented with full explanation. Usually the reasons made sense, at least to her. She came to every situation from a place of past pain and emotional damage. And yes, often the reasoning made no sense to his cop sensibility. September's PTSD set her apart, making her susceptible to, and a victim of, her own demons.

She had to know about this. Had she agreed to it, asked for it, been complicit, or something else? How long had she known? And why hadn't she said anything? He and September were as good as married!

Wait.

Kaliko Wong had targeted September for years, culminating in the wedding debacle. Had September's hidden relationship with Henry Wong fueled that vendetta? Had September known beforehand? Or only recently learned of the relationship?

His head hurt worse than his frigging leg. He shifted in the chair, and flinched, silently cursing his inability to go after September and demand answers. Ethel thought her trip to Dallas meant a romantic rendezvous, but maybe instead she planned to explain…or maybe to cut ties. If she couldn't justify the secrets this time, could they ever trust each other again? What future could you have without trust?

Cursing again, this time out loud, he waved away the nursing staff when they checked on his outburst. She might keep secrets from him, but he knew someone with an expertise in unraveling the most nefarious, and convoluted hidden mysteries. He dialed again.

"Teddy, I need your help."

Chapter Twenty-One: Willie

Willie sat in the back of Aunt Ethel's car, arms crossed hard against his narrow chest. She frowned on him listening in on grown-ups' conversation. But he couldn't help overhearing all the juicy stuff she and Mr. Williams talked about. He didn't know whether to be angry, sad, or worried. So he settled on all three.

He couldn't ask any questions, either. Not when he wasn't supposed to know about it. Grown-ups did that a lot: assumed kids wouldn't understand, didn't deserve to know the whole truth. He'd be glad when he got grown-up, and people wouldn't try to hide things from him. He wasn't a baby anymore! He'd been through stuff. He'd even helped September thwart bad guys. He liked that word. Sounded like the sound of a superhero weapon...*thwart-thwart-thwart!*

That's why this news worried him so much, making his

stomach hurt in a weird kind of way. September was one of
the good guys, even if she was a girl. Yet Aunt Ethel now
seemed to think she had something to do with Dad's
injuries.

The bad guys attacked the wedding to go after
September, but she didn't get hurt. Did keeping secrets from
Dad prove she was a nefarious bad guy? Maybe it was good
the wedding hadn't happened, so Dad could back out.

Tears welled at that thought. He really liked September.
Maybe even loved her. Not that he'd say that out loud—
definitely uncool to say to somebody who wasn't your
relative. Yet.

"Willie, my friend would welcome your help toting boxes
and such from her van; she can't walk very well after her
knee replacement." Aunt Ethel eyed him in the rear-view
mirror. He shrugged and nodded. He didn't trust himself to
speak or he might blurt questions she wouldn't want to
answer.

"Thanks. I knew we could count on your brawn." She
grinned. "Afterwards, you can check out the rest of the fair
while we set up. Some booths don't open until after the
parade, but it'll give you a taste."

"Sure." He stared out the window.

Aunt Ethel muttered under her breath. "Guess we better
park here, and hoof it in."

At least he didn't have to tote things from their car. The
plastic ribbon dividing up the parking area reminded Willie
of crime scene tape. He shivered. He'd seen that for real,
and it wasn't nearly as cool as TV shows made it out to be.

Lots of people already crowded the place, mostly retirees
and some kids since school didn't start for a while. Some
men walked around in kilts, showing bare knees, and high
socks with tassels. Furry purses hung down in front of their

privates. They'd be in the parade later. A skirl of plaintive music echoed; the droning haunting sound announced at least one nervous bagpiper practicing for the coming contest.

Willie ducked beneath one of the ribbon barriers and followed Aunt Ethel down a path already worn into the sod to reach the vendor area. Nearby, a large open field stood ready to welcome the Highland games, deeds of strength and dexterity.

A lady who looked a lot like Aunt Ethel with faded red hair wearing a blue skirt and yellow blouse waved at them. She stood at the end of a grassy corridor flanked on each side with white tent canopies. Aunt Ethel waved back and hurried to meet her friend. Willie lagged behind, taking in the displays.

Face painting looked pretty neat, except it was for little kids, and mostly appealed to girls. They had designs for comic faces, for adding snakes, and delicate blossom patterns, depending on the flavor of mystic fairy creature you wanted to be. Whatever.

He paused at another display, admiring the swirled pattern on one blade, which looked like gas shimmering on water. It decorated a wicked 18-inch knife, jagged teeth on one side, honed to a razor's edge on the other.

"Willie, come help." Aunt Ethel called from several booths away, and Willie jogged to reach her. Across the way, the blacksmith had fired up his bellows. In the August heat, it felt like H-E-double toothpicks to Willie.

The friend had backed her van right up to the rear of her canvas canopy, and already had tables set up. Willie ignored the boring chatter between the two—as they spread plaid cloths over the tables—picking up boxes as directed and setting them on the specified tables. The ladies unpacked and created an artistic display of silver and stone jewelry, colorful crystals, and paintings nestled in cardboard frames covered in protective plastic. Most of the pictures featured fantasy characters: fairies, unicorns, dragons, even a flying cat or two. An assortment of homemade candles, and jars of honey and jam, completed the offerings.

"Can I go now? That's all the boxes."

"Thanks, Willie. Yes, you can go explore for a while. We'll finish up and then visit. Check in every so often, okay?" Aunt Ethel gave him a hug, and he tolerated it briefly before pulling away.

He really wanted to go back and look closer at that knife. But he figured he'd check out other stuff along the way, so he didn't keep Aunt Ethel waiting. She had lots on her mind, after losing Uncle Stan and all. And now the business about September.

Or whatever her new name was.

He passed a booth displaying tooled leather bracelets and wallets. He saw an armband Melinda would love with Celtic knots embossed in the design. The man at the booth had the biggest arms Willie had ever seen, with massive tattoos featuring intricate knots that twisted and rolled across his flesh like a living sleeve. When the man saw him looking, he grinned and flexed his muscles, making the tattoo jump and dance. On the other arm, he glimpsed a dragon. *Awesomeness.*

Next, he passed a booth full of home canned vegetables. Yuck. Well the pickles looked pretty good, but gee, you could get that stuff at the grocery.

The booth next door sold sparkly fairy wings in cellophane wrapping, ready to strap on a little girl's back. Willie made a face. The masks looked great, though. Wolves, and dragons with teeth, and a massive lion head. And swords! He picked one up to look closer, and immediately set it down. Plastic and fake. No fun.

Not that Aunt Ethel would let him get a real sword. He might come back later for a mask. That could help with his acting, even though the director said he had to be good enough to convince the audience without a special costume. He'd still like a mask. Maybe the lion, or better yet the wolf. That would put him over the top. The director would see it and flip out—in a good way.

"Whoa." The glint of the sun sparkled on chain mail at the next display. He'd read stories about King Arthur and knights, paladins who fought for righteous causes, to thwart evil, but he'd never seen armor in person. It felt amazing, cool to the touch, with layered scales like a snake.

"Made it with a 3D printer." The owner of the booth grinned at him. "Go ahead and look. But they're pricey. Bring your mom or dad back and we'll make a deal."

The chain mail fit over and around the shoulders of a manikin. Willie looked at the price tag. "Whoa!" Way more than his piddly allowance could manage, and no way would any grown-up pay that for a costume. But maybe one of the dragon tails you could attach to a belt…they came in vibrant colors: green and silver and black.

Willie continued, giving short shrift to displays of decorated gourds, pottery with Celtic designs, embroidered tapestries featuring stylized trees, mythical beasts, and all kinds of Irish or Scottish coats of arms. One booth provided information about the Choctaw Tribe. He wondered what they had to do with the festival. He'd ask Aunt Ethel later.

At the end of the row sat a fully enclosed ominous red tent, with a narrow entrance. It seemed deserted, so he drew nearer to read the sign.

The Psychotic Psychic:
Magical Maeve's Tarot Readings.

Curiosity piqued, Willie crept up to the entrance to check it out. Inside the crimson tent, black lace wall hangings transformed the space into spiderweb shadows. He imagined ghostlike figures moving about inside. Dad said psychics were fakes, but Willie figured it was just grown-up pretend and kinda fun. Just like he did with acting at the theater.

The sign offered a whole list of prices for different kinds of readings. He didn't know what tarot was, but the prices didn't seem that bad. You could get a reading for ten to twenty bucks. Wouldn't hurt, as long as you knew it was fake. Maybe he could ask about September's fake name and see what the psychotic psychic said.

He stuck his head further inside. He heard a clink-clank sound, and jumped, startled by movement under one of those spiderwebby wall hangings.

A girl's face peered out, painted to look like a cat. She wore a skimpy blue dress with a sequined belt, fairy wings on her back, and a heavy chain binding one ankle to the table leg.

"You supposed to be a fairy?" He eyed the chain, and noticed the area around her ankle had calluses, like she'd worn that chain for more than a few hours. He raised his eyebrows.

She shook her head, bit her lip, and looked all around the tent as though fearful somebody watched. "She'll come back soon. You gotta go."

"Who? Magical Maeve? I can pay." He dug in one pocket and pulled out wadded bills. Not enough for the chain mail, but he could fund a so-called reading, if he wanted to.

"She's dangerous. No lie, you need to leave." Her wide eyes held a curious combination of resignation, fear, and desperation. "She'll hurt you, too."

Willie dared a glance outside of the tent. Nobody there. But that didn't mean the girl was wrong. He thought for a second, then grinned with delight. "It's an act. Right? You almost got me there, you're pretty good. I'm gonna be an actor, too."

Her breath quickened. "Not an act. She caught me, she could catch you."

He frowned and drew closer. "No lie?" He crouched down, took a closer look at the chain attached to leather bindings wrapped around her scarred ankle. Holy cats! It wasn't an act. He ran his hand down the links of the chain to reach where it connected to the table leg and discovered the small padlock that kept it attached. "Geeze Louise."

"What have we here? Alana, you telling this poor boy stories?" An imposing woman entered the tent, blocking the entrance. She wore a long silver-shot broomstick skirt with a ring of jangling keys hooked to her waist. A leather vest laced up her chest, complete with a knife in a sheath nestled in the cleavage of her ample figure. A sequined scarf bound the crown of her head, out of which sprouted gray braids that fell nearly to her waist.

Willie gasped and fell backwards on his butt, scooting away from her menacing figure.

"Kid, you should know better than to try to rescue a fairy princess. Only the iron chain binds her magic—and messing with fairy magic could get you killed." She reached for the knife sheathed at her bosom.

Choking back a scream, Willie backpedaled, fetching up against the red canvas at the rear of the booth and staked snuggly to the ground. He scooted around, hands behind his back seeking purchase. He finally got fingers under it, lifted the edge, and wriggled out.

He pelted away. He had to tell Aunt Ethel about the girl held captive in the psychotic psychic tent.

Chapter Twenty-Two: September

September hurried to the hotel, followed by Pierce and Shadow, clutching Alana's backpack in one hand, strap of her go bag over the other shoulder, and pressing her phone to her ear with the other hand. When it went to voice mail, she wrinkled her nose and debated what kind of message to leave.

"Lia, I need to pick your brain about last summer. The case you and Officer Teves were involved in about trafficked Hawaiian girls."

She paused as the hotel transport carrying Jared drove past. "I know you're busy with class and training, but please call back or text as soon as you can. Something's come up—related, I think."

She ignored Pierce's snort of amusement behind her.

"I'm mostly interested in anything about who ran the operation. Specifically, was it a Kaliko Wong operation? Any known associates, are they in custody? And identity of victims, especially any still missing." That would help verify Jared's story. She disconnected.

Pierce surged ahead to grab open the door. He held it, bowing his head slightly in a courtly gesture. She hesitated, then rushed through, Shadow in her wake.

She couldn't quite figure him out. Ready with his gun, but late to the party—and she'd done nothing special to evade him. Or had that been intentional?

Paranoid much? Her insecurity meant second-guessing everyone's actions and motives. September trusted Gabriel Pierce as far as she could throw him.

"Left a message for my cousin." Not quite accurate, now she knew her true parentage, but that didn't change how she felt. She'd choose Lia over these new relatives any day. "Lia's at the Dallas police academy, and kind of hard to reach. Last summer, she got dragged into the trafficking gang Jared says took his daughter."

Pierce collected a piece of hard candy from one coat pocket. He popped the mint into his mouth, returned the crinkly cellophane wrapper to his pocket then spoke around the candy. "Why not just call your cop husband?"

"He's not my husband." *Why did I say that?* "Yet. Jack briefed you on…everything." She glared. "Long as rehab lasts, the doctors want Combs away from any stress, anything work related, so he can concentrate on healing."

"Must be driving him crazy, getting shut out." Pierce smiled, and crunched the candy, renewing the scent of peppermint.

She really didn't like him.

Needing to burn off her own stress, they took the stairs. September wasn't surprised when Jack met them in the lobby.

"Hotel security sent an alert. You got accosted in the parking garage?" He whirled, getting in Pierce's face. "Where were you?" The men mirrored each other in height and build, a before-and-after picture: a youthful dark man squaring up to pale elder, fists ready and nostrils flaring.

September snorted. Let them whale on each other and leave her alone. "Come on Shadow." She strode past, pointedly ignoring their posturing. When they continued to growl at each other, September barked at them. "Fight later. Work now." When they didn't move, she turned with hands on hips. "Jack, you have your computer here?"

He nodded, and his white hair shimmered in the hotel lights. "Always. What's going on?"

He boasted his Internet skills made data dance to his tune. According to Jack, he'd had a back door into the Family's online dealings for years. Time to put that intel to the test.

Pierce scanned the lobby, documenting the army of uniformed employees pretending to ignore the raised voices: two behind the registration desk, more at the concierge podium, the high-end bling-centric gift shop, waiters hosting coffee and juice offerings, the valet stand, the elevator monitor, and lounging elsewhere ready to take care of any guest issues that might arise. His eyes narrowed. He took a step closer, bent to speak softly in September's ear. "We need a secure place. If you really want to do this, limit personnel involved."

"Conference room." Jack pointed, a key card already in his hand. "This better be good, Sorokin. Took me weeks to coordinate and get everybody here for your introduction." He led the way, muttering under his breath. "Whatever you're cooking better not derail things. First impressions matter. Careful you don't set things back months."

Her shoulders tightened at the sharp rebuke. Shadow whined and nosed her hand. "It's okay, baby dog. I'm here." *And thank God you're here too, Shadow.* She'd landed in a diamond-crusted world filled with vipers eager to strike. She trusted no one but her dog.

Jack's laptop was already set up at one end of the long table. Pads of paper with pens sat in front of each chair. This must be where her introduction to the board of directors would take place.

September dropped Alana's princess backpack onto the middle of the table, shrugged off her go bag onto a chair, then she and Pierce pulled chairs to either side of Jack, as took his place behind the computer. Shadow explored the room, performing his standard *check-it-out* without prompting. Once he finished, her shoulders relaxed as he settled at her feet and rested his chin on one foot.

"From the top. What happened in the garage?" Jack's uncanny pale eyes stared hard.

She took a deep breath, focusing her thoughts. "I need to start earlier. All the stories about me in the news, especially the flurry of propaganda…"

Jack raised his white eyebrows and cocked his head. "You mean the PR campaign about Sorokin Glass and her reappearance?" His voice, though mild, cautioned her to proceed carefully. He'd authored most of that propaganda.

"You have to admit to some poetic license, romanticizing my history, and everything about me. It's attracted attention."

"Good. It was meant to do that."

"Not all attention is good. I've gotten phone calls, dozens of letters and texts, emails filled with threats. Some plead for help, or demand *donations*, or want special attention paid to a friend, an enemy, and on and on. Everyone thinks

I'm this bottomless pit of money." She smoothed and tucked long hair behind each ear. "It's worse than when I won the lottery years ago." That small payout on the heels of her first husband's death proved small consolation to losing him. That, along with his insurance, funded her retreat to Texas, and purchase of the old Victorian.

Jack sighed, and leaned against the table, big hands flat on the tabletop. "We talked about this. You have nearly unlimited resources, Sorokin. People will reach out to you. They'll ask, even demand, more from you than you should ever give." He offered a smile. "Learn to say no. Politely. Firmly. Hire assistants to field the requests and say no for you. Ignore distractions, or you'll never survive emotionally—or otherwise. This isn't an easy game to play. You know that."

"Especially when it escalates to tracking you down and accosting you in the parking garage." Pierce leaned back, crossing his arms over his broad chest. "The man tried to kidnap her."

"But he didn't. I stopped him." She didn't hide her exasperation. "Yes, a determined petitioner, but harmless. I took him out with a handful of crap. Literally. *You* only showed up in time for cleanup."

September felt small satisfaction when Pierce winced at the barb.

"Look, from the beginning I have voiced my plan for changes in the Wong organization. Every big company makes mistakes. If what happened to that poor man's daughter connects to Kaliko and the Family, I'm now responsible." She flexed her neck and shoulders, trying to relieve the ache. "There's no better way to make my intentions clear. I want to get his daughter back and make restitution."

"You gonna bleed the company dry? Shut it down?" The two men looked at each other.

"Yes. Maybe. Why not?"

"Might want to rethink that. Certainly don't say it too loud in public."

She couldn't read Jack's expression. "I have no attachment to this…Family. Or the money. It's not real to me." She stood, unable to sit any longer. She paced the room, more and more determined to make this happen. She would not be handled.

"Every company decision impacts more than just the board. Or the boss." Pierce's deep voice stopped her for a moment. "Do you know how many people Wong Enterprises employs? Forget the off-the-books operations, think about the legit ones. The staff at this hotel, for instance. Blow everything up, and everyday Joes…and Jills…lose their jobs."

No. September shook her head. She couldn't think in those terms. Better to stay focused on black-and-white issues. Shades of gray distracted from what needed to happen.

But Pierce's gentle words, so logical, painted a more compelling reason to proceed with caution. "Jared"—he looked at Jack—"the guy in the parking garage, said he found you by visiting your house? Talking to somebody there."

September gasped, belatedly realizing the implications. He'd spoken to Willie, confronted Ethel. She must call them, make sure they were okay.

Quickly, she dialed while walking to the other end of the room. No answer. "Ethel, please check in. I just met a…well, unexpected visitor named Jared. He said you sent him. Are you and Willie okay? Please let me know."

What she'd worried about had already begun. This new life, her position, put her real family in danger. "Jared got a ransom demand. The kidnapper sicced him on me to fund the exchange."

Jack's pale eyes widened. "Interesting. Trolls stirring the pot."

She didn't know what that meant. "Alana disappeared last year. I think it might have been part of a case Combs worked on. I wasn't involved, although Shadow did some tracking during the case." She stopped when she felt Shadow shift and press harder against her leg. He'd suffered his own injuries in the fire due to Combs's lapse in judgment.

Jack knew her history. He'd studied it to tweak for those judging her fitness to run the family business—he pumped up exploits and played down insecurities and failures, painted the new boss of Wong Enterprises as resolute, ruthless, and savvy. Like Kaliko. And like Henry Wong, her father.

She felt none of those things. But she'd play the part. She had no choice.

"I left a message for Lia Corazon. She was involved in the case, too. I don't want Combs bothered by this. Do I make myself clear?" She stopped pacing long enough to nail each man with her gaze and waited for them to agree.

"This man accosted you in the parking garage, demanded you pay the ransom for his kidnapped daughter, and you agreed?" Jack waited to work his magic with the laptop.

"The Family ran the operation, making me responsible. It's up to me to make amends."

Jack shook his head. "I'm all for you wanting to set things right, Sorokin. But not like this. You don't even have the full backing of the Family yet."

"You told me that was automatic, said I had no choice. So which is it?" She breathed heavily.

"Pierce, can you talk some sense into her?" Jack stood as well, frustration clear in his stiff posture and clipped words.

"I'm just the help. She's the boss." He grinned at September, clearly enjoying the exchange. Pierce put his hands behind his head and leaned back in the chair.

Disgusted, September rummaged for her cell phone when it vibrated with an incoming text.

>Jared here. Message says Sorkin bring $ at kleptic festival in hartlind, time details later. You still help me? PLEASE!!!!

"Jared got a message from the kidnapper. They want me to deliver the ransom at...I think he means Heartland at some festival. He must mean..." Ethel always attended the Celtic Festival and planned to take Willie today. September needed to warn her.

And she needed trustworthy help. Her "boss" power over these two men—let alone anyone else in the organization—had little clout. She dialed, and her shoulders relaxed when he answered on the first ring. "Teddy, it's me. I need a favor—"

"That's a habit with you. Lots of favors. And lots of secrets, isn't that right?" The older man's voice trembled more than usual, clearly emotional about something.

She frowned, and walked to the other side of the room, lowering her voice. "What's wrong? Did something happen? Are Ethel and Willie okay?"

"They were just here. They're fine, no thanks to you." He cleared his throat, and she heard his cat meow in the background. "I've got to go. I can't help you this time, September. Not until you're honest with me. And, God help us, maybe not even then." He disconnected.

Chapter Twenty-Three: Jared

No matter what the doctor said, Jared would not be staying overnight. Forget about more tests. A few bruises couldn't compare with the pain of losing Alana. He planned to be out of here and on his way back to Heartland as soon as he could manage it. He was already feeling better after the food, but he still needed another Red Bull.

The fellow that brought him from the hotel had been cordial enough, even authorized payment for the medical attention, since the accident—that's what they were calling it—happened on the property. For that he was grateful.

Sorokin hadn't discounted his plea out of hand but had sidelined him. He texted her the kidnapper's latest message but had got no response. Had she changed her mind? Jared needed to be there for Alana. That was a father's job.

A quick phone search and Jared found the Celtic Festival

being held a short drive north of the fly speck town where Sorokin lived. He could find it. But not without a car. Uber, maybe?

Another text. His heart quickened. From Sorokin? The kidnapper said she'd use different phones, so maybe Sorokin did, too.

>Clocks ticking. Have the funds?

Kidnapper. He licked his lips.

<Soon. I met Sorokin

His leg jigged up and down with impatience, staring at the phone, willing the next text to come through. When it rang from an unknown caller, Jared didn't want to answer and miss reading the text. He gritted his teeth when the phone refused to give up its strident demand. "Hello?"

"Meeting Sorokin, good first step. Pray she works fast. Hear this?" The phone moved away.

Jared heard soft weeping in the background. A sudden loud cry, then muffled scream followed, and then louder sobbing. He'd wished to hear her voice...oh God!

"What'd you do?" He wanted to scream but kept his voice low to prevent hospital staff converging on him. "Alana, oh please *keiki*, don't cry. I'll come for you, Papa's coming."

The kidnapper came back on the line. "That's your fault. Every delay, every time your answers aren't satisfactory, your little one gets it. She's used to punishment, though, such a bad girl. Got toughened up over the past year. You wanna hear how she got toughened up?" A low chuckle. "Lots of people pay good money to make girls scream."

Jared choked on his own sobs. He whispered through the tears. "Why you doin' this? How could you..."

"I don't care about her. Or you. It's about the money. When you see Sorokin again, remember she made this happen, it's all her fault. She owes you. And I want my piece of the honey pot." Her mocking tone hardened to brittle venom. "The festival closes at 8:00 pm. I'll take the cash anytime, but deadline is 8:45 pm. I have eyes all over the festival. If I see anyone sticking noses into our arrangement, Alana disappears for good." Her voice growled, a rabid animal anxious to bite anyone within range.

He stifled his tears. Be strong for Alana. By tonight, he'd have her back. But the Celtic Festival covered several acres with hundreds of exhibits and events. "The trading place. Where should she come?" He tried to sound decisive, but he knew she held all the cards.

"All in good time. Just make sure she gets small used bills. Unmarked, from her stash, not from a bank. She'll need at least two bags."

Jared leaned forward putting one hand over his eyes while still clutching the phone. "But $500k, and not from the bank…"

"The Family has extra cash for emergencies." She laughed and repeated the word. "Emergencies. Bet she never predicted this when she decided to cancel my career, the son-of-a—"

He whispered, not wanting anyone outside of the room to overhear. "But she's here. I mean, here in Dallas. Takes time to get money, drive to the festival—"

"Not my problem. Tell her no cops." She snarled the words. "Not her boyfriend, not any of her friends. Sorokin and me, we meet alone to make the exchange, no later than 8:45. Tell her. I see anyone else sticking their noses into my beeswax, I'll finish my business with Alana the way I should have months ago. And leave her in pieces in the red tent."

Robin disconnected the phone, pleased she had put the fear of the devil into the man. She glared at the girl who cowered beneath the display table. Reaching down, she grabbed the chain manacled to the girl's ankle and yanked hard until Alana squealed.

The brat grew bolder by the minute. Shouldn't have let her talk to her daddy. "I dressed you up for the story you tell. You're a captured fairy, magic bound by the iron chain. If anyone shows up to investigate, I'll do them in like I did Maeve. And it'll be your fault. Your fault again, would you like that? They're dropping like flies, you're such bad luck."

Alana shuddered, squeezing her eyes shut, and whimpering like the baby she was.

Disgusted, Robin cleared her throat and spat. The pollen, dust, and heat did a number on her sinuses.

At Alana's age, Robin learned to stand up for herself, with nobody around to champion her. Not like Sorokin or September or whatever the Wong princess called herself. Robin turned her life around and became a winner. Now she had a chance to change her life again, to win the biggest jackpot of her life. She'd never be a loser again.

Chapter Twenty-Four: Shadow

Shadow watched September pace the long room. Her heart thumped fast, and her scent spoke of worry. He crouched beneath the big table, peering out between the many chairs.

He didn't care for Jack. The man tried to steal September after the blast. Shadow couldn't trust anyone who tried to steal his person.

Pierce puzzled Shadow, which made him want to get closer for better sniffs. The man kept his distance, didn't stare at Shadow, or approach too close. He knew how to treat good dogs in a polite way. But the man made September uneasy, so Shadow remained cautious.

He reached out to whiff Pierce's pant leg, inhaled deeply but detected no dog or cat. His brow wrinkled. Pierce had no contact with good dogs or special cat friends, like Macy. The people September—and Shadow—trusted most spent time with creatures. No animal smell worried him.

September called Teddy earlier. Usually, Teddy's gruff voice overflowed with affection, sarcasm, and humor. But this time, their talk stopped so quickly, September gasped with shock. She still sat collapsed in the chair beside Jack, propped her elbows on the table, and cradled her face in her hands.

Shadow knew Teddy had upset September. Her heartbeat galloped, and her scent turned acrid, a smell that predicted bad feelings—meant she could fall into that dark place inside herself. A scary place Shadow couldn't follow. It was his job to stop her from falling.

September hadn't fallen into that deep dark place in a long time, many days, more days than a good dog had paws. But he remained vigilant to guide her back to the real world. That was his job. And Shadow would do anything to keep her safe, not only from outside threats, but from those invisible bad feelings that made her sick. To do that, he must touch September, press hard into her arms, to keep her here. Shadow whined. He tried to climb into her lap, to offer a furry anchor to keep her in the here-and-now. But at his movement, she signaled him to *wait*.

The two men argued with September, voices raised with waving hands. Pierce stood up, pacing, while Jack yelled back. She raised her face and sat silent and still, a glazed expression on her face.

Shadow wanted to bark at them. Not with an inside voice, either! Tell them September was in charge, she knew things other people didn't, more than even a good dog could know. September was the smartest person ever. That's why he trusted her, and always followed her commands. Well, except when she got something wrong. Sometimes, good dogs could tell things about the world, like important smells and sounds that people couldn't detect.

He guessed people were smart in many ways, and dogs were smart in other, different ways. That's why he and September made such a good team.

She suddenly slapped both hands down hard on the surface. Shadow jumped. And gave in to his barking urge.

She shoved away from the table, and stood, out-shouting even the loudest barks. "Enough! I've had enough, gentlemen—and I use that term loosely. If you *won't* help me, you will *not* stand in my way." She strode to the door. "Let's go, Shadow. We're on our own. Again."

"No, wait." Jack jumped to his feet, and the rolling chair nearly tipped over. "If you're determined to act stupid about this, let us keep you safe."

Shadow pranced about, panting happily at this sudden action. Maybe they would get in the car and go home. Just him and September. He'd like that. A lot.

"Get me the info I need. Who ran the trafficking operation? If still active, who runs it now? Use that insider hacker genius skills you brag about"—sarcasm dripped from her voice—"and get it done." Her phone buzzed, and she grabbed it to stare at the tiny surface.

Shadow's wagging slowed, recognizing September's dismay. Deep furrows creased her brow. She licked her lips like Shadow did to calm himself. "Another text from Jared. Cash demand of $500K, small, unmarked bills. Deadline tonight, Sorokin to deliver by 8:45 or the child dies." Anguish filled her voice. "How in God's name can I get that much in time? Even if in the accounts, do banks keep so much cash on hand? The drive back to Heartland takes at least ninety minutes without traffic."

Jack crossed the room, gave her a hug.

September stiffened. Shadow growled at the man's

effrontery, but she didn't pull away so it must be okay. He spoke into the top of her head. "Oh, ye of little faith. You still don't understand the resources at your fingertips."

Pierce stood patiently. He glanced at Shadow, then politely away, and yawned without trying to hide it. Surprised, Shadow couldn't help yawning back. He felt his fur smooth along his top line. Pierce might not smell of dogs, but he knew the right signals. Shadow's ears came forward with approval.

Pierce unwrapped another peppermint. "Just gather the cash you need. Don't worry about driving. I've got a helicopter on call."

Chapter Twenty-Five: Lord Byron

L ord Byron watched from the window of the RV. He chirruped, eager to join his special human outside. He used to sneak outdoors to enjoy grass between his toes. But now that they traveled all over, the big man wanted him safe. So Byron learned how to walk on a leash.

The snug walking vest pressed against his long gray fur, but the green vest and leash meant a fun day meeting new people and making friends. Traveling around and perching on the dashboard gave him a nice view of the world. But nothing beat meeting people, enjoying their surprise and admiration at his tricks.

They weren't tricks to Byron. Playing fetch with fuzzy toys or other objects made the audience gasp and clap for more. He loved the games when Ian tossed things to stalk, pounce, subdue, and bring back for another game.

Byron relished chasing real prey more, like the elusive grasshoppers. They tasted bad, though. He'd learned the hard way not to crunch down on the bugs, only play and bat them around. Sometimes they jumped too high and flew away—tiny frustrating birdlike bugs. Lord Byron *ack-ack-acked* deep in his throat at the thought.

He trilled with excitement when Ian returned to the vehicle. Byron patiently waited when the big man climbed inside. "How's my handsome man-cat? Ready for some fun?" He caught Byron up in his massive, colorful bare arms.

Meowing and talking happily, Byron kept up his end of the conversation. He kept his claws retracted—humans, even big ones, squealed when their fragile skin got snagged. Byron pushed his head and chin hard against Ian's neck. Purring with happiness, he rub-rub-rubbed to share signature scent, marking the man as Byron's personal and beloved property.

Ian gently set Byron on the driver's seat, then hurried to the back of the RV. He returned with the cat's outside home, prompting an impatient meow.

"Let me get your condo set up. Got your name on it and everything. Then you can come outside safely and watch while I set up the booth. How's that?"

He meowed again with anticipation when the man also grabbed the bag that held treats. Byron always got full bowls of yummies for outside events. And he hadn't had third breakfast yet.

The collapsed wire cage quickly transformed into a two-level cat friendly condo. Byron watched the familiar set up. Ian placed it on grass in a shaded area under the booth canopy, filled the litter pan with fresh gravel, fastened the water bottle in place and—yes!—dished canned food into the shallow bowl. Byron licked his whiskers, and his purr grew louder.

Lord Byron couldn't help hugging the man hard, even with a bit of claw thrown in, as he rode Ian's bare shoulder from the RV to the condo. Ian grabbed hold of the fabric handle on Byron's walking jacket, catching him midair when he wanted to leap down.

"Grass and fetch later. For now, relax and watch while I finish the set up." Ian opened the wire door and urged Byron inside. The canned food smelled strong and tempting, so he happily crouched over the bowl.

He ignored the rest of the man's busyness. They traveled everywhere together—he remembered no other life—and the routine felt comforting. The bump-and-thump of boxes being moved, metal clanking on metal in cases, the flap and flutter of flags. Tummy full, Byron dozed.

Loud bangs and clangs reverberating beyond the red tent brought Robin up short. "Now what?" She glared at Alana and warned her with a gesture toward the knife holstered in her bodice. It actually made a nice touch to the hokey costume she put together from the dead fortuneteller's closet. "Stay here, and no noise, not even like a mouse. Got me?"

Alana nodded, eyes big.

It must be a vendor, running late, and setting up booth space. She better check out who drew the short straw as her neighbor, and make sure they wouldn't interfere. Maeve mentioned meeting relatives here. Robin fingered the long braids she'd attached to the sequined headscarf she wore, and whispered, "Surprise."

She ducked out beneath the swag opening, and carefully avoided the taut ropes and ground stakes that held the tent canopy in place. The soothsayer's booth squatted at the end of the long column of white tents, a bloody exclamation point for the rest of the line. How appropriate. Lucky for her, this end of the fairgrounds remained deserted. But that wouldn't last for long.

The spot next door remained open air with no confining sides below the shaded canopy. With grass as carpet, a tripod held a sign that announced the attraction: ax throwing.

Now this could be fun. Robin loved anything with blades.

A burly man wrestled a third large wooden box into an upright position. Each of the boxes had a large bull's-eye painted on it. At the front of the display squatted the trunk of a massive tree with a half-dozen sharp axes buried in its top. Next to the stump, and taking advantage of the shade, sat a large wire cat condo with a sleeping gray feline curled up inside on a soft bed.

Ah yes. Maeve mentioned the stupid cat.

He caught sight of her and did a double take. "For a minute there, I thought you was my cousin. You a friend of Maeve?" He nodded at the red tent and shaded his eyes with his hand. "She inside? Going fancy on us hiring extra help? Hey Maeve, you gonna introduce me to your cute friend?" He grinned. "I'm Ian, by the way."

Robin's eyes narrowed with calculation as her smile widened. She put hands on her hips, swaying them as she took a few steps closer. "I heard about you. The cousin?" She nodded at the sleeping feline. "That Lord Byron? Like literature, do you, along with cats?"

"That's right, cousin on her meemaw's side. Big family."

He looked her up and down, the tip of his tongue wetting his lower lips. "I'm told it takes a big man, a confident sensitive guy to appreciate pussy cats." He blinked, feigning innocence. "We're all of us big. All over." Ian flexed his bare sweaty arms, and a colorful snake tattoo undulated.

"And how big is that?" She walked closer, letting him ogle her low-cut bodice. Maeve wasn't small, but Robin's buxom figure trumped the dead woman's. She felt the heat of his eyes on her as she passed. Robin strutted around the three big wooden boxes, noting the backsides hinged open to prop them upright. In transit, they held equipment, nesting boxes for axes, swords, and miscellaneous items for his display and sales.

Ian followed her. "Want to find out how big?" His breath smelled of pizza and cigarettes. Heat radiated off him in waves. "Is Maeve in the tent, or somewheres else?" Fishing—he wondered if they'd have privacy.

She shrugged with coy invitation. "Haven't seen her since early this morning." *True.* "You want to check out the new…uhm, displays?" She stroked down the length of the plaited hair, brushed it against her flushed skin, and whirled, making the skirt swirl around her ankles. She didn't wait to see him follow, just hurried back to the front of the crimson tent and ducked inside.

Robin had the knife out of the sheath before he'd even crossed the threshold. As Ian blinked in the shuttered red gloom, she lured him to the back of the tent, pushing the table to one side. Alana squealed and pulled away the length of the chain.

"Wait. Who's she?" He balked, but his forward motion carried him close.

Her knife slashed his thick neck before he could back away. Blood splashed the back of the tent, the wet wash only darkening the fabric a darker crimson. He dropped to his knees, eyes wide, and mouth gaping. Ian fell forward hard on his face.

"Not a word, you." Robin glared at Alana. She wiped her blade on one of the tablecloths and re-sheathed it. Let him bleed out in here, into the ground where it wouldn't show. His bad luck to pick a spot too close to her action.

She bustled out of the tent, retracing steps to the three standing box targets. One still contained products he planned to sell. But the other two, aside from weights in the bottom for stability, stood empty.

Robin tipped the nearest onto its side, grabbed one end, and dragged it behind her red tent. She couldn't carry him, and didn't want to leave his body there—too easy for passersby to catch a glimpse. He'd fit inside, she just needed to get the box close enough to stuff him inside.

It took her several minutes struggling and manipulating to get the box in place. She positioned the box on its side with the open lid flat against the ground. Then she propped up the back of the tent siding just high enough to shove the cousin's body out. She positioned Ian, knees bent, on top of the flat lid. Robin wanted to roll the box onto its proper setting, so she could flip close the lid. But she wasn't strong enough. Instead, she lifted and pushed until the box fell over top of the man on the lid. It would have to do.

"Our family's big, too, and strong, with lots of cousins." But she got the brains in the family, not like her simple-minded cousin, Beebo. He chose his pets over family. Sure, she liked dogs well enough, but not if they stood in the way of business.

She grinned as a new thought occurred to her.

Robin hurried back to the front of the ax-throwing display and looked closer at the cat cage. Not bad. This would work. She opened the front, shaking the metal wire sides, and banged on the top to awaken the sleeping feline.

"Out, get out of there now." She didn't need someone seeing the caged cat and wondering who left a poor kitty unattended in the heat. "Go on now, scat."

The cat hissed, green eyes dilated with excitement. His back arched under the green walking vest. His long gray fur fluffed with aggravation. At a second round of banging on the top, the cat zoomed out the opening, flicked his funny-looking short, crooked tail, and disappeared.

With satisfaction, Robin grabbed the wire cage and grappled it back to the red tent. She ducked inside and set it up right on top of where the big cousin bled out. "Alana, look at what I got you. Now don't say I don't treat you well."

She grabbed the girl's arm, opened the cat cage, and shoved Alana inside. "That'll cool your urge to wander or attract attention. And remember, kid, you play your part as the captive fairy. Or else you'll be playing the part of the dead girl."

Lord Byron crouched beneath his RV, shivering with anxiety. He'd seen the swishy-skirt woman disappear into the tent next door with Ian and waited for him to come back. But he didn't.

Usually after setup, Ian attached the leash so Byron could safely perch on top of the cat condo, or even one of the big boxes. That way he could meet and greet new human friends but stay out of nose range of dogs. You couldn't trust what strange dogs might do.

But that swish-skirted woman moved one of the boxes,

tipped it over and dragged it away.

Byron hissed softly, not liking a stranger rearranging his furniture. He quickly groomed mussed fur back into place, playing particular attention to the crook in his bushy gray tail. Then he raised his head, sniffing delicately for any sign of his person. He meowed, and cried again and again, wanting Ian to come back and catch Byron up in his big arms.

The odd woman stole Byron's person, then the wooden box, and now dragged away his cat condo. What to do? He couldn't get back into the locked RV and had no safe place to sleep. And his person was nowhere to be seen.

Creeping from beneath the vehicle, Byron narrowed his eyes against the bright sunlight. Staying low to the ground, and slinking as quickly as possible, he raced to where the displaced box rested behind the swish-skirt woman's tent.

He carefully sniffed the wooden box from one end to the other. It looked different lying on its side, but still had the familiar odor of his person. Yet another more pungent aroma rose from within the box, something hidden to the eyes and ears but as clear as a moth on a lampshade to Byron's discerning nose: blood.

Lord Byron leaped atop the box, pacing back and forth, crying a haunting ululating song of feline loss and grief.

Chapter Twenty-Six: Alana

Alana tucked herself into a ball in the corner of the cage, scrunched down in an overlarge litter box. It was clean, but she wouldn't have cared if the cat had left stuff in it. She'd experienced worse.

She hid her face against her knees, wrapping her thin arms around her legs to hug herself. She had to duck her head or bump the underside of the second level, accessed only by a small cat size hole in the other end.

What Robin did no longer shocked her. She'd met the woman the girls called Boss last year, before Tony took her away. Tony's special attention to his favorites—including Alana—made her shudder. The older girls got passed around more frequently to Tony's *friends*. That's what he called them, but she'd seen the money change hands. And they didn't act like friends.

Then he disappeared, leaving them locked inside a dingy

place. Relief lasted only briefly when Boss showed up, bringing the starving girls food, until visits from *friends* increased.

Home and her parents seemed very far away. One by one the other girls disappeared. Boss said she sent 'em home where they belonged. But Alana knew the difference between truth and lies. She doubted everything after Boss said, "Never share the truth when a lie serves better."

Alana kept her eyes squeezed tightly shut. Boss didn't like girls to stare. She wanted girls scared and trembly. So Alana had learned to act the way Boss wanted—it sometimes stopped the slaps before they came or shortened the punishment. Now, with the coppery smell clogging the tent, and memory of the recent bloodletting, Alana had no trouble acting like a frightened mouse. She heard the woman bustle around and finally leave the red tent. Only then did she cautiously raise her face, peering through a messy curtain of long dark hair to take in her new surroundings.

The wire cage didn't feel cramped. In fact, Alana felt surprisingly comforted and protected within the enclosure. She picked up a neon yellow mouse toy, missing one button eye, and with a gnawed shortened leather tail. She held the toy like a treasure, stroking its soft short fur with one index finger. She hadn't had a toy in many months. It made her miss her stuffed kangaroo, and just like that, tears filled her eyes.

She wanted to believe the phone call came from Papa, and not some cruel trick arranged by Boss. Alana wanted to go home, like the other girls.

But Boss lied. She lied for fun, she lied for money, she lied cuz she didn't know or care about truth. So Alana figured she lied about the other girls going home. More likely, she kept her promised threats to dump 'em in a ditch somewhere.

She'd never had such a good opportunity to try and escape. With lots of strangers around, like that boy, Boss couldn't keep her dirty secrets so easy. And Papa might really come to find her.

Boss would use her knife on Papa…so she had to get away and go find him. She fingered the latch on the cage door. No way to get it free from this side. Maybe she could pull apart the wire enough to squeeze through, since she got so skinny. But she couldn't let Boss catch her trying.

Her tummy rumbled. She hadn't eaten since yesterday. Her mouth tasted like cotton. A large water bottle hung upside down from one corner of the cage, with a bendy straw at the bottom. She crawled out of the litter box to look closer. Tentatively she touched the tip of her finger to the end of the straw, and a few drops of water leaked out. Alana smiled. She peered around the outside to see how it attached, hoping to unhook the bottle for a long welcome drink. But when she moved the bottle and jiggled to pry it loose, more water leaked out. She whimpered, not wanting to waste a single drop. So she leaned forward, palms and elbows flat on the base, and fit her mouth to the tube and drank, gulping the sweet wet. She stopped only briefly, to catch her breath, and then drank the rest of the warm water. Bliss!

Alana sat up, arming the moisture off her chin. She sniffed. And sniffed again. Not the litter box. This pungent aroma made her tummy rumble again. Maybe something on the second level?

She moved to the small opening and poked her head through to see. Only her head cleared the opening. She couldn't force her shoulders through. But at the far end of the platform Alana saw a bowl. Food? Her mouth watered.

She lowered her head, and then pushed one arm and shoulder up through the hole as far as she could reach. Her fingers scrabbled on the surface of the platform but couldn't quite touch the bowl. Alana pulled her arm back, trembling with frustration. She spied the willow switch, the latest torture Boss used to discipline Alana's misdeeds. It sat on the table right next to the cat cage.

Alana reached through the wire barrier, pressing hard against the side of the cage to grab the end of the switch. She pulled it inside, afraid to smile and jinx the success. She fingered the flexible green stick, firm at one end and whip-thin at the other, that gave her such pain. And now, it would feed her.

She returned to the second-level opening, again pushed her hand through to reach with the long switch. She felt around to locate the dish. Slowly and with care she manipulated it, pushing and dragging until the dish finally came within finger reach.

Eagerly she checked the bowl. Remnants of canned cat food still stuck to the sides and bottom, some of it crusty from standing in the heat. Alana didn't care. She scooped with her fingers, bringing the cat food to her mouth, and cringing at the taste, yet swallowing eagerly.

Alana cleaned out the bowl, bringing it to her face to lick the last crusty pieces free. She'd made do with worse. At least the cat food seemed fresh. She wondered what happened to the cat that owned the food and crate.

She set the bowl down. Only then did she notice the dirty-furred little dog staring at her, pressing close to the side of the cage, sniffing for whiffs of the food bowl.

Chapter Twenty-Seven: September

S eptember leaned over Jack's shoulder, watching as his search unfolded on the small but powerful laptop. He accessed the Family's database—she didn't ask whether it was legit or hacked. Pierce had disappeared twenty minutes ago to make helicopter arrangements.

Pierce looked different when he reappeared. No longer wearing the button-down Wall Street attire, he wore loose-fitting cargo pants, all-terrain lace-up shoes, and a sleeveless V-neck T-shirt that showed more skin and tattoos than she expected. His left shoulder, arm, and back of his hand featured an intricate single wing, each feather rendered in exquisite detail. He clutched the straps of a small knapsack in one hand. Based on what Jack had shared about Pierce's resume, she felt sure the bag mirrored her own go bag, but augmented, in prep for anything they might face. He looked ready for battle, or ambush, and she shivered at the thought.

"I found several possible do-ers." Jack leaned back, flexing his shoulders and stretching his neck. "There's a woman called Sunny in the files. No last name. That could be a code, but she had something to do with drug running."

"Sunny *the Babe* Babcock." September fingered the quarter-sized bald spot at the top of her scalp that never went away. Her hair had regrown since the encounter with Sunny eighteen months ago, but September still remembered the murderous gleam in the killer's eyes, and how she fell into rushing floodwaters, never to be found. "She's alive?" God help her, but September had hoped the woman had drowned.

Jack shrugged. "Like I said, much of this off-the-books data appears in code. I can suss out some of it, but nothing's specific. I don't see any recent communications with that moniker, but that doesn't mean she's not directing operations on the dark side."

"Anyone else?" Maybe the kidnapper's identity didn't matter. Still, she didn't want to walk into this ransom exchange expecting a one-on-one swap and get ambushed by a force of twenty. It made sense that not everyone in the Family welcomed her running the show.

Jack finger-combed snow-white hair. He'd forgone any colored contacts, and his ice blue eyes held both hope and concern. He'd inherited the full effect of albinism, complete with eye issues, while his sister—her mother—had been more fortunate. She had only a *moon mark* of white that streaked her dark hair, which she passed on to September.

"Adding Sunny Babcock to the bad guy list. Also Gray Masterson, Shelley Savage, and Dewey Celeste. Names to monitor. They've variously headed up operations in a number of states, running guns, drugs, prostitution, gambling, and trafficking. Usually they partner with other shady operations, even canned hunts."

September closed her eyes and sucked in a breath. She'd seen the horrible consequences of dogfighting, and never wanted to witness a canned hunt. Such things often worked hand in paw with illegal guns, drugs, and other nefarious dealings.

Jack recited some history. "Antonio Kanoa ran the trafficking operation for Kaliko Wong. For years, Kali managed a baby selling business. She'd 'rescue' girls off the street then get rid of them after the baby was born and sell the baby to desperate people." He nodded at Pierce. "You know a bit about that."

She suspected Rose—the woman who raised her—had been a unicorn victim, that rare victim who escaped.

"Kanoa specialized in older girls, not the babies, selling to a specific market." Jack spoke dispassionately, as if trying to distance himself from the ugly story. "The Family tried to purge any records, coded or otherwise, of Kaliko's enterprises. But you can get to it, if you know where to look. Stuff on the 'net never dies."

"I know that name. Antonio Kanoa? Wait, Tony Kanoa!" She spoke quickly, trying to prime the pump of her memory. "I think he's the man from last summer, where Lia nearly died. Yes, that's gotta be the person behind all this."

Jack shook his head. "He's in prison awaiting trial. Even if he kidnapped Jared's little girl, unless he's pulling the strings from a cell, somebody else currently has her."

Pierce dropped his knapsack on the table, next to the girl's. "Did Kanoa work with anyone? You mentioned Babcock, Masterson, Savage, and Celeste."

Holding out his hands in a "who knows" gesture, Jack leaned closer to squint at the screen. "No references of

Kanoa associated with any of those. But this is strange."

September peered at the screen. Jack enlarged the size to make it easier to see and pointed. "Robbie Benson. Not the 70s teen idol. It's a woman."

She wrinkled her nose. "She worked with Kanoa?"

He pointed again, following several lines on the screen. "First mention right there, arrested in a roundup at a dogfight. Another one there, selling drugs—again, at a dogfight bust."

That ticked a memory. "I had a client once named Beebo Benson." A gentle soul, he had asked for her help introducing a rescue kitten to his pit bulls. She'd found him murdered. Beebo had been a simple and kind man, totally opposed to any kind of animal cruelty.

"That checks out." Jack clicked a few more keys. "Robbie Benson had a cousin named Beebo. Her married name was Gillette. Her husband went to prison and died there in a knife fight."

"Maybe Robin Gillette? She worked for Doc Eugene, Shadow's vet. He fired her. He couldn't prove it but suspected she stole veterinary drugs."

Jack's fingers clickety clacked over the keyboard, until a large grin widened his mouth. "Looks like she changes her name regularly. But here's a picture, with a.k.a. Dr. Robin Gillette. No guarantees she still goes by that, or looks the same."

Pierce joined them at the computer and stood too close to September for comfort. She took a half-step away, not liking the heat pouring off his big body.

Robin Gillette, wearing a polyester pant suit, was heavy set, with short graying hair, a wide grin, wider hips, and massive chunky glasses. She could be a mom going to the PTA meeting, or a pediatrician eager to help soothe a child's fever. But there was something cruel about the lift of her lips. Her hooded eyes hid horrible secrets no human should ever witness.

September studied the face, the broad shoulders, the thick neck and ample bosom, committing it to memory. She remembered meeting the woman at the vet clinic once or twice. Even then, Gillette's snarky attitude hadn't sat right with her, or the people she worked with. But September would never have imagined this placid unassuming face could hide such evil. "We're coming for you." She whispered the words and felt Pierce shift beside her as if agreeing.

"Can you check for wants and warrants?" Pierce added, "Better cancel the board meeting before everyone arrives. Say you had an emergency and will meet another time. That's better than hacking them off worse than they probably already are."

Irritated, Jack interrupted. "Not your problem, Pierce."

September raised her eyebrows. "You didn't reschedule, did you?" At her tone, Shadow nosed her hand, asking for contact she knew had more to do with lowering her blood pressure than to satisfy his itchy ear.

Jack didn't look at her, just kept running his search on the laptop. "Shouldn't be necessary." He glanced at Pierce. "With the angel Gabriel by your side, you'll have this little errand wrapped up in a couple hours." The barbed words found their mark.

Pierce took a step toward Jack, hands fisted.

September stepped between the men. With such acrimony between them, why had Jack hired Pierce to look out for her? A question for another day. "Any information on Gillette's last known location?"

Jack nodded. "Kanoa got picked up in California but

refused to say where he'd stashed his girls. Authorities assumed dark web connections facilitated their disappearance. About that same time, Gillette got a ticket on a big van in the same California town. She never paid the ticket."

Pierce filled in with his own speculation. "She collected the merchandise Kanoa left behind."

September hated his choice of words. "Merchandise? They're women, people, humans."

"Not to Kanoa, and not to Robin Gillette. They were a payday. That's the reality." Pierce shrugged, and the tattoo wing flexed like it might take flight. "If Jared's girl has survived this long, she's got an angel watching over her. Probably made of sterner stuff than her dad."

Jack sneered. "And I suppose that angel's name happens to be Gabriel—"

Pierce shook his head, and grinned. "Nope. Those wings belong to a Magpie. Right, boss?"

September didn't return his smile. She didn't feel like any kind of an angel, avenging or otherwise. She just wanted to do what was right. "We can flush this Gillette woman out of the sewer, but we need Heartland PD to lock her up."

The two men exchanged a look.

"We're not vigilantes. Do you hear me, Pierce? You too, Jack. The Family must fund the ransom, and we'll facilitate the exchange to get the child back safely. Beyond that, it's a no go. I don't need any more sins on my resume."

That made her question the provenance of easily available cash. While it surely included blood money and illegal activity, *she* hadn't done anything to earn it. Seemed poetic justice to use ill-gotten gains to right one of many wrongs perpetuated by the Family. "Do we have $500K in small, unmarked bills on hand?" That seemed an ungodly amount of money to her.

"Working on that." Jack looked up from his computer. "Got about a third of that here. The rest I'm coordinating with couriers. Might save time if you pick up on the way to the helicopter."

Couriers? She pictured a squad of bicycles speeding around the city with backpacks. And getting waylaid by robbers. Geeze, when you saw criminal minds up close and personal, it painted everything with a suspicious brush.

Pierce whistled. "500K in small bills won't fit in one tidy bag. Hard to move quick with that extra weight."

September quirked an eyebrow. She hadn't thought of space requirements.

Jack clarified the issue. "A stack of $20 bills equaling $500,000 would measure about 108 inches tall. That's with pristine bills. Used ones add volume. It'd weigh about 60 pounds, plus the bag or whatever carries it." He nodded at Pierce. "Two large duffel bags would work. Divide the weight, for ease of transport."

Jack looked at September. "But if she wants to meet you alone for the swap, how do you feel about lugging an extra sixty maybe seventy pounds?"

That much? "At least it's not coins." The joke fell flat. "No problem with the weight. But if I have to move fast, I'll drop it. Somebody finds it, they win the lottery."

"Then let's go." Pierce grabbed his backpack and shrugged the straps over his broad shoulders. "We'll get what's here and collect the rest on the way to the helio. We take your car. It beats anything I could get for horsepower and protection."

He'd been checking her out. She signaled Shadow, grabbed her go bag and Alana's tiny backpack, and followed Pierce out of the room. She offered one last instruction to

Jack. "Keep communication open. I want to know anything you find out, anything that gives us an edge with this Robin Gillette. I don't want any surprises. And Jack, alert Heartland PD."

September hurried to catch up to Pierce's long strides. The valet brought her car. "I loaded your package in the back." He didn't blink, as if delivering a shopping bag of money happened all the time.

Pierce held out his hand for the keys. "Faster if I drive. I know where we're going."

She didn't argue, just opened the rear door for Shadow to take his usual spot. On the floor sat a brown paper bag. September opened it, then quickly closed it over the tidy stacks of money.

September stashed the child's backpack and her go bag in the rear next to her bo staff. She quickly took her place in the passenger front seat. "I've never ridden in a helicopter before."

He didn't say anything, just quickly navigated away from the hotel and into traffic. She assumed they would head to DFW, but soon they were in an area she didn't know. The hair rose on the back of her neck.

Pierce stopped in front of a shotgun-style house, honked the horn in an odd pattern, then waited. Within seconds, a nondescript woman wearing an apron scurried out of the house. Without a word she handed another paper shopping bag to Pierce, who passed it to September. He rolled the window back up, preserving the air conditioning that had just started cooling the car.

September twisted in her seat and set the bag on the floor with the other. Shadow stuck his head down, exploring the smells with enthusiasm. His tail whapped the seat.

They made three more stops to pick up bundles of cash,

and a final stop at a sporting goods store to purchase two athletic bags. Pierce didn't seem fazed by the experience as he divided the shopping bags between the two duffels.

"I assume your dog's never been in a copter, either."

She started and shook her head. "But Shadow goes where I go. Don't you, baby dog?" He woofed, agreeing to anything she said. He trusted her. As long as September acted calm and confident, Shadow wouldn't question.

They pulled into a private drive, traveling down a long narrow lane to reach an open field. In front of two airplane hangars a small helicopter nested on a cement pad. Pierce parked her car inside one of the hangars and climbed out of the car.

September slammed her door, then let Shadow out. She grabbed Alana's backpack, her go bag, and the bo staff—which wouldn't draw undue attention at the fair. Many of the attendees carried walking sticks as part of their Celtic garb.

Pierce shouldered his own bag and grabbed the two duffle bags of money before heading toward the helicopter. She followed.

A flutter of anticipation and nervous energy made her both eager to have this over, and reluctant to begin this latest adventure. She'd always reacted to outside forces that pushed and pulled, shaking her like Shadow's bear-toy. This time, she wasn't the target. Not a reaction, this was action and must become her new normal. She had made the choice to move forward. No second-guessing to hamstring herself. This was right. She hadn't wanted this. But once forced upon her, by all that was holy, she'd see it through.

Pierce opened the passenger door on the helicopter and waited. September gave a silent hand signal for Shadow to *kennel up* and he leaped willingly into the glass bubble. She climbed in after, and at Pierce's gesture, strapped the seat belt harness and picked up ear coverings.

A man in coveralls approached from a nearby building. The pilot she assumed.

Pierce leaned in close. "Last chance, Sorokin." He climbed into the helicopter and took his seat next to her.

She cocked her head. "What you mean?"

He whispered. She felt his warm peppermint breath on her face. "With $500,000 we could fly away forever, disappear from everything your uncle has dragged you into."

Chapter Twenty-Eight: Willie

Willie watched the red tent from the small brick toilet building. This vantage gave him a direct line of sight to where the evil witch held the fairy girl captive.

He'd tried to tell Aunt Ethel. She thought he'd made it all up, or that Alana did.

Willie didn't care what grown-ups said, he believed Alana. She didn't want to be there. Heck-fire, she tried to protect him by warning him away before the witch showed up. At first, he thought it was an act, too, but he knew bad acting when he saw it. He might not be a very experienced actor yet, but Alana wasn't playing pretend.

Acting was supposed to be fun. If it wasn't fun, why bother?

No, something *nefarious* was happening in that red tent. He liked that word, had heard his acting coach say it several times, and it sure fit this situation.

The sun scorched the back of Willy's neck. He wished he'd worn one of his baseball caps. Aunt Ethel had insisted he rub sunscreen over his arms, and even on his legs below his shorts, but they forgot about his neck. His arms felt the sun's fiery kiss despite the lotion, and he worried Alana would melt inside the tent. At least out here, an indifferent breeze ruffled his hair now and then.

The big witchy woman with long gray braids strode out of the tent, ducking her head beneath the low sash of the entrance. Willie dodged out of sight when she started looking around.

Now was his chance to spring Alana; he'd take her back to Aunt Ethel to prove he wasn't imagining stuff. Then they'd call Dad. He didn't want to bother him too soon, though, cuz Dad had lots on his mind with re-habili-tation stuff. But a police detective always knew what to do.

The fairgrounds grew busier as vendors completed set up, and crowds gathered for the opening parade. Willie didn't have his own cell phone—for some reason Dad didn't think he needed one yet—so he didn't know the exact time. Aunt Ethel said opening happened about 4 o'clock. With extra people milling around, it'd be easier to sneak Alana away. He just needed witchy Maeve to leave the tent for a little while, maybe to take a potty break.

At the thought, Willie sucked in a breath. If she needed the toilet, she'd see him hiding here. He hazarded another quick look around the corner of the building and gasped when he saw her approaching, almost as if his thoughts summoned her.

Looking up, he found the Ladies sign and quickly scooted around the building, keeping it between himself and the approaching woman. By the time she pulled open the heavy door and entered, Willie had completely circled the building.

He waited until the door swung closed behind the woman's swishing skirt, then ran fast as he could to the tent. *Hope witchy Maeve gets constipation or diarrhea. That'd tie her up for a while.* He ducked under the canopy and blinked hard as his sun dazzled eyes adjusted to the red gloom. As he feared, he had trouble breathing in the sweltering heat, especially with air colored by some icky smell.

"Alana?" Willie whispered, afraid to speak too loudly.

Something rustled in the corner of the tent. A low growl sounded. Startled, Willie took a step back when he saw the dog standing between him and some kind of cage. That was new. "Alana? You still here?"

The rustling came again, this time from inside the wire cage. "In here. She shoved me in here. Look out for that bad dog, he wants to bite me!"

Willie crouched down and turned sideways to the dog. "Maybe not. I think I startled him. September says never do that. Even good dogs got to protect themselves if they feel threatened." He made a point of looking away from the dog, and even threw in a yawn. September said that told dogs you meant no harm and helped 'em relax.

The dog yawned back. *It worked!* Willie saw the hair on the back of the dog's neck smooth. His raised tail dropped into a low wag. A small tentative whine sounded.

"Good dog. You're not so scary, are you?" Willie made his voice soft and gentle, in a singsong that he knew Kinsler loved. He made brief eye contact, looked away again, and then spoke to Alana. "That lady? Is she your mom or what?" He didn't want to insult her momma, but geeze, who tied up their kids like this? He kept his attention split between the girl, the dirty white dog, and the entrance, worried the big woman would reappear at any moment.

Alana shook her head. "She won't let me go. Wants Papa to pay a bunch of money. I heard her on the phone." She spoke softly and quickly through tears. "But if Papa comes, she'll hurt him." She hesitated. Her lower lip trembled. "Please? You'll help me?"

Willie reached out to the dog. He placed just the flat of his hand on the dog shoulder and stroked slowly once. The dog whined again, and pushed his head and shoulders into Willy's chest, whimpers increasing and his tail sweeping the grass floor of the tent. Willie could feel the dog's bones through his fur. A tag hung from a worn collar; Willie read it aloud: "Noah."

Lots of dogs came to the Celtic Festival, especially the breeds famous from Scotland and Ireland. Maybe this dog got lost. "You're okay, Noah, good dog." The mostly white fur, stained with reddish mud, made it hard to tell his breed. He patted Noah one last time then stood to take a closer look at Alana's cage.

He'd seen plenty like this crate. Easy-peasy to open from the outside but designed to keep clever pets from escaping. Quickly he unlatched the door, and beckoned Alana to come out.

She scooted free of the cage, relief clear on her face. But then she motioned to the tether encircling her ankle.

Willie wrinkled his brow. No way to remove the padlock. But a knife could cut through the leather thong where it connected to the chain. The complicated knot had shrunk down and tightened upon itself. Willie thought back to the ginormous knife he'd seen earlier.

No time for that now. The witch woman would trudge her way back over here any minute.

The dog whined and stretched into the cage for the food

bowl. He licked and licked even though it looked clean. That gave Willie an idea. "You got anything to eat?"

Alana looked at him like he was the stupidest kid ever. She was right. He realized she'd cleaned out the cat food bowl. Ew.

He looked around the small enclosure and spied an insulated igloo cooler. He hurried over, pulled out a water bottle and a Tupperware bowl of tuna salad. Yuck, but it would work.

Alana's eyes grew large, and she licked her lips. He cocked his head. "Thirsty?"

She reached out a demanding hand. He unscrewed the lid and gave her the bottle. He grabbed another for himself as she drank. The heat really sucked the energy out of you.

"Bet you're hungry, too. But first we gotta get you outta here. This nice doggy is gonna help."

Noah sat as though anticipating the next move. He licked his lips and drooled, stretching his neck toward the scent of the tuna.

Willie had Alana move as far as she could away from the table, stretching the chain and leather tether. "His name's Noah. See, on the tag? He's a nice pup, and won't mean to, but he might hurt you just a little. Is it okay, to hurt just a little, so you can get away?"

She lowered the water bottle from her lips, half of it already gone. "I got hurt before, plenty bad. You'll help me get away?" Her eyes widened when he used two fingers to scoop a dollop of the pungent salad and smear it on the leather connecting her ankle to the chain.

The dog whimpered, but politely held his position. Somebody had taught Noah manners.

"Okay Noah, you get the treat, and help us at the same time, okay? Just work fast."

The dog moved forward, tail wagging in gratitude. He sniffed first, then licked the doctored leather. He whimpered for more after finishing the treat, looking at Willie with begging eyes.

Willie shook his head and pointed at the thong. "Chew, boy. Then you get more."

The dog returned his attention to the leather. He took it between his teeth and tugged.

Alana squealed. The pressure on her already raw and bruised flesh must hurt something fierce.

But when the dog realized tugging wouldn't release any more flavor, he turned his jaw sideways and began to gnaw, squeezing out every last bit of flavor from the treated restraint.

"Good dog. That's the way, Noah, good dog." Willie whispered, praying the dog's sharp teeth would do the job before the witch returned and killed them all.

Chapter Twenty-Nine: Ethel

They'd finished unpacking boxes and setting up the display hours ago. Ethel lost track of time, visiting with her friend. "Willie should've checked back by now. Is there anything else you need me to help you with?"

The other woman shook her head and gave Ethel a quick hug. "You and Willie were a big help. I hated to ask you, what with everything that happened."

Ethel pulled away, a tight smile stretching her face. "I needed to get my mind off things. Life goes on, isn't that what everyone says?" She couldn't suppress a bitter laugh. "Stan was big and loud and hard to live with, but I loved the big guy. And now the house feels so empty." She stiffened her back. "It helps to have something to do, like help you out here at the festival. I expected him back ages ago, complaining how he's starving to death." She laughed. "I'll be back later after feeding the boy and cleaning up a bit before the parade. Feel like I'm melting in this heat. I've got my outfit in the car and wouldn't miss it for the world."

Ethel glanced around. Willie turned up a while ago with a wild story about a kidnapped fairy princess. He wanted her to drop everything, and tag after him to see some fortuneteller. All that theatrical stuff had gone to the kid's head. She shrugged him off, told him to come back after she was done, and they'd explore together. It had taken longer than expected. She'd make it up to him, maybe even splurge on a gift. Now he had disappeared.

She hadn't noticed how busy the fairgrounds had become. Rows of white tents created dozens of rows of booth displays, many of them featured Scottish clans with the appropriate tartan, history information, and coat of arms. She already knew hers.

Willie had little interest in the historical aspects of the fair. He'd probably gravitate toward the open field where friendly competitors showed off feats of strength. She grabbed up a brochure from a booth and fanned herself with it as she hurried along the grassy pathway between booths to reach the competition.

Several contenders lined up to take their chances. Both men and women, and even a few youngsters, milled about, eager for their chance to throw the hammer. In his younger days, Stan tried his hand at caber toss, lifting and tossing massive logs as far as possible. No longer able to manage that, he'd still enjoyed last year competing in the tug o' war, a team sport that Willie and his dad joined. She frowned, disappointed she didn't see Willie anywhere around.

She nodded and waved back, but turned quickly away from a few familiar faces from Heartland PD. They wore bright yellow vests with "security" emblazoned across the chest. But she wasn't in the mood to chat with anyone about how much they respected and missed Stan.

She passed the main stage, where an announcer prepared to open the Celtic Fair officially. Representatives from the Choctaw Nation mounted the stage and began singing the Lord's Prayer in the Choctaw language. She waited, bowing her head in respect and speaking the words in her head until they finished. Then Ethel hurried on, past the rows and rows of folding chairs set up for the future entertainment of clogging, Irish dance, and bands.

Ethel continued to fan herself, her footsteps hurrying faster and faster. A niggling itch of worry caught her throat. Tables of sterling silver rings featuring Celtic knots, crystal jewelry, wooden dragon puzzles, and other talismans posed no interest to Willie, although some of the paintings might appeal. She paused and asked one of the vendors if he'd noticed the boy.

He shook his head, and made a dismissive gesture with one hand, waving to the growing crowds. Unless somebody actually purchased something, nobody would notice Willie. He had a few dollars, but that narrowed her focus. She could safely ignore the pricey wares.

She passed another booth that featured interesting masks, and neon colored fairy wings in cellophane, ready to be fixed to the back of any child interested. That reminded her of the fairy girl Willie mentioned. Maybe he'd seen something here that inspired the story. Again asking for any sightings of Willie, she came up lacking.

Booths featured leather armor in layers, with rivets decorating the embossed patterns. In the same display a large sign invited customers to design their own *sporran*—a traditional part of the men's Scottish Highland dress. They wore the sporran at the front of the kilt, and it served as a kind of pocket. Gorgeous examples offered intricately engraved pewter fastenings at the top, with the pouch made of fur. She'd purchased one last year to complete Stan's outfit. His featured an antlered deer in the center with figures of heather on each side worked in relief. If interested, she'd give it to Willie when he got older. Stan would like that... she pushed the thought away.

A line of children about Willie's age spilled out of the next booth, impatiently waiting their turn to have faces painted. But no Willie.

The next booth featured chain mail in bizarre neon colors. That would certainly attract Willie. The price, in the hundreds of dollars, counted Willie out. Next door, though, the handmade knives and swords would draw Willie like bees to heather.

"Sure, a young'un stopped by earlier before the crowds came. They's plenty sharp and not toys, nothing to mess with, but he sure drooled over one of 'em. Then some lady stopped by not ten minutes ago and bought his favorite." He smiled and leaned forward. "Good for ladies to have protection. I got more, if you want to look."

"Thanks. Just looking for my nephew. Which way did he go?"

He shook his head. "Sorry lady."

Another couple approached, potential customers, and he turned his back on Ethel before she could press for more.

Further down the line, she heard a hollow THUMP. Someone yelled. "Get away from there. We're not open for business yet."

She swiveled, and saw a young man, with an even younger girl clutching his arm, giggle and sprint away. Looked like they'd taken turns throwing axes at two upright targets. Two stuck in one of the targets, with a third in the grass below. A large woman in a broomstick skirt and keyring jingling at her waist swished around, collecting the axes, and dropping them into a large container. Her long gray braids with bells attached tinkled and swayed as she worked.

Butted up next door to the ax-throwing display squatted a blood-red tent. Huh. Must be the fortuneteller Willie mentioned. Ethel hurried to catch the woman, sure she'd have information, but she'd already ducked inside the small tent.

Ethel stopped to catch her breath. She'd quiz the woman, maybe have a sit down while they talked. She could use a rest.

Chapter Thirty: Jared

Wincing, Jared rolled out of the hospital bed. He'd been told he needed mental and physical rest, to drink lots of water, use OTC headache medicine if needed, and avoid bright lights and loud noises.

But Alana didn't have the luxury of Jared checking out for 24 hours or more. And he couldn't wait for some nebulous hero to rescue her. He was her father. He didn't have the ransom, but he had two legs, strong arms, and a father's wrath to fuel his next steps.

As far as he knew, Sorokin and her yes-men hadn't filed charges against him, or even reported the accident. When the so-called good guys didn't want the police involved, either, Jared figured he'd do as well on his own. Rescuing his daughter would not only save her life, it might redeem his soul.

He moved stiffly, aching muscles reacting to the airbag impact, as he shed the hospital gown. He quickly donned the fresh clothes, glad to find his wallet beneath them.

He prayed the wad of cash would be enough to get him to the Celtic Festival.

Jared moved to the door. He cracked it open and cautiously peered out, checking both directions. They had no reason to hold him, and no authority to do so, but he didn't need further delay, or argument and invented lies to explain his actions.

Quickly he slipped out of the hospital room and hurried down the open corridor. Nobody stopped him, but he thanked his lucky stars when the elevator doors opened to accommodate him. In less than two minutes, Jared exited the hospital, scanning the area for the Uber he had booked.

He had lied on the app, though, about his destination. He knew routes outside of the norm might be ignored, and he couldn't afford to be stood up.

Jared figured once the driver arrived, he could make other arrangements…

Chapter Thirty-One: Shadow

Shadow thought this was the strangest car he'd ever seen. Its three crooked spiderlike legs perched on the pavement, while a long tail with a spinner on the end stuck way out. He didn't see any eyelights, either, so maybe it never drove at night. Another spinner sat on the roof like a hat—it looked like one of Macy-cat's toys.

The leather seats smelled wonderful, and his nose read the story of those who had previously sat in them. September and Pierce sat in the front, leaving Shadow by himself behind the pair. He whined with a combination of frustration and concern.

Pierce leaned toward September. The man still hadn't offered Shadow any peppermint candy. "The $500K split two ways could last a long time."

September laughed, but she didn't sound happy. Her body stiffened. "Wait. I need to get Shadow in his hoodie.

For noise protection." September rummaged in her go bag and pulled out the black headgear Shadow recognized and didn't like. The hood kept out all the good sounds. When they visited the range where she practiced with her gun, she made him wear the hood.

"Looks like military." Pierce handed car keys to a man wearing coveralls. "Take care of the car." The stranger quickly ducked away and trotted back to one of the big buildings.

"It's called a Canine Auditory Protection System. CAPS. Yes, it's designed to protect military dogs. Lia got it for me." She turned in the seat, beckoning Shadow closer; he reluctantly obeyed.

Pierce raised his eyebrows, then turned his attention to the dashboard filled with colored lights. He fiddled with it, making some lights change color, and others make odd noises. "He shouldn't need protection. This is an Airbus H155 known for its quiet ride." He spoke with pride. "Has a top speed over 200 miles an hour. Police, hospitals, and EMTs love this aircraft. So do the Family VIPs." He grinned. "Lucky for us, I've got a license to fly. Easy-peasy for a solo pilot, too."

Shadow ignored the conversation. He knew lots of words—he was smart that way—but Pierce spoke strange ones that made no sense. And because September didn't say the words, Shadow knew they weren't important.

September tugged the snug padded cloth over Shadow's face, until it covered his ears and hugged tight to his neck. He shook himself hard to settle it more comfortably. He could still hear muffled conversation. Shadow listened carefully, in case September said something important.

"I won't risk his hearing." She stroked his muzzle, scratched his chest. "It's just like a car ride. You like car rides, don't you baby dog?"

He grinned happily and wanted to push up next to her in the front of the weird car. She and Pierce sat surrounded by clear glass, which offered a wide view of the pavement all around them.

September shook her head and gave the *wait* hand signal. Shadow gave an exaggerated sigh, letting her know his opinion of the instruction, but turned to take in the rest of the small vehicle.

He sniffed around several leather seats, many more than would fit in September's car. Shadow wondered if windows might roll down, so a good dog could stick his nose in the crack and drink the scent that always rode the wind. He'd like that.

"Don't you have to file a flight plan?" September craned her neck, looking around the small field. It held several other small vehicles, some with wings that Shadow knew were called airplanes. He'd been around them before, and September had taught him that with the name game, but he'd never gone inside one. When they flew in the sky, they looked much smaller than birds. Here on the ground, they looked even bigger than this funny car.

September wore a belt like she did in the car, and so did Pierce. They both put on ear muzzles, too. Shadow wondered if loud booming noises might come, like with fireworks. He didn't like fireworks. He especially disliked the big booming ones that blew up gardens, hurt people, and made September scared.

"We're using visual flight rules, so we just need to avoid high-traffic areas. We're far away from DFW and flying lower than planes. We just need a nice open space for landing."

"Hope you got enough gas to get there and back, or a

quick getaway if needed." Shadow could tell even with his ears muffled that September felt concerned about this whole situation.

Pierce grinned. "We're fully fueled, got a 500-mile range, so we're good to go. You strapped in? When she gets going, it's quite a rush."

A noise started and sounded very different than September's vehicle. The car vibrated. Shadow startled, then moved closer to one of the windows, searching for the noise.

Slowly the noise increased. Shadow could feel shaking that traveled from the pads of his feet clear up to the tips of his ears. Yet the car never moved forward. How strange! He noticed funny shadows racing around the ground outside. The weird flicker spun around and around, faster and faster, making a good dog's eyes feel funny.

With a sudden unexpected lurch, the floor tilted. The ground fell away beneath them.

Shadow yelped, immediately regained his footing. He barked and barked again. When September gave him the signal, he used his inside voice, boofing softly as he stared around the small cabin. He pressed his nose to the nearest window, enthralled as the ground fell away.

Chapter Thirty-Two: Combs

With exasperation, Combs answered the phone. "Yes, Tee, what else?" In a way, he resented her pointing out September's duplicity when he should have recognized it himself. As a detective, he prided himself on picking up on things everyday folks missed.

"Sorry to bother. Just got a hit on Robin."

"What about her?" At least Tee had better intel than he did. "She in Texas like your informant said?"

"In a way, yes. Found her in back of a Buc-ee's truck stop off of Hwy 75 just north of Dallas. What's left of her, anyway."

He sat up. "She's dead? Who's on the case?" Texas, a huge state by any standard, meant the dump location might as well be in his back pocket.

"Not your guys, that's why I called. The GPS in the

vehicle last synced directions to Heartland." She took a breath. "Evidence in the vehicle indicates she had someone with her. A kid."

A victim. Tee didn't have to say it. Combs winced. "Maybe the kid got away." Or got taken by whoever took her out.

"Still questioning staff at the gas station. Of course, the cameras don't work, they're just for show." Her disgust mirrored his own. "Anyway, let your wife know Robin Gillette won't bother her again. Somebody cut her throat, bashed her face, and took her fingers to delay identification. But working hypothesis ID's Robin Gillette. The license plates and vehicle registration list one of her known aliases, D'Andri. It's her."

He still couldn't bring himself to correct Tee that he and September weren't married. After what he'd found out about Sorokin Glass, maybe that wasn't a bad thing.

Disconnecting the call, he stopped himself from leaving September another message. It bothered him that Gillette got so close to home before someone stopped her. While her profession probably caused her death, he worried about who had taken her out. And why. And what had they done with the kid?

Combs placed another call, this time to Captain Felix Gregory. He still had his badge, dammit, even if sidelined temporarily. Heartland PD needed a head's up about Gillette and the unsub who slit her throat.

Not realizing he'd held his breath, Combs exhaled when the captain answered on the first ring.

"How're you holding up, Combs? On the mend, I hear. Acing the PT stuff. Never doubted for a minute. I've got a desk ready for you as soon as you can return—until you're up to speed."

He hated hearing that and answered stiffly. "Appreciate it, Captain. Not interested in the desk, no offense."

Gregory took it in stride. "I expected as much. We'll see how it goes. Thanks for checking in. And no, we don't have anyone in mind for the detective slot. Gonzalez left big shoes to fill."

The comment punched Combs where it hurt. He'd miss his partner forever. They'd worked together long enough to anticipate each other's thoughts. "Another reason to get me out of rehab and back on the job. I know you're short-handed."

The captain laughed ruefully. But Combs knew the humor didn't reach the man's piercing gray eyes. "Got that right. We got the annual Celtic Festival this weekend. We've got a team over there, with some of the off-duty officers helping out. Couldn't afford to send more than a couple on the clock. We never have problems with that group anyway, so it's good community outreach."

"Speaking of outreach, you remember Officer Tee Teves, the Chicago cop here on loan last summer?" *Awkward, Combs.* He rolled his eyes at himself.

Gregory grunted. "Yes. Got herself nearly froze to death, as I recall. Then sidelined for several months with some kinda tick disease, right?" He paused. "You're not suggesting we hire her? Too new, still too green to rank detective."

"No, not at all." Damn, he hadn't meant to put *that* thought into Gregory's head. New, green, hardheaded, and a rule breaker they didn't need. "She's happy in Chicago." A little creative license never hurt. "She just called me about a side project, a loose end from her time with us running down the kid trafficking ring. We identified the boss running the operation as Robin Gillette. Until now, she's been in the wind."

"Until now?" Gregory's tone turned grim.

"Tee…that is, Officer Teves, learned that a body tentatively ID'd as Gillette turned up at the Buc-ee's just north of Dallas. That's a stone's throw from y'all. Appears she was headed your way, according to her GPS, but got waylaid." He repeated the details Tee had shared.

"Thanks for the head's up. Don't like that she had business in Heartland." He growled. "I'll get on the horn and see what the fellas working the case care to share."

Combs felt his shoulders relax. "Thanks, Captain."

"Oh and Combs? Healing takes time. I heard tell you haven't met with the counselor yet. You know that's a prerequisite to returning."

His whole body stiffened. "I'm fine. Once my leg heals…"

"Cut the crap, Combs. I'm not a fan of all that woo-woo head shrinking, either. But you got the stuffing knocked outta you in the bomb blast. And your wife—girlfriend—September ain't an easy keeper, at least not up to now. I gotta know you're solid, and the department psychologist signs off that you're ready." He paused, waiting for an answer. When Combs remained silent, Gregory added, "That desk only stays empty so long. Don't want to lose you, Combs. Don't force my hand."

Chapter Thirty-Three: Robin

Robin admired the new blade. These festival folk knew how to fancy up the sharps. While it wasn't as functional as she liked for most of her jobs, you had to admire the artistry of the blade.

Close to two feet long, it had a smooth razor edge on one side and a jagged shark-toothed serrated spine on the other. The Damascus steel shined in the sun with iridescent whirls pounded deep into the metal itself. The blade bore a falcon stamp with the maker's mark: Frost Cutlery, designed by Jim Frost.

The swirl handle, of orange cocobolo wood, boasted a twisted spiral grip that felt made for her hand. The butt of the handle featured four animal faces in a circle: lion heads alternated with monkey faces, all with golden mouths wide open. The bolster attached blade to handle with a stylized bat-like gargoyle in intricate relief. She slipped the long thin rawhide tether that encircled the handle over her wrist. That allowed the knife to go from hanging in its sheath to easily gripped in seconds.

Not a subtle knife at all, Frost designed the ceremonial blade the size and weight of a machete. It'd strike fear in that devilish girl until she got unloaded to her father—or died on the edge of the blade itself. At the thought, Robin smiled and increased her pace, hurrying back to the red tent. She hadn't promised daddy-dear that the ransom bought a *living* child…

The fair now had long lines of eager attendees waiting to enter in the blistering heat. Robin purchased a soda, two bottles of water, and a large cup of ice along the way to restock her cooler. The girl hadn't eaten or had much to drink recently, and she needed to keep Alana vertical if Sorokin demanded proof of life before the exchange.

The crowds worked well for her purposes. Lots of people masked whatever needed to be done and offered Robin a head start to escape. Crowds also limited what any would-be do-gooder might try. Heroes had a weird hang-up about injuring bystanders.

Robin had no such limitations. The girl's father, September, or both would show up with the funds, and they'd make the exchange. If all went as planned with no cops in tow, she'd kill the Magpie, frame Jared, and celebrate in the next town. She'd need a less noticeable vehicle and plans to get out of the country.

Several more people gathered around the ax-throwing booth beside her tent. "When's the ax guy coming back? Been practicing, going to show my buddies."

Robin shrugged. "He wasn't feeling too good and ducked out. Go find something else to do." She took a few steps closer, widening her eyes, and half unsheathing the big knife.

The speaker's mouth dropped open, and then his shocked expression melted into giggles. "Good one. You got me there, fortuneteller. Spooky. Hey, I want to get my fortune read."

Cretin. They never saw the truth, always believed the surface lie. "Later. I've got spooky business to attend to first."

Another from the group spoke up. "Hey, I thought this was your business. We've got cash. And we may not be in the mood later..."

Robin pulled out the massive knife and brandished it in the sun. "I read your fortune in blood. If you don't want to wait, hold out your hand—"

Squealing with feigned fright, the trio scurried away, giggling and laughing but tossing suspicious glances back over shoulders.

Shaking her head, Robin strode to the red tent and ducked inside.

A small dog spun to face her. Fur rippled along his hackles; lips peeled back to show glistening fangs. Alana shivered and shrank against one side of the empty cat cage, clutching the boy's arm. The little urchin had returned.

"Son-of-a..." Robin drew back her arm and launched the huge knife. She didn't care if she hit the dog or one of the kids.

The blade struck the ground near Willie's feet. He yelped and jerked away. The witchy woman was evil. She'd had it in for Alana, and would get him, too, if they didn't get away.

The dog growled louder, ferocious despite his size, the

rumbles a welcome distraction. Noah made inroads on the rawhide, but not enough to break Alana's ankle free of the chain.

"Good dog. That's a good dog, don't let her get us." Afraid to lose eye contact with the furious woman, Willie reached forward and grabbed the handle of the big knife. He wrenched it from the ground. Damp soil splattered against his bare knee, leaving red bloody streaks as if the earth bled.

"Hurry, hurry, hurry!" Alana pulled on the tether, grabbing her own leg and yanking and pulling. Willie could tell it caused excruciating pain.

The dog moved forward, blocking the woman's approach. The air turned blue with curses; some words Willie had never heard before. But he understood the meaning. If they didn't get out, and get out quick, they were all dead.

Willie knifed the remaining portion of the rawhide. Alana fell backwards when it released.

"Go-go-go-go!" They couldn't get past the dog or witch blocking the entrance. Noah growled and lunged at the woman, keeping her out.

Like before, Willie grabbed the back edge of the tent and lifted it for Alana to roll under. He dragged the heavy knife with him, afraid the witch would get it and come after them. Willie wriggled out, following Alana to freedom.

The knife—the one he had drooled over—weighed about a million pounds. If they got caught with it, that witchy woman could say he robbed her. So when they ran by the two big bull's-eye ax targets, Willie shoved the knife inside one of the empty wooden boxes.

The dog yelped and barked. Willie hoped Noah wouldn't get hurt.

Chapter Thirty-Four: Lord Byron

Byron hissed when the two children snuck out the back of the tent right beside where he perched atop Ian's wooden box. They didn't see him.

Inside the tent, the strange dog kept barking. Byron's ears flattened to the top of his head, and a low growl grew. He readied himself to sprint away if the dog squeezed out to follow the kids.

More and more people gathered. He could hear them, and sometimes glimpse them as they wandered past. Usually that enthralled Lord Byron. He loved to greet an admiring throng. But Ian's absence left him unsettled, and the blood smell emanating from the box made his long gray fur frizz and stand up, the way lightning charged the air. The aroma of his beloved owner's pungent fear clung to the area, invisible to the eye but shouting louder than growls.

The boy threw something that THUMPED inside one of

the targets as they raced by. Byron hopped down from his perch, shook himself hard, then slunk slowly and carefully away from the bad-smelling perch. He didn't want the dog to notice. Or the woman who stole his cat's condo. Staying to the shadows and crouching low in the grass kept him invisible to all but the most discerning human.

Maybe Ian was playing a game, hiding away only to hop out to surprise Byron? He loved that hide and seek game. And the chase game, and eye-tag where Ian peered around corners and waited for Byron to paw-whap him.

Oh, but the blood smells scared him!

If only he'd reappear, catch Byron up into his broad arms, speak in his beloved rumbly voice once more. They'd play chase the feather, or maybe fetch with a furry mouse toy.

Ian called Byron his *kitty-dog*, he wasn't sure why. Noisy creatures they were, and smelled funny, and sometimes dangerous like the barking dog in the nearby tent. Dogs offered lots of mixed signals like waving tails that warned smart cats away.

Byron carefully sniffed the base of the wooden box the boy had touched. He found his own signature odor, and refreshed it with cheek rubs. He walked around the box and put paws-up to stare at the top. The high perch tempted Byron, but first he thoroughly reviewed ground level for safety. Byron circled the box, and at the backside, found a split wood opening where the boy's scent smelled strongest.

Holes were fun. Byron peered inside, the narrow pupils of his eyes widening to full circles to see into the dark interior. Threads of light reached through the wooden slats forming the box. There! Something glinted inside. The object that THUMPED.

He tentatively poked one paw through the gap, pushing

forward and extending his foreleg to reach inside. His paw spread wide, the sensitive pads patting the bottom of the crate to test and feel the shape and identity of the object.

Claws hooked on something loose. Byron withdrew his paw, grappling the string into view until it hung out of the opening. He sniffed it, batted it as it swung against the wooden crate, and fell on his side to paw dance with the string-like material. He sniffed it again, tasted with a cautious nibble. Rawhide, like some of the small chewy treats his special person sometimes offered.

Lord Byron stood, grabbed the rawhide in his mouth, and backed away, growling with ferocious determination. A large object bumped against the interior of the wooden box. It took three tries for Byron to drag it through the opening, and into the light.

The glistening 18-inch blade shined brightly in the sun.

Chapter Thirty-Five: Willie

"C ome on! This way." Willie grabbed Alana's hand,
dodging between people in the growing crowd.
He slowed to match her shorter stride and bare
feet. At least they ran on grass, not gravel or asphalt. The
August sun raised pavement to blistering temperatures.

He grabbed a quick look over one shoulder, still hearing
Noah's bark behind them. So far, the witchy woman hadn't
appeared, but it was only a matter of time before Magical
Maeve came after them. He tried to remember the location
of Aunt Ethel's friend's booth. Maybe over there?

Tugging at Alana's hand again, the pair set off in the new
direction. At first Willie worried grown-ups might look at
them strangely, but nobody seemed to blink at the sight of
Alana's fairy wings, cat face, or the rawhide anklet that
remained.

After making sure they still weren't being followed, Willie

dug money from his pocket and bought two bottles of water. Alana already ate a bunch of the smelly tuna, so she should be good for a minute. He pulled her into the shade of a picnic area.

"We gotta hide." Her shoulders hunched, Alana this time drank only a few swallows before recapping the bottle. She cupped the cool plastic like it was the most precious jewel in the universe.

"I met your dad. He got into our house this morning, talked to me and my Aunt Ethel." He took a gulp of his own water and wiped his mouth with the back of one hand. "You'll like her, my Aunt Ethel I mean. We just gotta find her and she'll help get you back to your dad. I know she will."

Alana's eyes welled with tears. "Boss didn't lie?"

"The boss? Oh, you mean that nasty woman who tied you up. We showed her, huh? Got clean away." He had rescued her, just like a hero. Willie couldn't wait to tell Dad. He hoped Noah escaped, too. "No lie, your dad wanted to get money to swap for you—a ransom."

She hugged herself, shivering even in the terrible heat. "Papa's got no money."

"Like I said, we just need to find my Aunt Ethel. She'll call Dad. He's a cop, a police detective and a real hero."

Alana froze. She made whimpering noises, and slowly stood and backed away from Willie. "No… No, no!" The water bottle slipped from her hand.

"Hey, what'd I say?"

She shook her head again and again, lower lip trembling and face draining of color. "No cops. Boss says cops will arrest me an' throw me inna black hole. I'd never see Papa again!" Her voice rose an octave, and strangers turned to look.

He wrinkled his brow. "What're you talking about? Dad would never do that. Cops don't throw kids in jail. That's just one of those evil Boss lies."

"No cops. Please, please, no cops, Willie.

"Okay, okay. No cops. Geez. Let's just find Aunt Ethel. She'll know what to do."

Men and women fidgeted in ragged lines, taking their places for the parade. Ladies in long skirts with hair twisted with ribbons and men in kilts holding bagpipes, drums, and fife. Each group identified by clan tartans held banners showcasing the coat of arms and piper insignia.

At some unknown signal, the parade began to march, each group playing signature snarly music. Willie grimaced, not caring for the obnoxious drone sound. But at least the concerted movement of the crowd gave them cover.

Spectators lined each side of the parade path, as the march snaked between booth displays on the way to the stage. He guessed judges would calculate awards or something. Aunt Ethel planned to march in the parade. Maybe that's why he hadn't seen her?

Willie leaned forward, and patted Alana on her shoulder. "Ready?" If they joined the parade line, mixed in with the crowd, then even if the witchy woman saw them, she couldn't do anything.

The pair matched steps with the parade. Willie caught sight of the candle and preserves booth he'd helped with set up. "Come on, betcha Aunt Ethel's waiting over there."

Alana nodded and followed him like a puppy right up to the entrance. Then she twisted her head sharply upward. She pointed at the sky. "Cops! Boss called the cops!" She dashed away, weaving between adult legs, and disappeared into the crowd.

Willie's mouth dropped open, staring after the panicked girl. He looked skyward. Overhead, a sleek black-and-white helicopter with a nose like a dolphin swam in the sky.

Chapter Thirty-Six: Ethel

E thel berated herself, limping toward the red tent, hoping to get a clue where next to look. She'd let time get away from her, and now she'd miss marching in the parade. He'd come back with his wild story, and she hadn't taken Willie seriously. Boys his age, full of imagination, got distracted. She should know better. Her clothes stuck to her damp flesh. She wanted to sit down somewhere, unscrew her feet (gosh, they hurt), and soak them in cool water.

Her phone buzzed. "Teddy? Can we talk later? I'm at the festival. Willie came to help, but now I can't find him." Her voice trembled a bit on the last words.

His gravelly voice felt like a bracing cool breeze. "Stay calm. When he gets hungry enough, he'll turn up." He cleared his throat. "Have you reported it to the authorities?"

"Not yet. I've only been looking for a short time. You

think I should?" *Of course I should.* She'd do that, head over to the stage to ask them to make an announcement, soon as she got off the phone. It'd embarrass the boy no end, but she'd make it up to him later. "Willie mentioned visiting a fortuneteller's red tent. He acted worried about some girl pretending to be a captured fairy princess. I should have paid closer attention." She sighed. "He's too young for girlfriends. Isn't he?" She palmed tears away from her face. "He's so dramatic lately. Everything's a soap opera."

"Well, wouldn't hurt to check it out I suppose."

She nodded, although he couldn't see it. Maybe she worried for nothing, and he'd made friends with a girl inside the tent. Once she found him, she'd give him a piece of her mind—that is, after she hugged his neck. "Why'd you call?"

He sighed. "I've been digging, Ethel. Don't know how I missed it before, but we've all been distracted these past few weeks." He cleared his throat.

Distraction was one word for it. "You've been digging? What'd you find?"

A commotion disturbed the red tent opening. The woman with long braids backed out, waving her hands at something inside.

"It's true. September Day is the natural daughter of Henry Wong."

She nearly dropped her phone. "That Kaliko person is September's birth mother?" She nearly spat the words.

"No. Heavens no! Wong remarried that snake after his first wife and babies disappeared nearly thirty years ago. The daughter, named Sorokin Glass, resurfaced right after Kaliko's death."

"Why didn't September say anything? How long has she known?" Nearly six weeks had passed. Ethel had to steady the phone with both trembling hands.

"I don't know." Deep sorrow, disappointment, and anger shook his voice.

Maeve backed the rest of the way out of the tent entrance, waving her hands in a warding off gesture. A little dog followed her out, leaping and yapping, tail wagging furiously. Ethel couldn't tell if the dog—it looked sort of like a Shih Tzu—meant to snap at Maeve, or simply wanted attention. Once clear of the tent, the dog whirled and raced away, chased by a cloud of invective from Maeve.

"Teddy, I've got to go. Keep me posted. I'll let you know as soon as I find Willie." She quickly added, "Don't you dare tell Jeff about this. *Any* of this." She couldn't bear for him to know she'd lost Willie. "Give me a little time before you call the police."

As if she'd invoked them, a helicopter buzzed by overhead. On closer look, though, it had no PD designation.

She pocketed her phone and walked toward the fortuneteller. "Are you okay? That dog didn't bite you, did it?" Ethel considered herself a cat person.

The lady shook her head, still glaring after where the dog disappeared. "Damn stray sniffing around. Probably after food." She turned to go back inside the tent.

"Excuse me. I hope you can help me out. I'm looking for a boy about this tall…" She held her hand to the appropriate height. "He's eleven, but small for his age. Strawberry blond hair, medium length, and wearing—"

The woman smiled, and cut her off, offering a detailed description of what Willie wore. "He came by earlier today to visit my little girl. She's helping with my act. I got her all dolled up in a fairy costume. I'm afraid it freaked out your son. Sorry about that." She took a step closer to Ethel, still smiling. Rather, she showed teeth in what looked more daunting than the dog's display.

Ethel took a step back and laughed nervously.

"He returned to apologize—you raised him right. They're getting acquainted over cookies and lemonade. So sorry to scare you if he's late getting back."

Ethel breathed with relief. "Oh thank God. I'd never forgive myself if I had to tell his father and September I lost him."

The woman's eyes widened. "September? Unusual name." Her grin widened, if that was possible. She beckoned Ethel forward. "Come on in, you look like you could use some lemonade, too."

Chapter Thirty-Seven: Combs

C ombs's brain had become a hamster wheel of worry. He didn't want another partner—would always miss Gonzalez—and the good Lord preserve him from Tee and her side projects.

Look at all the angst she'd stirred up over nothing. Even if the Gillette woman was heading to Heartland, it didn't mean it had anything to do with September. With Gillette presumably dead, there was nothing to worry about. Well, except for the long, hard talk he planned to have with September as soon as she returned his call. If she called back...

Of course she'd call.

This felt worse than jail. At least perps did something to deserve getting locked up. The only thing Combs did wrong was love the wrong woman—

No. Stop it. Don't think that way.

"Trust her, Combs. She's trusted you with her past." A past filled with ugliness and secrets that humiliated, and still haunted, her. Trust worked both ways. This Sorokin Glass stuff, they'd talk, she'd explain, and they'd figure it out. No doubt she had her reasons. *Probably wanting to protect the invalid.* The idea twisted his gut. His hands clenched tight.

He wished he could double up on PT, get home twice as fast. Never mind the psych stuff. Talking to counselors helped people with problems, couldn't argue with that. If he had to jump through that hoop, he'd grit his teeth and do it. But he didn't have problems. He had everything under control.

The phone tweedled. *September!*

Combs grabbed at the phone so quickly he knocked it on the floor. Cursing under his breath, he twisted into a pretzel to retrieve it and fell heavily onto the floor. His injured leg remained stuck, propped up on the extender.

He yelled, more with frustration than pain, and grabbed his injured leg with both hands. The phone tweedled another half-dozen times before he got his leg dismounted from the chair stirrup. Crap. He'd need help getting back into the contraption.

He hated this!

He lay on his side and answered the call without looking. "September! I really need to see you—"

"Combs, it's Teddy. You called me earlier."

"Yeah, right. Teddy." Combs rolled onto his back, and stared at the ceiling, where a crack spidered across the plaster, a symptom of the North Texas shifting ground. Like his emotions. Did he want to bring up the Magpie stuff with Teddy, before September had a chance to explain? That didn't feel right, spreading suspicion and distrust. He remembered how it felt to be the innocent target of accusations. It took forever to dig out of the mess when a hurt kid spread lies about him. He owed September the benefit of the doubt.

Teddy always sounded like he'd swallowed broken glass. "Ethel called. She had a run-in this morning with a fella who broke into your house looking for September. She and Willie are fine," Teddy hastened to add.

"Wait, Willie was there, too?" Combs tried to sit up and winced at the strain it put on his leg. He collapsed, resting impatiently on his back.

"Like I said, everyone's okay. The man's gone. Ethel didn't want me to worry you…"

He held something back. Combs could tell. But he waited. Silence prompted people to talk, often when they didn't want to, just to fill the void.

Sure enough, Teddy rushed on. "They're at the Celtic Festival now, and absolutely fine. Both of them. Ethel. And Willie." He cleared his throat.

His tone said otherwise. "What is it? There's something else."

The man sounded miserable. "Maybe nothing. Just wondered if you've talked to September today?"

Combs wanted to reach through the phone and strangle the man. "Tell me."

"The guy who broke into the house wanted September's help. More precisely, Ethel said he wanted help from Sorokin Glass."

Chapter Thirty-Eight: September

September stared at the crowd gathered in the fairground as the helicopter made a wide circuit overhead. "Not the subtle approach I had in mind." She gritted her teeth, twisting her fingers in her lap until she made a conscious effort to calm her anger. She needed all her wits for this operation, and resented the stress spurred on by this man's pointed aggravations.

Pierce hadn't said much since she laughed in his face. Taking off with the cash? He'd meant it as a joke, right?

She didn't trust Jack; she hated the crazy family business; and while running away had its appeal, it would put Combs, his kids, and her brother at risk. Besides, disappearing with Pierce? Hell, no!

She hadn't heard from her brother Mark since Jack saved him that tragic day at the lake. He'd done his own disappearing act, but no doubt the Family could find him should they wish.

Pierce continued to ignore her as he scanned the ground below. "What are you doing?" Shadow poked his nose forward between the front seats, just like he did in her car. She absently stroked his face. Shadow licked his lips, revealing his own nerves.

"Looking for a safe place to set down." Pierce made a beeline for a cove of trees that separated the fairgrounds from the city proper. "I'd prefer our landing spot stays somewhat hidden. Don't want every Tom, Dick, and Larry-the-loser checking her out."

"Did you have to buzz the fairgrounds? Sure you don't want to take another pass and make sure Gillette knows were coming?" She didn't hide her sarcasm.

He had his own agenda, but she was stuck with him. She worried the stark black-and-white helicopter looked like a police vehicle, after Jared explicitly warned to keep them away.

He met her sarcasm with his own. "She knows you're coming. That's why she sicced Jared on you." He spied an opening in the thick cover of trees and pointed the helicopter's nose. "We hike in. We're fat on time. We're way early." He finally turned and met her eyes with a flinty glare. "She chose this venue on purpose. Knows we won't risk hurting any bystanders."

"Of course we won't. And the less attention, the better. I told you…"

"The pilot makes flight decisions. Get it straight, Sorokin. Gillette won't care about bystanders. She's all about the money. And revenge."

"Revenge for what?" If anybody had a reason for vengeance it was September.

"You, of course."

They hovered over the grassy space as he manipulated the controls to slowly descend. The helicopter landed dead center of the clearing with a soft bump.

Shadow sprang to his feet and barked with excitement as he ran from one side of the helicopter to the other, smearing nose prints against the windows.

"Shadow, *chill.*" Revenge against her? "I had no part investigating that operation. What's she got against me?" She unbuckled the safety harness and climbed to the rear area. Quickly, she divested Shadow of his head gear, and he shook himself with relief.

"You're the universal target. Anyone loyal to Kali won't like the rules changing."

Just one more reason to get rid of anyone loyal to Kali.

Pierce hopped out first, taking his go bag. September handed him the money bags then slipped the strap of her own go bag over her shoulder, so it rode out of the way on one hip, which helped conceal the bulge of her gun. She rummaged inside the child's knapsack and transferred the bandanna-wearing kangaroo toy to her own bag.

Once out of the helicopter, she signaled Shadow to join her. September caught up her bo staff in one hand and grabbed one of the bags of money with the other. Pierce shouldered the other money bag, and his own satchel. She didn't want to think about what might be inside.

They headed through the scrubby trees, weaving between stands of burr oak, cedars, mountain ash, and cedar elms, the ubiquitous volunteers crowding North Texas farmlands. September figured they had maybe a quarter mile to reach the edge of the fairgrounds. They were so early she hoped to catch the woman unprepared. While September would love to put away Robin Gillette, she prioritized the safety of a little girl. If swapping the money got Alana back, she'd consider it a win. Later, they could set the police on her trail.

Soon they reached a small man-made lake, a tank, in Texas parlance. Typically created to water cattle, the city made it a feature of this park. On Sunday night, if the weather held with no fire hazard warnings, revelers would enjoy a bonfire on the shore.

On the far side of the lake, fairgoers rambled. A few children competed in the shallows with homemade boats and water races.

September and Pierce's phones buzzed in tandem with an incoming text. She also noticed missed calls and texts from Combs. Her jaw tightened. That conversation must come later. For now, Jack's message took precedence.

>Call immediately. New info re: target.

Without waiting for Pierce, September dropped her bag of bills and dialed, putting it on speaker. "What've you got? Good timing, we're just approaching the fair."

"Took a while to comb through the records, but figured you'd want to know before you make contact. Might help decide how to proceed."

"We go in, make the exchange, and get out."

"Up to you. But Sorokin has it in her head to clean the slate. That doesn't necessarily mean termination of the current target."

Termination? September looked up sharply. "I never agreed to that." She'd put the bad actors behind bars, sure. But she had no intention of perpetuating Kaliko's killer methodology.

"Just saying... After reviewing the audio, we've got strong indication Kaliko contracted a team to terminate her husband. And to set up Wayne Teves for the murder." He paused. "Gillette was part of the assassination team."

Chapter Thirty-Nine: Robin

Robin followed the smaller woman into the red tent, blinking rapidly to adjust her eyes to the dim light. She'd wanted to destroy the stupid dog that let the kids get away, but now fortune smiled.

The older woman stumbled against the animal cage, caught herself before she went to her knees. "I thought you said Willie was—"

"Oh the scamps. The kids must've snuck out. I'm sure they'll be back soon." She pulled out a chair and gestured for the older woman to seat herself. "I'm Maeve. Your name is…?"

"Ethel Combs. Thanks for your help but I can't stay. I'd better ask the fair to make an announcement." Her eyes narrowed. "Aren't you worried about your daughter?"

Willie *Combs*? Detective Jeff Combs's son. This got better and better. The kids had slipped away, but she still had

Ethel—and she wasn't going to get away.

"What's that smell?" Ethel turned in the small space, eyes taking in the odd assortment of animal cage, table chain, crystal ball, tarot cards, and assorted amulets and knives. "Some special kind of incense?"

Robin didn't bother answering. Ethel stood in the soggy area where the ax cousin bled out. Confining an adult took more skill than cowing an underweight kid. She needed Ethel's compliance, at least momentarily. Fortunately, Robin had ample experience arranging such things.

"What a happy accident we met. I'm afraid, Ethel Combs, I haven't been completely truthful with you."

"What do you mean?" Ethel's shoulders hunched, lips tightened. She straightened and took a hesitant step toward the entrance.

People really should heed that mysterious *feeling* warning them of danger. Lucky for Robin, most folks dismissed such things.

Ethel's eyes widened when she saw Robin's gun. She froze.

"We have a situation here. I have a business meeting soon. Your kiddo threw a wrench in my plans, so you get to fix it for me." She preferred knives, but some situations called for bigger guns. Literally. She brandished the weapon, indicating the overlarge animal cage. "Don't think you'll fit inside as well as a kid. So we'll just improvise, shall we?"

"What have you done?" Ethel crossed her arms across her chest. Her voice, initially so assertive, turned quavery like an old woman.

"Nothing. Yet. But if you value Willie's life, do exactly what I say."

"Where is he? Is Willie okay?"

Robin hesitated, and then smiled broadly. "I have the

kids stashed somewhere safe. For now. Don't want damaged goods before the final sale, although what comes after…" She shrugged, enjoying Ethel's look of shocked realization.

Outside, the skirl of bagpipes rose and fell as the clan and piper parade marched by. Robin detested the sound. But the noise would cover gunshots, if need be.

"I'm in sales. My customer picks up the merchandise very soon. Your Willie sweetens the offer." She shrugged, grinning. "There's no accounting for taste."

Ethel took two hurried steps toward the exit.

Robin followed and jammed the gun into her ribs. "With all the clamor outside, nobody will hear. Don't make me waste ammunition." The clock was ticking. The kid might call his cop father to step in. She needed a body to swap for the ransom.

"Sit. Don't make me say that again." Robin shoved Ethel toward the chair, and the woman obediently sat. "Turn around, hands behind your back." Ethel complied, shuddering breaths the only sound as Robin quickly bound her wrists. "I'm going to gag you, too, because I just flat out don't trust you to keep your mouth shut. Don't struggle, or it'll make it that much harder to breathe. You gotta stay alive until Sorokin brings my money."

At the name, Ethel whimpered. Her shoulders slumped when Robin stuffed the gag in her mouth and knotted it behind her neck.

Even bound hands and feet wouldn't confine her for long. Ethel could squirm off the chair or worm out of the tent for do-gooders to see and rescue. Robin needed a better way to confine her out of sight.

Robin kept the gun trained on Ethel as she quickly checked outside. The parade continued past the tent. Crowds lined both sides of the path, facing away to watch the procession. "Perfect." Nobody paid attention to anything else. She unsheathed the knife nested between her breasts. Ethel watched, nostrils flaring, and shrinking away when she saw the blade.

"Don't worry sweetie, I won't stick you as long as you follow the rules. Do exactly what I say." Robin crossed to the rear of the tent, stabbed the knife through the crimson fabric at shoulder height and slit the tent open to the ground. She parted the fabric and peered one direction and then the other. Deserted. Next door, the two remaining coffin-size crates stood tall, bull's eye targets brightly painted to face the crowd.

She grabbed Ethel's arm and levered her upright. "Run, and I'll slit your throat." She pulled and pushed until they stepped through the slit, then led her to the closest crate.

The obnoxious gray cat crouched on top of the box, hissing. Robin hissed back and jabbed her knife at it. The lithe creature sprang away, not a whisker disturbed. Her lip curled. She hated cats. They creeped her out. Robin pushed Ethel inside the open box. "Sit."

Ethel slid down the interior, tears flowing freely down her face. The gag had already soaked through with spit, snot, and tears. Disgusting.

Robin squatted beside her to quickly loop bindings around the woman's ankles. She stood, put a finger to her lips, and swung closed the lid of the wooden box, shooting the thumb bolt that held it shut. It was unlikely the petite Ethel could knock it open while scrunched down in the bottom of the heavy container, but for good measure, she secured it with one of the decorative locks strung amid the ring of keys at her hip.

Satisfied, Robin sheathed the knife in her bosom and grabbed a handful of her skirt to dab the sweat from her face and neck. The sequined head rag with attached gray braids helped change her appearance—not Robin D'Andri, or Gillette, or any of the other aliases she'd used. The Magical Maeve costume increased the heat level, though. A cool bottle of water had her name on it. And later, a beer. Or five. After she took care of the ransom exchange and the gadfly delivering it.

Ethel Combs better hope September-Sorokin appeared on time. The wooden coffin had no ventilation. Robin didn't need her alive, only the threat in her presence as a backup. She'd learned to build in redundancy whenever possible.

Four young men with pretty girls hanging on their muscular arms lounged near the front of her red tent as she walked around it. As she came into view, one called out.

"Where's the guy for the ax throwing? I got a bet with my buddy I can make four out of five bull's-eyes." He pointed to the wooden casket where Ethel's hidden form now waited.

Robin shrugged. "Haven't seen the ax man in hours." *Not a lie.*

"So it's free. You don't care if we toss some blades?" Another of the young men called to her back, but she didn't bother to acknowledge him. *Knock yourself out.*

She smiled, as she heard the first THUMP! of an ax find the target.

Chapter Forty: Shadow

Shadow always enjoyed car rides. But this ride gave him views out the many windows he'd never seen before. They had been as high in the sky as some of the scruffy birds he chased out of September's garden.

Back on the ground, he followed close beside September, keeping himself between her and Pierce, who hadn't proven himself yet to Shadow's satisfaction. The man carried a bag that smelled oily, which meant a gun. He hated guns, not only their smell, but their ability to reach out and bite a good dog with no warning. September also carried one, but that was different. He trusted her.

In the distance, Shadow heard the murmur of many people, funny loud music, shouts, and laughter. Pungent cooking smells made his mouth water and tummy rumble. He wondered if September had brought along treats for a good dog. He'd like that.

"I checked if the kidnapper had contacted Jared again."
September increased her pace, following a well-worn path
that snaked through the trees. "Just before we landed, but
he hasn't replied." She adjusted the bags that carried the
supplies they needed.

Pierce led the way. "Have to wait on the exchange
location?"

"The details help, but I don't plan to follow her
directions. She probably has an ambush waiting. I'll track
her another way."

"Really? How?" He stopped and turned so quickly that
September nearly ran into him.

Shadow growled, hackles rising. Pierce made September's
heart beat fast, not in a good way.

"I have been stalked, hunted, hounded, and attacked
multiple times by people just like her. If she's worked for
the Family for years she won't change tactics overnight.
She'll dangle the child like a trophy to get what she wants.
This won't be some easy-peasy swap. It's gonna get nasty."

"So what's your plan?"

They broke free of the tree line and stood atop a slight
rise. A sometime water runoff, dry in the August heat,
snaked a path to a roped off section of land. Beyond that,
many people walked, talked, and laughed. Shadow sniffed:
grilled meat, sugary pastry, human body stink. Lovely!

September stroked his head, and Shadow's tail moved as
though she switched on the wag. "We have the girl's toy.
Shadow's trained to track missing pets. More recently he's
also shown aptitude to track humans, once he knows what I
want and has the right cue."

Shadow wagged again, understanding she talked about
him. He'd do whatever she asked.

"You telling me your dog can sniff out and track one

child in the middle of all this mix of humanity?" Pierce shook his head, doubt clear in his voice. "How're you going to do that without shining a spotlight on yourself?"

She laughed. "You've never been to a Celtic Festival, have you? You'll see loads of dogs performing work demos, competing in pet parades, or hanging with their people. Shadow will fit right in, sniffing around the front of each and every booth." She pulled out her phone, did something with it Shadow couldn't see, and then held it out to show Pierce. "You should have one, too. It's an official pass, gives us all access, if we get stopped and they ask."

He smiled. "Courtesy of your Uncle Jack, I suppose."

She nodded. "The security folks wear clearly marked smocks. Some are local PD and might recognize me. Best to avoid them to cut down on questions that might delay the search."

September skidded down the steep runoff, quickly running up the other side, then stepping over the barrier rope. Shadow leaped ahead and waited beside her. Pierce quickly joined them but shoved his money bag underneath the rope barrier.

"Any idea what to do with our luggage? Shadow sniffing around might not draw attention, but I guarantee lugging these bags will raise eyebrows."

"Way ahead of you. We'll stash the cash where no one will look, or at least Gillette won't discover. There's plenty of space under the grandstand, directly below the stage. Two extra bags won't be noticed. We find Alana, tell Gillette where to collect the reward, and hightail it out of there. And if needed, we have the money at hand if things go sideways."

Shadow took in the extraordinary sights. He licked his lips and slowed with a plaintive whine when they passed roasting wieners. Sometimes September used those during training lessons. Almost as good as bacon. She ignored the enticing aroma, though, and with a sigh he kept pace.

They approached rows of folding chairs in front of a large platform. People on the stage milled around, spinning and stamping their feet to strange music. Shadow cocked his head, wondering why they bounced around like clueless puppies. But the rhythm and coordinated movement felt oddly pleasing and exciting. He barked once, but then shushed immediately when September placed one finger to her lips.

She showed her phone to a person wearing official bibs. Pierce did the same, and they hurried to the back of the stage. "Shadow, *wait.*"

He whined under his breath, but didn't disobey. Shadow watched the pair disappear underneath the platform, lugging the bags of money with them.

A tantalizing scent caught Shadow's attention. He stared across an open field. Woolly creatures ran in tightly packed groups. Sheep! Close enough for a good dog to meet and sniff. Hectoring black-and-white dogs drove them hither and yon as birdlike, the sheep swooped and flocked across the field.

What fun! The dogs chased and the creatures ran wherever those good dogs told them to go. Shadow whined again, wanting to join the fun.

The wind shifted, and Shadow's attention shifted with it. His nose wasn't mistaken: Willie… Dodging between people, and racing toward the herding trial.

Chapter Forty-One: Alana

Alana ran and ran and ran some more. The big helicopter, black-and-white like cop cars, made true Boss's dire warnings. Run away, and cops would come. They'd take her away. Lock Alana in a black hole, never to see the sun again, send more men to do hurtful things. Because she deserved it. Alana, a nasty, terrible, ugly little girl, brought everything on herself. That's why Papa gave her away to Tony Kanoa, he didn't want such a terrible bad girl.

Boss treated her awful, and Alana knew she couldn't survive something worse when the police punished her badness.

The tiny flame of hope she'd see Papa again and he'd forgive her flickered out. His voice on the phone, just a trick. Maybe Willie tricked her, too. Even though he seemed nice…If Willie hadn't helped her, she never would've got away. And getting away meant cops punishing her.

Whimpering, and trying to choke back sobs, Alana dodged between grown-up legs, ducking into and back out of canopied booth spaces. She tipped over a display of beautiful crystal rocks, and the owner shouted bad words, and chased her.

One of her fairy wings ripped off when she ducked beneath a picnic table to hide. A big woman with a greasy smile and four squalling kids sat down with spicy food. Alana scooted away before the woman could tell the cops on her.

Bare feet stung on grass burned crispy dry in the summer heat, but the hard packed dirt raised blisters if she stood in one place. Alana hopped from one foot to the other, then rushed to a shady spot beside the toilet. She stood silent, gasping for breath, and shuddering with fear.

The helicopter disappeared. They probably had rules about squashing honest, innocent people or else they would have landed right on top of her and taken her away in chains. Alana scrubbed the tears from her face.

Alana peered around the corner of the toilet, not even minding the bad smell. She'd smelled worse, seen worse like the Boss's most recent sacrifice. Her fault—always her fault—that the lady with pretty braids got killed. She wondered what the tattooed man had done wrong? Alana knew it was only a matter of time before she became Boss's latest sacrifice.

Across the way she saw an open field with tree trunks scattered here and there. Small groups of people gathered in lines to watch something, but she couldn't tell what. Alana crept closer. A small lake glittered on the other side of the field.

If she could cross the field, and wade in the water for just a little bit, her feet wouldn't sting so bad. Oh, to soak in the cool water up to her neck. She hadn't taken a bath since…forever. Maybe cops wouldn't see her hidden in the water. She bet helicopters couldn't land there, either.

Or she could float away and die. That wouldn't be so bad, better than if the cops caught her.

Impulsively, Alana dashed for the field. She aimed for a place where no onlookers stood, just in case one of those cops hid ready to snatch and grab bad girls. She ducked under a rope barrier and sprinted across the empty field on sore feet.

The roar of several voices rose behind her. Individual shouts yelled for her to stop. She took a quick look over one shoulder and gasped. A huge man lumbered after her, waving massive arms, bare legs pumping under a plaid skirt. His long, braided hair hung down his back, and his painted face looked like a monster. Oh, she didn't want to be caught by that man, he would really hurt her!

She screamed and ran faster. Then tripped, falling face down in the middle of the field. When she looked up, dozens and dozens of woolly sheep pounded all around her, their pointed hooves tearing up the grass as barky dogs harried them in a cluster ever closer to her prone figure.

Chapter Forty-Two: September

September ducked under the four-foot height of the modular stage. A fabric skirt curtained the edge all the way around, to hide the storage space beneath. Multiple large metal boxes filled much of the area, some stacked, but most too large to fit into any organized display.

Overhead, pounding feet danced in syncopated rhythm, making the platform shudder. September wedged her bag between two of the nearest boxes. Turning, she motioned Pierce to do the same. With the jumbled containers, and no expectation of hidden bounty, the money should be safe.

As she left the storage area, she pushed Shadow's inquisitive nose out of her face. He whined, and aimed a slurp at her face before she could straighten. September took a moment to press her forehead against his, smoothing his cheeks with a hand on each side of his handsome face. "Good dog, Shadow." She could tell the stress, and intense heat had the big dog concerned. *Me, too.*

September pulled a large thermos of cold water from her go bag and poured some into the doggy drinking cup, then held it for Shadow to drink his fill. She took a swig of cool water herself, swished it in her mouth, then spat it onto the grass before taking another long swallow. "Better get started. Lots of ground to cover. You ready, baby dog?"

Shadow woofed, tail waving with eagerness. He paw-danced in the shriveled grass. Maybe she should have brought his protective booties. Fur offered sun protection, but the black color absorbed heat. Wetting him down would help keep him cool. She cupped water from the thermos, applying it to his head and face, before closing and replacing the canister.

"Now what?" Pierce stood relaxed but ready to spring into action. "We can cover more ground by splitting up." He smiled, teeth bright against his dark complexion. He pulled a battered ball cap from his own bag, adjusting it so the bill shaded his face.

She read the lettering—*shitake happens*—surprised they shared the same sarcastic sense of humor. She liked that even if she still didn't trust him. "You kind of stand out in this forever-plaid crowd." Pierce moved like a panther in a herd of buffalo. "Gillette wants to meet me alone."

"How about I disappear, shadow you, and lend a hand if you need it."

She doubted Pierce could ever *disappear.*

"If the Robin woman sees anything suspicious, she'll cut and run. Or worse, do something to the girl before you can stop her," Pierce continued.

September tightened her lips. Maybe it was superstitious, but she hated hearing the worst case spoken aloud. "There's plenty of security around." She pointed at a nearby figure wearing a neon yellow smock with *security* written across the front and back. She wished things hadn't escalated so quickly before being able to loop in the authorities. And Combs. She figured Pierce would do whatever he wanted anyway.

"Good to know." He grinned, touched his hand to the cap brim, and ducked away around the stage. By the time she and Shadow followed, he'd disappeared into the crowd.

She'd had time to reflect during the helicopter ride. Her whole life pre-Sorokin had been one coincidence after another. This situation had the same stench of wheels within wheels.

Too late to change course now. No way to back out. Her only hope to survive the pending collision with the Family was to keep her eyes wide open and race forward. If she could reunite a father with his little girl, maybe some of the stink would fade.

She pulled out her phone to check for text messages. Nothing from Jared, or anyone else.

September took in the multiple rows of exhibitors. "Wanna play *seek?*" She asked Shadow, using the command for search work. His head tilted to one side, panting jaws snapping shut as he met her eyes with sharp attention. His tail moved faster, eager to begin the job.

Shadow already wore his tracking halter. With this crowded venue, she couldn't use the long lead. She placed him in a sit-stay then pulled out the stuffed kangaroo toy. She held it below nose level for Shadow to get a good whiff.

He snorted and snuffled several places on the fabric toy. Then he looked up at her with a happy grin. He knew what scent to follow, if he could find it.

Success depended on Alana having walked at least a short distance outside wherever she was being held. All bets were off if the kidnapper kept her hidden in a car off-site. But at least this initial search would eliminate areas and narrow the focus.

Usually Shadow had a starting point, a known location from where the lost individual had disappeared. He'd cast back and forth in a zigzag pattern to search for the scent. Once found, he could follow the missing's path.

But in this case, they had no starting point. Instead, September acted like everyone else attending the Celtic Festival. She walked along the grassy aisles, go bag over her shoulder, bo staff in one hand, and Shadow's leash in the other. Stopping at each canopied exhibit, she pretended to check out the wares. She avoided conversation that could sidetrack them from their purpose. While she stood, Shadow put his nose to work, casting around the booth space for the right scent.

Shadow's efficient detection quickly eliminated the first dozen booths. But it had taken them close to two hours to cover the majority of the rest of the booths. Still no luck. When September's phone rang, she eagerly pulled it out of her pocket, expecting Jared or maybe Jack with details that would cut short their search. Instead, she recognized Teddy's number.

She rolled her eyes. Horrible timing for him to offer an apology, or at least an explanation. She refused the call, and then sent him a quick text.

<Busy, talk later.

In the distance, the crowd murmured with concern, surging toward an open field. A flock of sheep raced around, driven by a team of dogs. They clustered at one

point, then schooled like fish pooling to the other side of
the field. Her phone buzzed again, answering her text.

>SOS! Pick up now

The message raised goosebumps, despite the heat. When
the phone rang, she answered.

"What's wrong?"

Teddy nearly shouted over the phone. Shadow whined,
recognizing fear in the familiar voice. "Ethel called. Said she
took Willie to the fair and he went missing. Now Ethel
won't answer her phone."

Pierce smiled and nodded affably, perused vendor wares,
exchanging pleasantries with everyone he met. Blending in
meant more than hiding in the shadows. In his line of work,
you only truly disappeared by standing out in the crowd like
you belonged. September, bless her clueless little heart, gave
him the ideal option.

He kept an eye out for the neon-garbed security
personnel. His intel gave no concrete numbers, no database,
no names. He'd have to make decisions on a case-by-case
basis.

He struck up a conversation with the first target when
the man sneaked off for a smoke behind a line of Porta
Potties. Pierce caught him from behind, hooking one arm
around his neck and the other bracing the pressure for a few
seconds. Fortunately, nobody seemed to notice when the
poor fellow collapsed. Pierce had an explanation ready just
in case—*heatstroke, he'll be fine.*

Pierce dragged the man into the chemical-smelling
cubical, zip-tied his wrists and ankles, then closed the door.

He noticed the "green" vacant sign on the door, and quicky popped a peppermint into his mouth, chewing it into a mush. Then he thumbed the mess onto the door lock slider. The red color indicated "occupied" and would work in a pinch. He didn't want the guy discovered too soon.

Pierce donned the neon vest and strolled on. Now one of the many no-name security hires, he had free rein to continue his assignment.

Chapter Forty-Three: Ethel

Ethel flinched when the first THUMP shook her coffin-like prison. She flexed her jaw against the nasty cloth gag but couldn't loosen the knot. She tried to yell, but her voice sounded muffled even to her own ears. It was doubtful anyone could hear her past the muzzle and through the thick wood.

She remembered the bull's-eye, so leaned away from the target side to put distance between herself and whatever pummeled the target surface, which wasn't harmless cornhole bags. Ethel shuddered and tried to loosen the bonds that imprisoned her wrists behind her back.

THUMP! Laughter followed the impact.

The fortuneteller had boxed her up, threatened her life, just for mentioning September... Or Sorokin, whatever the hell she called herself. Bile rose in the back of her throat and Ethel struggled to tamp it down. With the cloth stuffed into her mouth, she'd suffocate.

THUMP! THUMP! She gasped when a sharp metal edge penetrated the wood. Not enough, though, to use to cut her bonds. Solid planks kept the ax from jutting completely through, unless it hit just right in a narrow gap between boards.

She'd felt sorry for September, and the tragedy that stalked her like a vulture scenting decay. She'd quietly celebrated when Jeff's broken heart healed as his love for September grew.

But now this. So much pain, betrayal, losing her dear Stan in such a horrific way. Why the hell was September—*Sorokin*—working with this Maeve creature? And what about Willie?

Ethel's eyes flooded. Maeve had him stowed away somewhere, too. *Please God, not in the other box!* Shame on her for dismissing his story about a shackled fairy. The evil woman admitted keeping the girl captive. How could she?

September would never risk Willie. Ethel had seen them together, and they loved each other. Melinda, too, though that was a more challenging relationship.

Maeve grabbed Willie to get back at September, the reason didn't matter. Ethel had to escape, she must protect Willie.

Tentatively at first, and then with more resolve, Ethel leaned away from the side of the box, and then rammed her shoulder against it. She shifted and repeated the exercise in the other direction. First one way, then the other, she hit the sides over and over, pinballing back and forth. Rocking the box might tip it over. Anything to draw attention and get her help.

Another THUMP! And someone screamed. "Stop it! You're gonna hit that big cat."

Ethel redoubled her efforts, but she only managed a slight shuddering of the box with each shoulder slam.

"I wasn't aiming for it. Look, it jumped off. Let's go get something to eat."

The voices squabbled as they faded away. She'd missed her chance.

Her shoulders ached from the futile battering. The heat made her dizzy, and her nose ran from weeping. Nobody knew she was here. She'd told her neighbor she'd be gone until Monday. She'd either succumb to heatstroke, another ax, or the fortunetellers blade.

Get a grip, woman. She couldn't get out, but Magical Maeve had threatened to return. She had to prepare, surprise the woman with swift kicks when she opened the box. Ethel flexed her calf muscles, it could work if her legs didn't cramp or go to sleep. If Maeve returned at all...

No! She wouldn't die, not like this. Stan went out like a hero. She hadn't been a cop's wife for nothing. He'd always said her stubborn streak made her irresistible.

Oh Stanley, I miss you so much...even the blarney.

Ethel slouched against the side of the box. Her bound hands explored the splintery sides and floor of the box. When something soft and furry touched her wrist, she froze. With a sad, muffled laugh, Ethel realized the cat the kids scared away had noticed her and must be poking through a gap between the planks.

Her eyes widened. People couldn't see her, but they noticed the cat. Anyone with a feline affinity would pay attention to the cat's antics, might even investigate what had the kitty enthralled.

Even mind-your-own-business folks made exceptions for animals needing proper care in this horrendous heat. With luck, the stray cat just might save her life.

Chapter Forty-Four: Willie

W illie dashed after Alana, weaving between the grown-ups. For a kid in bare feet, she sure ran fast—fear turbo-charged her.

He knew it hadn't been a police copter, it didn't have the right markings. Magical Maeve sure brainwashed her, though. He saw a movie once where they brainwashed people, and it gave him nightmares. Dad got mad Melinda let him watch. Anyway, the police were there to protect and serve, just like Dad. They weren't about hurting little girls. Or brainwashing people.

He waited politely for a group of ginormous men to get out of his way. The tats they wore looked dangerous, but in a good way. When he got big, he wanted some rad ink just like that. He'd have to wait until he was at least a teenager before Dad would consider it.

Finally the muscled, kilted men moved aside, and Willie

took off past them down the row of booths. He'd lost sight of Alana. So he paused at the outdoor water fountain to take a long slurp and refill the water bottle.

A cold nose brushed his bare calf, followed by a quick licking tongue. Willie looked down, surprised and pleased the dog had got away and followed him. Daylight revealed the poor dog needed a bath, as clumps of dirt, leaves, burrs, and stick-tights matted his white coat.

"Bet you're thirsty, too." He cupped his hand and poured water from the bottle into it for the dog to drink. Eagerly, with tail wagging, the dog slurped up the liquid. Willie examined the collar tag, checking for an owner name and address, but saw nothing. Noah nosed and sniffed Willie's hand, the way Shadow did before going to work. That gave Willie an idea.

He offered Noah the empty water bottle to sniff. Alana had touched the bottle, and drunk from it, too. He didn't know if it would work, but it was worth a shot. The festival was jam-packed with people, all of them sweaty and smelly and crowding pathways. But a dog could track her down. Even little dogs like Noah had great sniffers.

Instead of sniffing the bottle, though, Noah grabbed it in his jaws. He crunched it happily, making a loud crinkly noise.

Willie silently called himself all kinds of stupid. Kinsler did the same thing. September always made him take the lid and plastic ring off to prevent choking. He didn't want Noah to choke, even if he didn't know how to track. The stray did help Alana escape.

Willie reached for the bottle. Noah dodged away, play bowing in the universal invitation. "No, wait. Give me the bottle."

Instead, Noah whirled and zoomed away. Willie

followed. Yelling wouldn't make the dog come, and besides, he didn't want to draw the witch's attention. Also, stray dogs got caught and sent to the pound. A hero dog like Noah had no place in the dog pound.

He heard the crowd yelling by the big empty field he'd passed earlier. The dog ran that way, so Willie followed. He pushed and shoved his way between clots of onlookers until he reached the rope barrier. Someone caught hold of Noah's collar to keep him from dashing onto the field. Willie hooked his own hand through the collar and tugged the dog away.

"Get that dog on a leash, kid." A big guy wearing a neon security vest admonished Willie. He recognized one of Dad's policeman friends, and blushed. Willie looked away and nodded without answering. He didn't need anyone tattling on him.

Willie stared into the field where everyone watched. His mouth dropped open. Alana crumpled in the brown grass, only one fairy wing left. All around her, disgruntled sheep bawled and milled, while frustrated herding dogs nipped and chastised the outer stragglers. Sharp hooves tiptoed around her form, and sometimes landed on her.

Noah whined and gargled with excitement, still clutching the empty water bottle. He pulled against Willie's hand on the collar, paw-dancing and clearly eager to do more than watch. It was as if the dog thought, *those other dogs weren't doing a good job.*

Willie considered the stray's rapt attention on the girl. Before he could make an impulsive decision, the collar decided for him by tearing away. He stuffed the collar and tag in his pocket. "Go get her, boy. Keep her safe."

Noah dropped the bottle and launched himself across the field, short legs a blur of motion. Willie followed, ducking under the restraining line and pelting across the field in the dog's wake.

The crowd roared. The sheep froze for three heartbeats. They scattered, woolly dandelion fluff riding a frenetic breeze.

Relieved the sheep abandoned Alana, Willie worried when she didn't move. The dog reached her first. Noah belly flopped and crawled to her, licking her face, whimpering and wagging. Willie arrived seconds later and helped her sit up.

More people ran across the field. The handler redirected his dogs to regroup the herd of sheep. Baa-ing and barks mixed with angry shouts, the noise worse than braying bagpipes.

"Get up, get up now. They're coming." Willie grabbed Alana's hand, and the pair raced in the other direction across the field. Noah barked with happy excitement, keeping pace.

"Hide! We got to hide. Those cops are coming to get me, Willie, let's hide!"

He let Alana lead the way. They circled the grandstand, staying as far from the crowed as possible. When Alana ducked under the stage skirt into the storage area, Willie followed.

Pierce jogged across the field with two security and a woman volunteer. The trio complained loudly about recalcitrant kids messing with the herding demo. The woman tried to placate the irate shepherd. Everyone stood with red faces streaming with sweat. And now, the poor herding dogs had a massive do-over to gather the straying sheep.

The security men left. Pierce followed, delighted when they headed to the nearby lake instead of back to the fairgrounds.

"Hate public bathrooms. Those porta jon things are nasty."

Pierce nodded. "Got that right. Me, I'm a nature lover. How 'bout you?"

The men laughed with good ol' boy humor and hurried to the brushy trees.

Once out of sight of any onlookers, Pierce waited until the men posed. Like kids, they each bet on which could reach the farthest.

Pierce caught the first man from behind. The choke hold put the man to sleep in less than five seconds. Pierce let him drop to the ground.

The second security guard turned. "What the hell? Is he okay?"

Pierce shrugged. "Heat stroke. Awful weather today." He stood back, expecting the man to kneel and check his friend.

Instead, the man came at Pierce, fists raised. "What'd you do to him?!"

Pierce held out the flat of his left hand and slapped against the other's chest. In the same motion, his right hand grabbed the security guard's shoulder and yanked. The push/pull flipped the man around. No longer facing each other, Pierce repeated the choke hold. Unconscious in three seconds, the second man also dropped to the hard ground.

He quickly bound them, then collected weapons, tossing them into the water. The men would revive quickly on their own, none the worse for wear, but he didn't want them found too soon. Gags took care of that.

Leaving the shelter of the scrubby trees, Pierce jogged

back to the main festival grounds. The sheep, dogs, and shepherd had left, and now caber tossing prompted shouts from spectators. Scanning the surroundings, he looked for the last volunteer. She stood guard by the rope that separated the spectators from the field.

The more security neutralized, the better. She armed perspiration away from her red face. *Left hand, no wedding ring. Perfect.* He pulled a cool bottle of water out of the bag slung over his shoulder and pasted on his most charming smile. On the way, he unwrapped and crunched another peppermint candy. She wouldn't know what hit her.

Chapter Forty-Five: Jared

After showing the Uber driver his thick fold of cash, Jared had breathed with relief when the man agreed to drive him to Heartland. The man shut off the service then turned in his seat.

"Half now. The rest when I get there."

Jared couldn't argue. He handed over the bills and waited impatiently as the man counted. Thankfully, the driver asked no questions, just tightened his lips and shoved the car into gear.

The man took his time, but Jared couldn't complain. An accident would further delay the trip. One-and-a-half hours later, the Uber turned off Highway 75 to the designated farm-to-market road; he slowed to check his phone map. "The fairgrounds are another three-odd miles up this road. Pay me now. Or you can walk the rest of the way."

Without argument, Jared handed over the rest of the fee.

"Just hurry, will ya?"

The man grunted, taking his time to count the other half of the cash. He stuck it into one pocket of his cargo shorts before pressing on the gas. He expertly weaved in and out of traffic, hitting the gas to beat yellow lights. Soon they reached the intersection with the temporary placard announcing Heartland Celtic Festival. "Better get out here. Parking's full."

Jared stepped out then slammed the door hard. The driver sped away without a backward glance.

Despite the lateness of the day, the sidewalk still held dozens of people, in pairs or family groups. They strode purposefully up the sidewalk past hundreds of parked cars filling nearby fields. Jared checked his phone for the hundredth time, praying for a message that Sorokin already had Alana safe.

His head throbbed, but the minor aches and bruising from the car accident paled before the imperative to find his daughter. He hurried along the sidewalk wishing he had a weapon. He'd never owned a gun in his life, hadn't a clue how to use one, or where to get one. The kidnapper mentioned a red tent. He'd find it, and take his daughter home, or die trying.

The entry line moved slowly as the crowd purchased tickets. Jared threw cash at the attendant and waved away the change. He pushed through people, nearly knocking a teenager off his feet in his rush. Jared had no confidence Sorokin would follow through with her promise. Talk was cheap, and Alana's life was at stake.

He stopped at the first exhibit booth. "I'm lookin' for a red tent." He waved vaguely at the rest of the exhibits.

"Dunno, man, I just got here. Relieving my mom, she wanted to see the last show on the stage." The kid shrugged and gestured toward the display. "Want to buy something?"

Jared rushed on. He jogged to the end of the first row of exhibits and stopped to ask again. The proprietors barely glanced up, intent on eating supper. Most of the attendees pooled around the stage at the other end of the fairgrounds. The woman pointed vaguely across the way, speaking past a mouthful of funnel cake. "Fortuneteller has a red tent, I think. Over that way, a few columns across, then back toward the entrance."

Finally! Jared dodged under ropes holding tent awnings in place, leaped across chairs left in pathways, until he reached the correct row. Without slowing, he turned and saw the blood-red tent. His head pounded in rhythm with his feet as he closed on the goal.

Jared only made it halfway before he went sprawling to the ground. "What the…"

"Thought you might pull something like this." A woman with twin gray braids had stepped from behind another exhibit and tripped him She stuck out her hand to offer help up, but only as cover for any watchers. Her other hand caressed the hilt of a knife nestled conveniently in her bodice. "We have a problem, Papa, and you need to fix it."

"Let me go, lady, I got my own problems —"

She leaned down, got right in his face. Garlic and body odor made him gag. "Sorokin broke the rules. She's got my money but is playing games with your kid's life. You're going to make her pay me, or never see Alana again."

From beneath her skirt, she pulled out a gun and pressed it into his hands. "Find the money she brought. Then kill her. Or I will take apart sweet little Alana while you watch. Look at me, Jared. *Look at me!* Do you believe me? You better. Say it back."

He nodded and gulped. "I believe you." He'd do whatever he needed to get his daughter safe.

Chapter Forty-Six: September

Heat rushed to September's face. Her pulse thrummed in her temple, and she closed her eyes to focus her bearings. The sounds of the fair dimmed. The ground beneath her feet tilted suddenly and she had to take a step to catch her balance. Shadow leaned against her legs, bracing her without need for her to ask.

"What do you mean Willie's missing?" September looked around. "They're here?"

"You're at the festival, too?" Teddy's gravelly voice settled her, and she took a breath. "Thought you were in Dallas."

"Change of plans." The crowd had thinned. Most remaining spectators surrounded the stage for final acts. The festival closed in half an hour. Shadow still had more than a dozen booths to scent. That no longer took precedence.

"Ethel mentioned helping a friend. Do you know what exhibit? Candles and jam, I think." She'd take Shadow there, and he'd switch to tracking Willie.

Teddy gave her the name and location. "There's a map schematic on the festival's web page. Texting you a screenshot. The friend doesn't answer her cell, either."

Teddy was a talented white hat hacker, and his skills had come in handy more than once. She oriented herself, noting a large red tent at the far end of this pathway. Next door sat an ax-throwing booth—sure to attract Willie—deserted but for a very large gray cat playing around the base of one of the bull's-eye targets.

"What are you doing at the festival, September? Or should I call you Sorokin Glass?" Teddy's voice grated.

She flinched. "I'll explain later." She disconnected. According to Teddy's directions they needed to cross two rows and walk toward the stage to find the friend's candle and jam display.

September cautiously approached the woman seated in a folding chair in the far corner of the booth. She had a battery-powered fan, and a cold drink next to her. September idly wondered why the candles hadn't melted in this heat.

"Can I help you? Candles, preserves, the sweetest honey you'll ever taste." The woman pushed herself upright in the chair, a fixed smile on her face in salesperson mode.

"I'm looking for Ethel Combs. Have you seen either her or Willie lately?"

The woman glanced from September to Shadow's dark figure, and recognition bloomed. "You must be September. Ethel left to find Willie." She chuckled. "Willie came back looking for her, with a girl in the cutest fairy outfit. But Ethel was gone by then."

"Which way did they go?"

She pointed. "Ethel said they had to park in the second field area." She sipped her drink.

"No, I mean Willie. Which way did he go?" That would give Shadow a good starting point, if he could pick up the trail from here.

As though reading her mind, Shadow reached up to nose-poke the kangaroo toy that peeked out of her go bag. He dropped his nose to the ground to snuffle around, then abruptly lay down to signal he found the target scent.

She hadn't told him to find Willie yet. He'd alerted on Alana's scent.

"Which way? Willie and the girl, where'd they go?" September wanted to shake the woman's bemused expression off her face.

"Don't know, got a customer about that time. Hey, you want to taste a sample? Ethel says my preserves beat everyone else's..."

With exasperation, September signaled Shadow. She pulled out the kangaroo for a refresher sniff. "Good dog, Shadow. Let's play hide and seek. Seek, Shadow, *seek*!"

He sprang to his feet, and without hesitation headed across the fairgrounds, moving so quickly September had to jog to keep from slowing him down. His eagerness told her the scent remained fresh. Alana had got away from her abductor. Now to find the kids and spirit them away from the danger zone. Then she'd send Heartland PD to take care of Gillette. And find Ethel.

Willie's involvement worried and exasperated her. The boy had a streak of his father in him, always ready to run to the rescue. But Willie was in over his head.

Shadow led her back toward the open competition field. The caber tossing event was in full swing. At the rope barrier, she stopped. Shadow looked up with confusion.

"Glad yours is on a leash." An onlooker nodded. "You missed a big mess that could've turned tragic. Stray dog ran onto the field and chased after the sheep during the herding demo."

September turned to go. The field held no trace of either child. She'd have to run Shadow around the perimeter to find where the kids came out.

A quickening breeze stirred the air, hot gusts lifting dry leaves into flurries. Shadow's head came up. His tail raised and began wagging, clearly detecting something else on the wind.

September followed the dog's gaze, and sucked in a breath of relief, a smile softening the tension in her face. Dodging between spectators, and making a beeline for the stage, ran Willie hand-in-hand with a little girl wearing bedraggled fairy wings. A dog followed them.

Robin spied from a distance. She'd spotted Sorokin with her big black beast when they approached the red tent. If Sorokin had come two steps closer, she'd have buried her blade in the woman's throat and happily sacrificed the money she deserved. The satisfaction, with deferred benefits, trumped the ransom.

But fortune favored the brave...and the patient. Sometimes she let immediate gratification overrule good sense. Robin couldn't resist cheesy-puff snacks, or cherry licorice whips—would eat 'em until sick—but vengeance tasted even better.

Bingeing spoiled revenge best savored one small bite at a

time. The delay would be worth it.

Besides, the woman only carried a long stick in one hand and the dog's leash with the other. Her shoulder bag probably held a gun but couldn't hold all the cash she'd demanded. Sorokin had stashed it somewhere. Robin couldn't trust Jared to do the job, but if she followed Sorokin long enough, the right opportunity would present itself. For the cash, and sweet revenge.

Sorokin suddenly stopped and swiveled with rapt attention. Robin grinned, recognizing the same running figures. She couldn't contain the gleeful laugh that made those nearby flinch and move away. She ignored them and continued following her nemesis. Protecting the kids would demand all of Sorokin's attention. Robin could finish her business, then escape without a scratch to start her life anew.

Chapter Forty-Seven: Willie

Willie held the curtain aside for Alana, and then followed her into the space under the stage. He expected it to be cooler in the shade, but the drapes cut off all air circulation. Stacks and jumbles of storage boxes filled the space, making it a good spot to hide from evil Magical Maeve.

"Over here." He wove between the piles, while on the other side of the ceiling—the stage floor, he guessed—there were noisy feet and movement as the next act prepared.

Alana joined him. Noah pressed close. The three huddled together behind a stack of containers.

He wished they had more water. Noah panted, tongue lolling in the heat, despite drinking up Alana's bottle of water before using it to track her. September had told him that's how dogs cooled off, using evaporation off the tongue instead of sweating. His damp skin didn't seem to help much, though. Sweat just made him feel icky. "Only one bottle left to share. Take sips. We'd better make it last."

"We gotta stay for how long? How will we find my papa?" Alana handed back the water, and rubbed her eyes, smearing the dirt and cat face paint across tear-streaked cheeks.

"Aunt Ethel wasn't at her friend's booth, so betcha she's hissed off and looking for me. Let's rest here until the crowd starts to leave. Then we sneak out with them and find her car."

Alana didn't want anything to do with the police. But if he got the chance, Willie would stop one of the security people. Or sneak up on stage and ask the MC to page Aunt Ethel.

Willie settled on the grass next to Alana, crossing his legs and leaning against one of the storage containers. Noah pushed up between them, wriggling until he could rest his head in her lap.

Alana gently stroked the dog's ears, watching with brightening eyes when Noah gurgled with delight and wagged his tail. "Thought dogs were scary. Papa got bit once. But he's not scary. He likes me."

Grinning, Willie added a few scratches to the dog's chest. The dog moaned in happy response. "He's a hero, helped you get away from that mean lady. And kept you from getting trampled by the sheep."

She stuck out her thin ankle, fingering the leather circlet that remained. "He chewed me free. He's a good dog. Noah." She tasted the name and nodded in approval. Alana leaned back, resting her head against the nearest bin, and yawned deeply. Her eyes fluttered closed.

Willie yawned in reply. He felt drained, too, from the heat and excitement. Alana probably finally felt safe away from the witch, so she could rest. She'd already fallen asleep. And like a hero, he'd stand watch. He blinked, blinked again, just resting his eyes for a moment. The heat made you feel sleepy, but he wouldn't doze off. No, he had to guard their hideaway.

Despite himself, Willie drifted off...

Sudden loud, brash music thundered the air, with bass notes vibrating the stage overhead. Alana clamped her hands over both ears, shrinking into herself. Willie blinked and came fully awake. How much time had passed?

Noah jumped to his feet, tail waving with excitement, and barked loudly—not at the noise, but at the storage entrance behind them. Willie gulped with fear, expecting the witch to appear.

Instead, a big black dog leaped into view. A zigzag white scar on one cheek, and missing ear tip meant they were safe.

"Shadow!" Willie's hands unclenched. His smile widened, staring beyond the German Shepherd for September. She'd take care of everything: get them home safe, and maybe even kick some fortuneteller butt. The huge relief made tears threaten. He tamped them down. *Heroes don't cry.*

The dog approached Shadow, stiff-legged with a warning growl gargling his throat. In answer, Shadow licked his lips and turned his head away, and canine signal to chill. It worked.

Willie grinned when September's tall slim form finally appeared. He took two quick steps toward her. "Am I glad to see you!"

Before she could speak, a big dark man tackled

September. She dropped her bo staff, and something fell out of her bag. The man straddled her prone figure, pointing a gun at her face.

Willie screamed. He grabbed Alana's arm and pulled her out of sight into the maze of jumbled boxes. Noah followed, standing guard with filthy white fur bristled and teeth at the ready.

Chapter Forty-Eight: Shadow

Jared's abrupt appearance startled Shadow. He yelped and darted sideways when September went down. Her head thumped one of the boxes as the man straddled September and pointed the gun. She bucked Jared off sideways, continued the roll, and instantly regained her feet. Her shoulder bag slipped off, and she stayed in a crouch, both hands raised in supplication to show no threat. Her long stick had fallen out of reach.

Jared crouched in front of her, a gun held with two shaking hands pointing at September.

"What are you doing?" September's words were lost beneath the cacophony of bandstand noise, but Shadow still heard. "I'm here. Just as promised, I'm here for you and your daughter."

Shadow readied himself to *guard*. Maybe to *bite*. Or even to *show-me gun*. He gathered haunches to spring and take

Jared down.

September met his eyes and shook her head. He whined, but waited, trembling with the need to protect.

Jared licked his lips, steadied his hands, then took careful aim. A tear rolled down the corner of one eye. "I got no money, so I got no choice. Kidnapper says this is only way to get her back."

Shadow knew the whispered words couldn't be heard by human ears.

"Shadow, *show-me gun!*"

He didn't hesitate. Shadow leaped. He nose-punched the weapon as he flew by. The gun spun away. It spat when it hit the ground.

At the same time, September swept one leg out, tumbling Jared to the ground. Shadow danced about the pair, reaching to snap at the man's raised fists.

"Stop fighting, Jared. We want the same thing."

He wailed, scooting on his butt to get away. "She'll kill her, it's too late, she has Alana. *You* were the only price I could pay."

Shadow placed himself between September and the scary man, telling himself to *guard*. He knew the kids still listened and watched. Willie peered around one of the boxes. September saw them, too. Why didn't they all leave together now they'd found each other?

September told Jared about the children, making motions at their hiding place. She had to shout over the noise and the man couldn't understand. She blew out a breath, clearly frustrated.

Then, in a brief abatement of noise, a new voice. The woman ducked into the cramped space under the stage. "You have the cash? Then let's make a deal, Sorokin."

Shadow growled and took a step forward.

The stranger-woman scooped up Jared's fallen gun. But her hands didn't shake when they pointed it at September's face.

"I saw the dog's gun trick. Try that with me, and I'll blow his furry head off."

Chapter Forty-Nine: September

In the dim light September wouldn't have recognized Robin Gillette, but she knew the voice. Robin would have no hesitation to put kids at risk to get what she wanted. Fortunately, she had no clue the two children were nearby. She prayed Willie understood he must stay hidden at all costs. She'd play the game Gillette expected, let her think she still had bargaining chips. Pay the ransom, send her on her way, then spirit the kids to safety.

No guarantees she or Jared would survive. If the worst happened, their bodies might not be found until Sunday night when the festival ended, and staff needed to put equipment to bed.

The woman wanted the cash. Play that card, September. Then get her to leave.

"Robin Gillette."

Her nostrils flared. "Names don't matter."

"You signed me up for this game. Sent Jared to guilt me into paying your ransom. I'm ready to pay, happy to hand over the cash. If you change the rules and take us out, you get nothing. No money, no way to get away clean from the Family. Don't think they won't come after you."

"You think I care? You destroyed every good thing in my life. First play-acting the part of naïve innocent September Day. Now the Magpie swooping in to destroy everything."

September cocked her head. "I haven't destroyed the organization."

Robin cackled as if September had told a hilarious joke. "The Family never recognized my worth, not until Kaliko gave me a chance. After that, she owed me—because I helped make her the queen." Her breath quickened. "She's dead, and you're in charge, or I'd still have the life I earned!"

September frowned. Gillette didn't want excuses or explanations. She wanted cash or blood—maybe both. "You can still have your best life, with the money. That's really what you want, isn't it? I played your game. I'm ready to pay. You still want the money, don't you? In exchange for Jared's daughter." The man sat motionless in the corner, silent and looking shell shocked.

The noise overhead resumed, but September could still make out the woman's shouted comment. "I got his kid in a safe place."

Suppressing a smile, September nodded. "And I've got your money in a safe place." She could feel the weight of her gun beneath the loose blouse. She'd never be able to draw it before Gillette killed her. Then Jared—and maybe the children.

September came to the realization that handing over the cash—secreted so close—wouldn't send the woman packing. Gillette hungered to torture her, punish September.

To keep the kids safe, she needed to get them all away from this deathtrap so Willie could run to find one of the security team. At least he and Alana would survive.

She raised her voice to send a message to the boy. "Alana survived this long because she's smart. Knows to stay out of reach. To run and ask any adult—or a smart kid—for help. A very wise woman I know named Ethel, taught me that."

"Enough playing around." Robin pointed the gun at Jared. "You, get over here."

He didn't move.

As the music swelled, Robin pulled the trigger. Jared screamed when dirt poofed between his knees. "Get up, get over here, or the next bullet makes sure you never have another kid."

Jared crab-walked to her.

"Let's just call this a practice, shall we? To prove to Sorokin I'm serious." She glared at September. "I don't need him anymore." She brought the gun to his head.

September shook her head, hand clenched in Shadow's harness to keep them from shaking. She released her grip, started to command him to take out the gun.

A scream cut through the din, freezing all action for a heartbeat.

"No, no, no, Papa, don't hurt Papa!"

Alana dashed from her hiding place and threw herself into her father's arms.

Chapter Fifty: Willie

Willie gasped when Alana left their hiding spot. September's message—in a kind of cool code—expected them to stay there. Now the witch could use Alana against September all over again.

He peered out of his hidey-hole. Sure enough, Magical Maeve pushed Jared out of the way, trading him for Alana.

"See? Told you I had her nearby." The woman snickered. She stopped laughing long enough to aim the gun at Jared when he scrambled to reach his daughter. It stopped him in his tracks.

The witch held Alana by the hair. The girl made no effort to struggle.

"I've got the ransom close, too. Let's make the deal and everyone walks away." September stayed motionless, holding Shadow's halter.

Shadow stood his ground. Willie knew the dog would

take a bullet for September, or even for him. He didn't want anybody to take a bullet.

Overhead, the stage shook.

Willie gulped, mouth dry, afraid to breathe and give himself away. His hand clutched the matted fur on Noah's neck. The dog trembled beneath his hand, and Willie figured they felt the same thing: frustration, and eagerness to do the right thing.

He wanted to rush out and save September, even if she had a new name. And Alana, too. He could surprise the nasty woman, so September got the drop on her. But fear kept him nailed in place. And, he realized he really had to pee...

"You, Mister Daddy? Tie her up and take her gun. I'm sure she has one on her." Magical Maeve tossed zip ties to Jared and motioned for September to hold out her wrists as he secured them. Jared found the bulge of her gun and flinched.

"Take it out and toss her gun here. Don't try anything."

Willie held his breath. He'd seen September practice bunches of self-defense moves. He'd learned a few himself. So he expected her to quickly reverse the situation.

But Alana's dad followed instructions. When the witch pointed to the bungee cords and snarled, "Wrap her up tight," Jared scurried to do her bidding.

"Hard to deliver the cash with my hands tied." September didn't fight. She kept her eyes focused on Alana as though willing her to stay calm and do nothing to disrupt the situation.

Willie shifted to take pressure off his bladder. He bumped a storage box. Luckily, the witchy woman had her back to him, but September made brief eye contact. She closed her eyes, and gave a slight shake of her head, telling him to stay put.

The witch hissed between her teeth. "I can't count on any of you to play by my rules."

How could he just watch and wait? Sit here like a scaredy cat until Alana got stolen again? Or somebody got shot? Heck, Dad wouldn't just sit and wait. Dad showed him some cool moves. What good were they, if you never used them?

Maeve shook Alana by the hair, making the girl squeal. "She's a bad seed, a liar, a black sheep. Liable to do something stupid again, like scream and draw attention from the cops. Too many security guys roaming around out there." She rolled her eyes. "Tie up the mutt—hold them long enough for me to get to my RV. Deliver the money there. It's parked behind the red tent."

September had three bungee cords holding her arms tight to her body. Willie watched as Jared, clearly scared of Shadow, looped another bungee cord through his harness, and attached it to September's binding.

"What if I give you the money now? Make the exchange, you take the cash and leave the girl." September's voice remained even, but her figure shook with anger. "No need to delay. Take it and go." She took a deep breath and finished in a rush. "It's over there."

A pause, then the nasty woman laughed. "How convenient!" Willie sneaked another peek. Maeve released Alana briefly to heft a bag over her head, strap crossing her body, her left hand still juggling the gun. When Alana would have scurried away to reach her dad, the witch stomped the dragging ankle tether to stop her. Her right hand again firmly entwined in the girl's hair.

"Very generous for a black sheep...two bags full! So Daddy Jared, you grab the other bag and tote it along. This

little money muffin"—she tugged Alana's hair again—
"leaves with me to make sure you do the right thing and
don't try anything stupid."

Jared reached for a second bag.

Alana screamed.

Noah exploded into action, a streak of dingy white jetting
to Alana's aid.

Willie reached to stop him. He tumbled into view.

The witch bared her teeth. She shoved Alana into the
dog's snarling face.

Noah licked the girl's face, trying to wriggle into her
arms.

Willie didn't think. He scrambled into position, and slid
feet first like his favorite base-stealing ballplayers. He aimed
one deft kick at the back of Maeve's long skirt, hoping for
contact with the back of her knees.

The bag pulled her off balance. She tumbled to the
ground. The gun spun away. Success!

Alana briefly hugged Noah. Then she pushed him away
and raced to her father.

Jared scooped the girl into his arms, and they
disappeared. Noah hesitated, then scampered after them.

Willie grinned, pumped his arm in the air, wanted to
shout. Wait till he told Dad—

September screamed. She struggled with the elastic cords
binding her in place. "Run, Willie, run! Get out of here, go,
go-go-go."

Too late.

A claw-like hand clamped the back of his neck. The
witch shook him, then looped her arm around his neck.
Black sparklies glittered before his eyes. "This one's worth
more than that feral girl."

"Let him go. Take your money and run. He's got nothing

to do with this."

"He does now."

Willie struggled as hard as he could. He tried to bite the arm. Her arm tightened, cutting off his air.

"Stop fighting. Or I'll shoot you both and call it good." She bent to recover her gun. He nearly blacked out, barely registered when the muzzle pressed against his side.

"What do you want?" September vibrated with impotent rage.

"Satisfaction. I want you to pay for everything you've cost me!" The witch breathed heavily. "I'll keep this troublemaker long enough for a head start, then dump him where you can find him. Maybe he'll live to thank me."

Maeve kicked the second money bag, and with the gun, she urged Willie to pick it up. He looped the shoulder straps over his head, and it cut into his throat. He gagged, and grabbed each side, lifting to relieve the pressure.

"If you come after me, you'll only find pieces. A finger here, an ear there…" Clutching one of his arms with a hard fist, she backed away toward the exit, pulling Willie with her.

Willie couldn't believe how badly he'd messed up. He mouthed *I'm sorry* to September, as Maeve, or Robin, dragged him from beneath the stage. He'd made everything worse.

Chapter Fifty-One: Ethel

E thel panted inside the wooden box and her nostrils flared, trying to take in more oxygen. She didn't know how much time had passed. The sun must have fallen below the tree line, because the temperature had dropped. She felt chilly. Or maybe heat stroke had finally taken its toll. Her clothing stuck to her drenched skin. Ethel waited to die.

The furry paw pats at her back had subsided. Probably the heat had grown too much for the playful cat, too. The decrease in noise outside told Ethel the crowd was thinning. She closed her eyes and prayed.

This was September's fault. Young people sometimes made bad choices. But this went beyond a mistake. It had left her and Willie at that terrible woman's mercy.

Ethel passed out again. She came to when the paw pat returned to nudge her wrist. Ethel struggled to manipulate her fingers. The bindings had put most of her fingers to sleep.

She felt a string, or a shoelace perhaps. She rolled her eyes. The cat wanted to play? He stuffed the string into the hole in the box. With no one around to see, Ethel had no reason to continue the game. She'd already exhausted herself with the futile attempt to rock her prison. Nobody noticed. Now, with the fair shutting down for the night, would she live to see the dawn?

Ouch! Likely frustrated by being ignored, the cat had clawed her hand.

Did she hear voices outside? Or imagine them? Maybe a last chance to engage the cat. "Help. Help, help." But her voice, hoarse from previous efforts and still muffled by the gag, barely carried. She struggled to catch her breath.

In desperation, Ethel grasped the cat's cord with numb fingers and reeled it inside. *Please let the cat follow, make noise, act goofy.*

Delighted, the cat stuck a paw inside, chasing the disappearing string.

Please let someone notice, please-please-please.

The string stopped. Attached to something outside, the object stopped the string's progress. It bumped and clattered outside against the wood. Ethel yanked and pulled, again and again, the thumping sound clear and strident to her ears. *Couldn't they see? Didn't they hear?*

The voices faded. Frantic, Ethel's muffled scream partnered a yanking tug on the string.

The cat screamed and hissed, then abruptly retracted his paws from the hidey-hole.

Had they seen? Would they come check? Oh please… Ethel strained for a long moment, praying someone would approach.

Hope turned into fear. Was her captor standing close, watching and savoring Ethel's panic? Blinding anger shook her body and Ethel yanked with all her might. *Arggg!*

The object attached to the tether splintered the small opening. It pulled partway into the box. She fingered it, testing its outline, its shape, and its thick spiral handle. It felt like...?

Ethel scrunched to one side to make room, then yanked the rest of it inside. She couldn't see the object, but her numb fingers could still feel the razor edge. That told her all she needed to know.

Chapter Fifty-Two: Jared

Jared's arms tightened around his daughter. The reality of her, the warmth of her fragile body in his arms…he kept waiting for the dream to disappear—the way it had so many times before. "Alana, oh my *keiki*, Alana."

The stage noise played a counterpoint to the painful rhythm of his aching head. None of that mattered now, and he rained kisses on the top of his little girl's head, all the while running, running, running, getting as far from the area as possible.

The dog leaped and pranced, chasing and bumping against at his feet like the sheep dogs in the field. No! He couldn't let it hurt Alana.

"Get! Get out of here, leave us alone!" He kicked at the dog.

The dog yelped. He tucked his tail, and ran, whimpering.

Alana first hugged him as though she'd never let go, but then pushed away. She had no shoes but wanted down. He looped one hand around her tiny wrist and kept tugging to guide her away from danger. They must head back to the parking area, where he could call another Uber. They'd run far, far away before the universe changed its mind.

He glanced over his shoulders. The stage skirt twitched, and Jared quickly pulled Alana behind a Porta Potty to hide. The big woman backed out from the storage space, a bag slung over one shoulder. The boy, toting an identical bag, followed in the grip of the kidnapper's iron hand. Jared bet she held a weapon for him to act so compliant.

Jared waited until she'd disappeared with Willie. The audience gathered belongings and left en masse. Closing time—the best possible way to sneak out, under the cover of the exiting fair goers.

He pulled Alana after him, quashing guilt over leaving Sorokin behind. Alana took precedence. He'd call his wife. They'd rebuild their lives. Alana had other ideas. "Papa, help Willie. He saved me. Now we save him!" She tugged at his hand, trying to pull him in the wrong direction.

"Alana, no. Sorokin, she'll take care of him. I gotta take care of us." He grasped her wrist but was afraid he would hurt her by gripping too hard. "We'll go away, see your mama again. It's our chance to get away."

Alana yanked away and stared up at him. "But that's her little boy. She wants to save him, like you wanted to save me. We gotta help." Alana dashed back to the stage.

Cursing under his breath, Jared followed. He couldn't force her, have her scream and have strangers see her mistreatment. He'd lose her all over again.

Sorokin, still bound with the bungee cords, crouched in the shadows between two large boxes. Her big black dog had already escaped his bindings and stood before her, whining and nosing her cheek. A dust-stained toy sat forgotten in the gloom.

"Shadow, find Willie, keep him safe. *Guard* Willie."

The dog's ears slicked back against his head, and he yawned. Even Jared could see the dog didn't want to go. But he obeyed, and raced out of the storage area, apparently tracking the boy.

At Alana's urging, Jared hurried to Sorokin's side. He struggled with the first of the bungee cords. Untangling a couple would give the woman enough wiggle room to release herself, then he could get them out of this godforsaken place.

He unhooked the first, and most of the stretchy material quickly unraveled.

"Thank you."

The second cord, much tighter than the first, cut into Sorokin's bare arms, bruising the woman, but she didn't flinch as the bonds loosened. The stage, now silent, felt ominous as the last cord snaked free, unfurling onto the ground.

"You know where she went?" Her hands, still zip-tied in front of her, didn't seem to bother Sorokin.

"The red tent. I'll show you." Alana scooped up her kangaroo stuffie, spun and dashed out of the crawlspace.

"No!" Jared pounded after the girl, amazed at her foolish dedication to a boy she'd only just met.

Chapter Fifty-Three: Shadow

Shadow raced across the uneven ground. Willie's signature odor shouted—as bright as fireworks—excitement, boy dirt, pain, fear. Shadow's paws galloped faster. The sun was setting, but warmth still radiated from the ground. He panted loudly, black fur holding heat close.

September told him to *guard*. That meant to protect Willie from outsiders, or any who would do the boy harm. Shadow's tummy hurt, worrying he'd already let September and Willie down. He'd failed by letting the strange woman take the boy.

In the before times, Shadow failed another boy. He had tried his best, especially tried to love Steven, but in the end he failed. Only September's love saved Shadow.

Now Shadow had another chance to save a boy. One equally important, because September loved Willie. Shadow liked Willie very much, but more than anything else, he wanted to make September happy, chase away her worries like sheep shooed away by smart dogs.

He had his own worries. The scary woman took a gun with her, so Shadow must be extra careful to avoid those long-distance stings.

He skidded around a corner, kicking up dirt to keep his balance, and caught sight of the woman's swishy-skirt. She gripped Willie, making him go where she wanted. Shadow glanced around, but his nose had already told him no onlookers tarried nearby.

She paused, glaring over her shoulder. He froze. He knew motion betrayed his presence to people the same way it did squirrels and rabbits. To Shadow, she was prey.

The woman scanned her surroundings before roughly shoving Willie into a tent. Only after she disappeared from view did Shadow dare move again.

Deserted booths had canvas flaps rolled down to hide inside spaces. He sniffed and listened. Nobody there, although owner scents remained. His tail fell with disappointment. People could help good dogs and boys in trouble, but Shadow was alone. Shadow's sharp teeth and loud growl helped him guard and keep danger away. They couldn't help against the bad woman's gun, though.

Shadow crept quickly from one booth space to the next, to keep hidden from the scary woman's prying eyes. Soon, only the display with tall wooden target boxes separated him from the tent where Willie hid.

The breeze shifted. Movement caught Shadow's attention. He cocked his head, licked his nose, inhaled and read cat on the scented breeze. And something more.

The familiar scent of Aunt Ethel mixed with fear, sweat, and blood…She'd been here. *Was* here. Somewhere…but hidden away?

The big gray cat sensed Shadow, too. He slunk several body lengths from the box, then, from a standing start, leaped to perch on top, just like Macy-cat jumped to the refrigerator. He swished his funny foreshortened tail, extra-long gray fur swishing in the air. Shadow whined with uncertainty. *Check-it-out* to find Aunt Ethel? Or *guard* Willie?

Willie screamed.

Guard Willie! That was Shadow's job!

He dashed to the tent's opening, skidded to a stop, and more cautiously crept closer, one slow paw step at a time. He sniffed, confirming Willie's presence. The bad woman's smell clogged the area. Her rage intensifying the aroma.

She emerged from the tent, gun in one hand and knife in the other. Shadow shrank out of sight around the corner of the tent, only the tip of his nose questing and gathering information. He watched her sneak away. She crossed to a shuttered booth opposite the red tent.

"Hello? Anyone there?" She grabbed one of the tent poles, and shook it, and when no one answered, she hid inside.

Shadow waited a dozen heartbeats. When she didn't reappear, he slipped into the red tent. The near darkness inside didn't bother him. His ears flicked this way and that, immediately focusing on the soft breathing in the corner of the room.

Willie crouched, bent almost double inside a wire animal cage. He pillowed his face against his knees, arms wrapped around and hugging his legs. Shadow extended his nose to touch the boy's bare leg through the wire mesh.

The boy squeaked, jerked away, eyes flicking open then widening with surprise. "Shadow!" He whispered with urgency, unfurling himself and looking around. "Is she gone?"

Shadow whined, just the end of his tail flicked. He kept one ear cocked toward the opening of the tent, in case the bad woman returned. He sniffed the wire, noting her scent, the girl's, Willie's, and a strange cat.

"She locked me in." Willie grabbed the front of the cage, and rattled it, shaking it hard. He reached his hand through the bars to manipulate what looked like the catch. Shadow sniffed the fastener. Although very similar to those he'd seen before, this one had something added to keep it from opening. "You need a key to open it."

Shadow's ears flicked at the word. He knew that word. He whined and pawed the door.

"That won't work, Shadow. I tried. I can't bend it."

Shadow had seen Kinsler get out of his crate by sliding the bottom tray out and squeezing his smallish body underneath. But Willie wouldn't fit, even if they pulled out the tray.

"Where's September? She'd know what to do." Willie sat back down and rubbed his face. "Guess I really messed things up." He sighed. "Without the keys, I'm not going anywhere."

Shadow woofed under his breath at the use of the word again.

Willie cocked his head. "Keys?"

Reaching through the wire, Shadow licked Willie's knee and wagged happily.

"Oh my gosh. September taught you that, didn't she? *Show-me key?*"

Jumping up, Shadow sniffed the air and did a cursory search around the tent. Keys came in different shapes and sizes. He did a paws-up against the table, nosed the contents, and scrounged underneath and all around the perimeter. His hackles bristled at the pool of drying blood.

Willie groaned. "It's no use. That witchy woman, she has the keys. A whole bunch of them, hooked on her belt. I'm sunk."

Shadow returned to Willie and sat before the boy. He pressed his paw against the metal grating. He whined. No keys. He'd failed. *Bad dog!*

"Good boy, Shadow. It's not your fault you can't find the key. Heck, you'd have to be super dog to find the key and bring it here."

Shadow woofed under his breath.

Find key, bring key, show-me key.

The words, the commands, chained the behavior needed. He knew what Willie meant. He was smart that way.

Shadow bounded to his feet and dashed out of the tent. He knew where to find the woman with the keys. He'd use his bright teeth and scary growl to make her to give them back.

Chapter Fifty-Four: September

September gritted her teeth and followed Jared from beneath the stage. He and Alana had disappeared. She wasn't surprised, and didn't begrudge him the chance to escape. "Safe travels, Jared." She hoped the family could find a way to heal.

She stood upright, held her zip-tied hands before her, out as far as they'd go—then pulled them back against her midriff as hard as she could. It took three tries, and not a little pain, for the plastic to break.

She ducked back under the stage to grab her go bag and bo staff, then texted Pierce. Where was he? He'd promised to have her back but disappeared.

<Target at red tent—need location from stage

The fairgrounds were nearly empty. Even security had disappeared, just when she would welcome the support.

September stopped a couple. "Have you seen a red tent

anywhere?"

The woman nodded and pointed. "Near the parking area. Go three rows across, and then at the end. Wasn't this a glorious first day?" She hugged her companion's arm as they hurried away.

September thumbed her phone and texted Pierce again. <ETA

September's nerves, jangled as much by Shadow's absence as the task at hand, quickened her pulse and hardened her purpose. *Willie, find Willie.* Within seconds, she'd traversed the three rows and lengthened her stride to an all-out sprint. Forget about counting on anyone from the Family.

Deja vu. She and Shadow had nearly reached the red tent before getting sidetracked. By now Shadow should have found Willie. She had to trust the dog would keep the boy safe until she found them both.

September picked up an ax, testing the weight like a spectator ready to throw. Might come in handy. A huge longhaired gray cat perched atop the closest target.

She kept the ax. September walked swiftly to the booth directly across from the tent, now shuttered, and pretended to browse the signage. From there, she could scope out the red tent, see if Gillette showed her face, or whether she should risk sneaking a look inside. She continued hefting the ax, getting herself familiar with the weight and feel. Without her gun she had to rely on the bo staff and make do with whatever came to hand to protect herself, and free Willie.

Behind her in the closed booth, the canvas drape twitched.

Pierce ignored the text from September. No cavalry would ride to her rescue this time. He'd neutralized as many neon-wearing security guards as possible. Now, with the fair closed, and crowd dispersed, it was time to take his bird into the sky.

Shooting from the air got tricky when piloting your own copter. But he'd done it before.

And if necessary, he'd do it tonight. That was the job.

Chapter Fifty-Five: Shadow

Shadow stalked the bad woman to her hiding place, slipping around to the back side of the booth. He stuck his nose through a gap in the canvas, far enough to see her back.

She clutched a long leather strap like a dog collar but squinted out the front, unaware of a good dog behind her.

Perfect! Scent-blind and hearing-deaf people made it easier for a good dog to do his job: *guard* Willie. And *show-me keys.*

He silently squeezed through the flexible opening. The material shuddered and quivered. Shadow froze. The woman didn't notice. One careful paw step at a time brought him closer to her. He focused on the bright shiny bundle swinging from her belt.

Bring keys.

Her hands spread apart, pulling the belt taut between

them. Breathing quickened. Shoulders stiffened. She stepped forward, reaching through the front of the booth, extending the stiff loop of leather. Stalking something. Or someone.

Just like Shadow. He must leap quickly before she moved beyond a good dog's reach.

He gathered his haunches, then sprang, jaws wide, closing hard on the bundle of keys.

They clacked against his teeth. Shadow's weight pulled her off balance just as she lunged at her own prey. She shouted. He yanked the keys free, and with his prize held firmly in his jaws, Shadow dashed to *bring keys* back to Willie. Panting happily, he skidded to a stop before the wire cage and pushed them against the grillwork until Willie took them.

Key by key, the boy checked each for a fit.

"Good dog, Shadow! You really are super dog."

Chapter Fifty-Six: Lord Byron

Once the knife disappeared into the wooden box, Lord Byron lost interest in the fetch game. Dinnertime had passed, and he yearned for a cool drink. Usually, the big man left a water fountain for him to drink. But Ian couldn't help, and neither could the woman in the box.

Another game would help him forget the scary stuff. Byron flicked his tail with aggravation and wished for another game of fetch.

When the big black dog showed up, Byron had warned him off. But the dog ignored Byron's hisses, and didn't seem interested in him at all. He felt better once ensconced on top of the box, out of nose poking and chasing range. Dogs smelled funny. They made loud noises, and had big teeth he didn't want to tempt.

The big black dog stalked around, hunting with his nose

to the ground. How odd, to rely so much on sniffing to hunt. When Byron hunted, he watched for sudden movement and listened for squeaks of yummy prey. Poor dog didn't know how to hunt.

He'd have to hunt soon, since his bowl had been stolen along with the cat condo.

The sky darkened. Everyone had left, except for a woman carrying a long stick and a bag on her shoulder. She stopped to pick up an ax and let the shoulder bag fall to the ground. Byron stared back, flicking his bushy gray tail, and debated whether to hop off the box to greet her, or to hide until she went away.

Instead, the dark-haired woman jerked and stumbled backwards. She disappeared into the shuttered booth.

At the same time, the black dog reappeared from around the back of the booth. He clutched something in his mouth that jittered and jangled. The dog dashed back to the scary tent and disappeared inside.

How exciting! Hunger and thirst temporarily forgotten, Lord Byron abandoned the perch to race toward the drama. Unnoticed by the two struggling women, he slipped through an opening and found a good lookout inside to watch the drama with interest.

When the belt tightened around September's neck, she dropped ax and bo staff as both hands grappled the binding at her throat. Garlic breath, tinkling bells...Robin dragged her backwards into the shuttered booth space.

September tipped her head up. Falling backwards risked knocking herself out, making it easy for Robin to finish the job. With fingers slipped under the throttling strap, she tried to flip around to face her attacker. She'd practiced the maneuver over and over: rotate her body and lift the belt over her head in the same motion. Mastered in practice, but not so easy when murder became reality. Robin yanked harder, tightening the belt to stop September's breath and voice.

"Figured you'd ignore my warning. Thank you for making my decision for me." The woman's words hissed in September's ears, her pungent breath spoke of bad teeth.

Tamping down panic, September forced herself to recall her lessons. Her fingers screamed, cramping as they buffered the strangling pressure on her fragile throat.

With the next vicious yank, September let herself fall. At the same time, she pushed backwards to increase the velocity and threw Robin off balance.

Together they crashed into a table. It rammed the side of the booth, punching the canvas lopsided. Anyone outside—security personnel—should see and investigate.

When she hit the ground, September flipped to spin horizontally. In the same motion she thrust up with both hands, lifting the noose over her head and away. She sprang to her feet, hands still gripping the belt. With adrenaline-fueled energy, she yanked it free of Robin's hands and turned it into a whip, whirling the heavy belt through the air until it whistled. September aimed the ornate silver buckle at Robin's face.

The woman dodged away, just out of reach. The buckle clanked on a tent pole, the belt wrapping around it and negating any defense.

Cagey as a feral cat, Robin drew the knife sheathed in her bodice. She slashed the air as she advanced step by step.

September backed away.

The knife was a blur as Gillette stalked her prey.

"You got your cash. Give me the boy." September grabbed display items and lobbed them at the woman. She had to get out of this closeted space. She could outrun the woman.

Needing all her breath for the battle, September refused to call for Shadow. His job was to protect Willie. She must fight this battle alone. She caught up an elegant silver-clasped sporran and shoved it into Robin's face.

Gillette batted it out of the air. "I'm taking the boy with me. Got the RV all ready to roll with the money. You did this to yourself, and to him. Gonna leave you bleeding out, then dribble him out in pieces along the way." She feinted with the knife.

September backed up against the table. She caught up a fist sized purple geode in each hand, then threw them—one caught Robin on the arm, the other she batted away.

Robin charged, knife raised.

September grappled her wrist. She thrust one leg between Robin's skirted legs, flipping her off her feet.

They fell to the ground, wrestling for the weapon. Robin wrenched the knife away, held it high. September scrabbled in the dirt for anything, and her hand closed again on the sporran. She held it like a shield.

The stabbing blade pierced the furry purse and caught on the filigreed fastening. September wrenched sideways with all her strength and threw the sporran—blade still lodged in the pewter work—out of reach.

Gillette bared her teeth. She mounted September's prone form and punched at her face.

September shielded her face with forearms clenched tight, then arched her back, bucked to throw Gillette off, and rolled. *Out, she had to get to Willie.*

She rolled beneath a table, grabbed two of the legs and tipped it over. The shining display of reproduction swords and leather armor spilled. She huddled behind the barrier.

A gunshot split the air. "I'm done playing." Two more shots rang out, punching through the tabletop.

September flinched, backing away from the meager shelter. Her hand found one end of the oaken staff that had fallen outside, with just its head peeking into the shelter. She dragged the bo staff the rest of the way into the area. It offered no protection from bullets, but she immediately felt calmer with it in her hands. A flicker of motion from the corner of her eye tempted September to glance that way, but she remained focused, counting the shots. When the gunfire stopped, September made her move.

She scrambled on all fours, looking for the slit in the canvas to escape from the booth. September kept the toppled table between her and Gillette to hide her retreat although the bullet holes clearly showed it offered no protection.

Robin's voice held gleeful grim satisfaction. "Time to pay, Sorokin."

The flickered motion came into focus. The big gray cat stared at Gillette's long swinging braids…

September grabbed a sword from the ground, swung it hard. It slit open the canvas, and she leaped through with her bo staff in the other hand.

The last rays of the setting sun glinted off the jingle bells dangling on the end of each braid, casting fairy-like twinkles.

Gillette pointed the gun.

September dropped the sword.

The cat leaped. Paws yearned for the belled braids.

Braids yanked off Robin's head. Robin screamed, aim gone wild.

September spun the bo staff. Made hard contact.

The gun spun away.

The cat grabbed the new jingle-toys and darted away.

Chapter Fifty-Seven: Ethel

E thel had never met a cat that played fetch. *God bless the little beast…* She manipulated the huge knife. So big, she had trouble propping it at the right angle to cut her wrist restraints.

She didn't question provenance, how or why the cat brought her the weapon. Some things you couldn't explain or understand. Like how the fine young woman she knew morphed into Sorokin Glass and spawned this mess. Time enough to get answers, once she got out of this.

By heaven, Stan wouldn't give up! Neither would she.

She carefully positioned her wrists over the blade. With little feeling in her fingers, Ethel feared she might cut her wrists without feeling it. She pressed against the blade, and started moving her arms slowly, sawing back and forth.

The box prison gave little room to move. The knife slipped more than once. She felt wet on her skin, knew the blade cut more than bindings, but couldn't stop. Even if she could cut herself free, she didn't know how to get out of the box. All that mattered was getting hands free, and the detested gag out of her mouth so she could breathe freely—and yell louder for help.

Sooner than she expected, the knife severed the bindings. Ethel whimpered with relief. Hands and fingers tingled with pain as feeling slowly returned. Once her fingers worked, she fumbled the gag from her mouth. She couldn't get it untied but by flexing her jaw and pulling Ethel managed to spit it out and pull it down around her neck.

Her mouth tasted like straw. Her tongue stuck to the roof of her mouth. *So thirsty.* She swallowed over and over again trying to conjure enough spit to get rid of the feeling. Her throat felt like broken glass from screaming. She had little voice left. But without the muzzle she had a better chance someone could hear.

Gunshots! Ethel flinched. You never forgot that sound, or what it meant. The evil woman could shoot through the wood, no need to open up the box—a DIY casket. They wouldn't find her until Lughnasa ended.

No! Ethel pushed those thoughts away. She'd come this far. For Stan. For Willie. And for September, who she still loved despite everything.

Grasping the big handle of the knife, Ethel sawed through her ankle bindings. She flexed her feet and legs, rubbed her hands and arms, urging circulation to return. She couldn't risk crying out for help with gunshots so near. Her tormentor might answer. No, she'd bide her time.

When Magical Maeve showed up, Ethel had her own plan. With the miracle knife on her side, she'd strike before the fortuneteller could prophesy her end.

Noah raced to find his safe place by the lake. The scary POP-POP-POP sounds followed, even though no lights splashed across the darkening sky. He whimpered, wondering what he'd done wrong for the man to scare him away. Maybe a long drink from the cool water would help. He'd belly flop into the water, and let the wet soothe his sore paws.

For the first time in many days, he'd felt happy. Not lost. And brave, even if he hated loud scary sounds. He wanted to stay with the girl. But that man took her, and made Noah go away.

Why? What would happen to the girl? Should he go back, show his teeth to help her again? He really liked the girl. The boy was nice, too.

But grown-ups—he didn't like them at all.

He stopped short. Two people—grown-ups!—lolled on the ground in his spot. His fur stood up on his back. His tail stuck out stiff, and his lips raised to show teeth, without even thinking about it. This was his spot! He wouldn't let anyone chase him away.

But they didn't jump up and yell. Or throw things. Or move much at all. One of the men groaned and sat up. He flexed his jaw. The man wore something in his mouth. How odd. He managed to spit it out, breathing heavy just like Noah trying to cool off. And he poked the other man with his feet. Both his feet and hands moved together, bound by something.

"Hey bro, you okay?"

The other man stirred and also sat up.

They couldn't stand with feet tied. So neither could chase

him or throw hurtful things at Noah. His hackles smoothed, and he yawned loudly, immediately feeling better.

The first man noticed and turned a hard stare his direction. Noah couldn't help it, he lowered his head, slicked back his ears, and wagged.

"That's the dog chased the sheep away from that little kid. Hey, dog! Here, pup."

Noah listened and watched, cocking his head first one way, then the other. At least the man talked nice. So he walked past the pair to reach the water and drank long and deep.

The other man groaned and tried to talk past the cloth in his mouth. Noah ignored the mouth noise he couldn't understand. He only knew a few words, like *food, hungry* and *get-outta-here* and *bad dog*. Sometimes he thought *bad dog* might be his name. But he liked *stick*. He remembered having toys—Noah loved playing—but toys went away, he didn't know why. And he remembered getting pets and happy laughs from the neighbor girl when she threw a stick for him to bring back. Sort of like a toy. He'd turn anything into a toy if it meant a game. A *stick* toy. He wagged at the thought.

The man poked his friend again. "We gotta get loose and call the cops." He wriggled on the ground, falling onto his side. "Hey, I see my knife! It's right there, caught in that *stick* by the water."

Noah raised his head at the word. How'd the man know about *stick* toy? His tail began to wag faster. Maybe some grown-ups weren't so bad after all. He looked around, and yes! Right there, by the water, a *stick*. Maybe if he brought it to the man, they'd play?

He dipped his head and carefully grasped the branch.

"Good dog! Holy crow, look at that. Good dog!"

Noah wagged some more. He liked *good dog* lots better than *get-outta-here*. He pulled the branch harder, tugging it out of the water until it reached the two men. He watched with interest as they scrambled to retrieve the knife to cut themselves free. He couldn't wait to play—

More POP-POP-POP noise ripped the quiet air. Shouts and screams, too. It sounded like the girl.

Noah yelped, stick toy forgotten. More important to find her, never mind the scary people and sounds. Tired of running, Noah wanted her soft touch again, to lick clean the salty wet from her face, just spend *more time* with her. Even if it meant kicks and yells of *get-outta-here*.

Chapter Fifty-Eight: Shadow

G unshot…Shadow whirled, placing himself between the threat and the boy. *Guard Willie.* September told him that. But now Willie had keys. His clever boy fingers worked the lock.

Another shot. He whined, hackles bristled and glanced back at Willie. The boy found the right key. Soon, the boy would break free of the cage.

September needed him. Guns could hurt her. He'd done as she asked. Now Shadow must stand with September and keep her safe. He couldn't lose her! They were part of each other.

He crept to the tent entrance. He tested the air with quivering nose, pricking ears for clues to understand what to do.

A *screeeeee* ripping sound. The booth from which he'd stolen the keys shuddered. Would it yank stakes from the

ground and scuttle beetle-like to attack a good dog? He
barked and barked again as a shiny long blade slit an exit in
the shuttered tent. Then September burst into view.

His tail whipped back and forth. Safe! Excited cries and
yelps made gargling sounds in Shadow's throat.

"That's it." Behind him, Willie banged open the wire
door and crawled out. "Let's get outta here." The boy stood,
and quickly joined Shadow at the tent entrance. He looked
both ways and drew in a surprised breath. "Holy crow, that's
September…with a sword? Sick!" He started across the
grassy barrier, eager to get closer.

Shadow galloped after the boy to push in front of him.
He leaned hard against Willie's legs to block him from
danger. *Guard Willie.* Do his job.

"Shadow, stop it!" Willie yelled with frustration. "We've
gotta help her, we can't let that old witch hurt September."

September heard him. She screamed. "Go, get out of
here, run! Willie, find security. Shadow, *guard Willie!*" She
turned back just as the bad woman, minus braids and keys,
emerged, with a knife.

"Out of bullets?" September danced out of reach,
holding the bo staff in a protective stance. She whirled the
stick through the air in blur of motion. He'd seen September
disarm sparing partners with that trick.

With the flick of a wrist, the bad woman threw the knife.
September screamed and dropped her staff.

Shadow howled. He left Willie—*bad dog!*—to rush to her
side. Sometimes dogs had to disobey.

September rolled away, keeping distance between herself and Gillette. The knife, still stuck in her left bicep, hurt like fury. She gritted her teeth and scrabbled in the grass for the dropped staff.

Gillette stalked her, grinning with malice, taking her time closing in for the kill. She stooped, straightening immediately with the ax September had dropped. Robin hefted it and laughed out loud. She loomed over September.

Holding the staff before her, September struggled to center herself. She set herself in defensive stance, swung the staff, but her left arm failed.

Robin wound up, drew back her arm.

Flat on her back, September raised her arms, staff extended to protect herself—

The ax cleaved the staff in two.

Shocked, September dropped half the stick, still brandishing the other part in her right hand. She whipped it through the air, rolling away from Gillette, and prepared for the next ax strike.

A black wraith bowled into Gillette and knocked the ax away. She shrieked.

Shadow danced away. He dove in and out to nip at the woman's flowing skirt.

September's heart swelled with pride and admiration. He'd generalized the behavior from a gun to any weapon. But Robin managed to scramble and recover the ax. She flailed at Shadow, her broomstick skirt swirled.

"Shadow, *play tug!*"

He immediately grabbed Robin's skirt. Shadow pulled the fabric hard, head-shaking with massive ferocious growls. Gillette outweighed Shadow but his zealous energy pulled her this way and that, keeping her off balance. He yelped when the ax caught him a glancing blow.

"Shadow, *bite!*"

Without hesitation Shadow jumped high and crunched Gillette's wrist. She dropped the ax, and screamed, an ululating siren that should bring security running.

Scrambling to her feet, September abandoned the shattered sabotaged staff and reclaimed the decorative sword. Better to retreat to fight another day. "C'mon, Shadow. Let's go find Willie."

Shadow took up his position to guard her back as they retreated. Willie should have run for help. He should have hidden somewhere. Instead, he and Alana stood in full view next to one of the bullseye targets, playing with the crazy gray cat that ran off with Robin's hair.

Chapter Fifty-Nine: Willie

Willie pressed his ear to the box. He'd started to run, like September said, but Alana showed up, snuggling a stuffed toy. Then Noah reappeared and made a huge racket pawing and barking at one of the target boxes. Willie thought Noah wanted to catch the cat, until he heard the noise inside.

"Honey, are you safe? Is she…that woman…anywhere around?" Aunt Ethel's voice sounded funny, but he could hear her clearly. She sounded pissed, too. You didn't want to mess with Aunt Ethel when she got her back up—that's what Uncle Stan used to say.

"What are you doing in there?" Willie looked over his shoulder as Shadow disarmed the witch—he bit her! Willie didn't know Shadow did that, totally rad. But they needed to get outta here quick. It took a lot to stop a witch.

"I'm okay. September's fighting her." She'd kick the

witch's ass-ets!

He circled the box, and found the padlock holding the lid shut, just like the lock that imprisoned him in the cat cage. "There's a lock. I can get the keys." He'd left them in the tent, and he really didn't want to go back inside that creepy place.

Before he could move, Alana shrieked.

The witch had picked up the ax with her uninjured hand and was running right at Willie, a snarl twisting her face into a goblin mask.

"What's happening? Willie, are you all right?" Aunt Ethel's voice shook with outrage. "Run, child, get away from here! Run!"

Alana darted away.

The ax flew. Willie watched it whiz past his head. He gasped when it hit with a solid THUNK into the box. Aunt Ethel squealed. Her cries unlocked his legs, and he sprang away.

Too late.

The witch caught Willie by one wrist and swung him around like the crack-the-whip game. His arm nearly wrenched from his shoulder. He screamed more with fear than pain. Willie gasped when she twisted his arm up hard behind his back and wrapped her bloody bitten wrist around his neck. She smelled of B.O. and garlic, and a weird coppery odor. He gagged.

"Let him go." September approached, the long sword dragging on the ground. "Walk away, take the cash stashed in your RV, just disappear." Shadow's eyes followed every movement.

"Aunt Ethel's inside the box!" Willie yelled before a hand clamped across his mouth and squeezed his nose shut.

"Shut your pie hole, or I'll shut it for you, son-of-a…!"

She hissed at him. "Sorokin or September, or whatever you call yourself—you made this happen! *You* could have walked away. But no, sticking your nose where it doesn't belong. Hurts you worse to see him die, I bet. You'll have to live with that and tell his cop daddy."

Willie pried at the hand stopping his breath. He saw the witch reach up to the target with the bloody arm Shadow bit. She yanked free the ax she'd just thrown and hefted it. "How about I just cut off his head, and save us all the misery of his jibber-jabber?"

Struggling, kicking his feet to get away, Willie saw September running toward them. She raised the sword again, wielding it like Aragon in *Lord of the Rings*—never mind she was a girl. He felt the witch stiffen, ready to hit September with the ax.

"Willie, knock her into the box!" He heard Aunt Ethel's cry, but the witch ignored everything but September.

Shadow stared, waiting for direction. September raced toward certain death—to save him.

No!

In desperation, with his free hand, Willie patted his own chest. He couldn't speak the words, but inside his head he screamed it. "Shadow, *Ka-pow!*"

Everything slowed down—*just like in the theater*—then Shadow obeyed Willie's prompt. The big dog outraced September and performed a perfect paws-up punch against Willie's chest.

The ninety-pound weight of the big dog shoved Willie back so hard he knocked the witch off balance. She staggered and fell hard against the wooden target.

She shrieked louder than any bagpipe chorus. Dropped the ax and released Willie.

He staggered out of reach, sucking in air. Willie watched as the witch writhed against the display, a weird human bug pinned tight against its surface.

Chapter Sixty: Jared

J ared panicked, running in circles looking for Alana.
They'd come so close to getting away. Why had she
run? They owed that boy nothing, they could have
been miles away by now. With darkness falling, it grew
harder to see and find her. Then he heard her scream.

He arrived just in time to see the kidnapper holding the
boy and threatening him with an ax, but what could he do?
He saw no sign of Alana. Then Sorokin's big black dog
leaped up and paw-thumped the boy.

His mouth dropped open when the kidnapper screamed
a siren wail covering two octaves. Both her arms sprang out
to her sides, flinging the ax one way while the boy wriggled
beyond reach in the other direction. She keened and tried to
reach something behind her back.

Alana appeared from the red tent, her kangaroo still
under one arm, with a jangling keyring clutched in the other

hand. She darted close to the gyrating woman as she circled behind the box.

"Alana! No, come away." Jared forgot about playing it safe. He ran to reach the girl, wary of the evil woman's odd gyrations.

Alana fumbled with the keys. She stood on tiptoe to reach the padlock securing the lid of the wooden target box.

"We've got to get away." He caught her hand, tugging at Alana to guide her to safety. The police would descend soon, and he had no answers to the questions they'd ask.

"Papa, unlock the box. Willie's auntie is inside." She held out the keys, eyes imploring.

He wanted to lob them far away and drag Alana after him. But Willie had helped Alana. He grabbed the keys and fumbled with the padlock. Something rubbed against his ankle, and he flinched before recognizing a stray cat.

From inside the box, a woman called, voice so hoarse he could barely understand. "Hello? Please get me out of here!"

He didn't answer, wanted to know nothing about any of these people. He'd open the damn lock, but then they were outta here. He gently nudged the cat away with one foot and tried one key after another. The sixth opened the padlock. He swung the wooden cover open, dropped the keys to the ground, then he grabbed Alana's arm. Her toy fell to the ground.

"This way, Papa!" She stopped him long enough to scoop up the keys again, then tugged his hand. "C'mon. She always hides her money in the RV." The girl pulled his hand.

The stray dog followed. He whined, ears slicked to his head, and tail wagging fast as though asking questions, begging for something, a wish Jared couldn't understand.

He prepared to kick, but Alana stopped him. "He saved me. Good dog, come on Noah."

Noah yelped with delight. He hesitated, sniffed, then grabbed up the bandanna-wearing kangaroo and raced to keep up with Alana.

Chapter Sixty-One: September

September scooped an arm around Willie's shoulders. She lifted him as Shadow danced all around, making happy noises. "Let's go! Hurry!"

The Gillette woman took staggering steps forward, wrenching herself away from the target. The box wobbled when she pulled free of a long blade that stuck out, dripping crimson where it had skewered her back.

Ethel lurched into view. "I stuck her, oh God, I stabbed her."

Robin grimaced, eyes wide with pain. She spun to confront Ethel.

September pushed Willie behind her. She still held the Celtic sword.

Ethel stooped to retrieve the ax and brandished it. Shadow growled, coming abreast of September. They formed a circle around Robin, hopefully holding her until security arrived.

She caught up her own replacement weapons from those spilled on the ground. Knife in each hand, Gillette spun, keeping her back to the wooden box. She threatened first one, and then another, keeping the trio at bay.

Keep her distracted, protect others from further injury. "The police will arrive any minute." September wondered why they hadn't yet swarmed the place.

Spinning, Gillette hiked her skirt and lashed out with a roundhouse kick at the wooden box. It toppled and Robin leaped over it, grimacing with pain. Before she'd taken three steps, her RV rumbled to life. Gears crunched, and the motor home roared away.

Robin screamed. The cat hissed. It grappled her ankles, tried to climb the broomstick skirt, shredding it. Robin tripped, groaning from the repeated impact to her wounds. She grabbed the box to drag herself upright.

September dashed forward, eager to take advantage of Robin's weakened position. But the woman wouldn't give up.

Robin grabbed the handle of the deadly machete-like knife that had impaled her. It shrieked as Gillette yanked it from its wooden casing, emerging like Excalibur pried from the stone. She clutched the haft with both hands and whirled the blade in a figure-8 pattern, aiming for the cat hectoring her ankles. One sandaled foot lofted the yowling feline several feet through the air.

"No! Don't let her hurt it!" Willie shouted, voice a metallic shriek from the woman's throttling. "Scat, kitty, run, run away…"

The big cat hissed, then dashed away. September's attention didn't waver from Gillette and her blade. *Make do with what you've got.* "Ethel, get Willie away from here." His risk increased by the second. "Our friends from Heartland's finest should show up anytime."

"Help me, Willie, my legs don't wanna work." Ethel rested one arm across Willie's shoulders. Thankfully, he didn't argue, just looped his arm about her waist. Together, they staggered away, leaving September and Shadow to deal with the woman.

Shadow barked, running back and forth from September's side to snap at Gillette. "No, Shadow! *Guard Willie. Guard!*"

He paused to stare briefly after the limping Ethel and boy. Then with a decidedly defiant expression, Shadow returned to her side. September groaned.

Why wouldn't Robin take the money and run? Now September had no choice but to try and hold her here. No way would she turn her back on Robin.

And where the hell was Pierce? For a man tasked as her bodyguard, he'd done little but set her up for this mess. Had that been his intent all along?

The two women squared off. September's long sword looked flimsy compared to the other's massive hacking knife. And despite the older woman's stabbing injury she hadn't slowed. Desperation and vengeance fueled Robin's actions.

"Put down the knife." September hated losing her bo staff. She could use similar technique with the long Celtic blade.

Robin swung the massive knife, slashing at September and blocking any advance. Dancing away, September spun, but the knife creased her right forearm, drawing a bloody exclamation in the flesh. She hissed with the pain but tightened her grip. Blood dripped down both arms, greasing the haft of the sword. She fell back, ceding territory while glancing around for help that didn't come.

"Nobody to hear you. So tell me why? Why not just walk away?" September grit her teeth, and signaled Shadow to keep his distance. She worried that he'd dash in, try to nose-punch Robin's blade and end up with mortally slashed jaws and tongue.

September turned and ran a short distance to a shuttered booth, ducked around the side. *Where is Pierce?*

Robin thundered after September, the woman's own wound and larger size slowing her down, but she was implacable, a rhino intent on destruction. "They said you were clueless. I thought it was an act." She panted, steadying herself against the booth pole.

"Clueless?" September threw gas on the woman's ire, mocking her. "Who's clueless? Failed kidnapping, failed ransom...failed murder. Just in the last 48 hours, that's not counting the years of mayhem that got you here. Keep standing there, the police will collect you shortly." She couldn't arrest the woman. Robin's injury meant she'd eventually wear out.

"Money means nothing. Nothing!" She spewed hatred, so angry spittle flew. "You're worth more to me dead, you freakin' pretender! Taking over, attacking me and everyone—killing Kaliko, the one who made the Family a success!" She lumbered forward, swinging the knife with both hands. "I freakin' took out your daddy, cupcake. I made it happen. Kaliko planned it, but I put it together, created the team and made it happen. Now it's your turn!" She wound up and swung the knife like a double-bladed hatchet at September.

September ducked. She held the sword overhead to block the downward-slashing blow. A showy reproduction at best, it shattered. She fell backwards, and, panting, crabbed backwards in the grass.

September rolled then squirmed into the next booth. Her foot caught one side of the canvas, and she kicked to get free. The tented canted to one side, opening one side wide. She rolled to her feet in one motion and swept the cover off a table, searching for her next weapon of opportunity.

Robin's blade stabbed through the canvas, ripping downward with a snarling sound. She stepped through. She'd gathered and tied up the skirt, tucking it into her waistband. "They put me on notice, you know. Me, and everyone else, knows it's your fault. Sorokin withdrew protection, Sorokin rescinded agreements. Do you know what that means? Do you?" She slashed at September.

September upended the nearest table, spilling whimsical toys over the ground.

Shadow leaped at Robin, bit her ankle, and received a glancing blow from the butt end of the knife.

"No, Shadow! Stay back!" She couldn't stand it if he got hurt.

"It means hiding." Robin panted. "Running forever. And if I don't run, it means prison, or death. You son-of-a—!" She slashed, and the knife took a chunk out of the table.

September grabbed kiddy shields, stacked four deep for a semblance of protection against the frenzied blade. "I never—"

"You're not from our world. They'll use you, discredit you, run the Family how they want anyway—and in the end, they'll kill you." Robin laughed. "Don't you get it? This test"—she waved her hand to encompass the festival, herself, and the whole situation—"was set up by the Family to prove you're not worthy of your father's legacy. Alive and shamed, or dead and gone, they can run things the way they want. If I were you, I'd prefer dead."

September ran at Robin, so fast she couldn't escape, and punched the woman hard in the face with the plastic shield. Robin nearly fell but stoically remained on her feet.

A test. *A friggin' test?* September staggered out of the booth. *Pierce helped set this up… and maybe her uncle?* The whole tent canted sideways and toppled over.

From beneath the remaining table the gray cat watched with narrowed green eyes. His gaze followed the swinging leather loop hanging from the fetch-knife. Slowly, he stalked after Robin.

Chapter Sixty-Two: Shadow

Shadow yelped, dodging to stay out of the way as September continued to fight. The blood stank in the hot air. September's arms streamed with the dark wet, and the back of the older woman's clothes were soaked through with blood.

When the tent overturned, Shadow ignored the cat to help September. She commanded him to stay back. And he wanted to make her say *good dog* but sometimes dogs knew better than people. She wanted to protect him but had no stick. And the long knife broke, too.

Shadow hated guns. But now he wished September still had hers. Sometimes just showing a gun stopped everything. Shadow had to do something. But what?

The two women staggered and chased through the open spaces, knocking into vendor displays. The bad woman slash with her big knife. September held plastic shields, and the big knife stabbed holes and divots in the surface. Soon, the knife would chew up September's protection like Shadow's jaws did his toys. She'd have nothing to defend her. No protection except a good dog with bright teeth and a ferocious growl.

The bad woman yelled sour words. She hacked at the shield. He had to do something! Shadow moved through the scattered objects from the tent display.

And then he knew what to do.

Lord Byron kept his distance but watched with avid interest. He tracked the hurky-gurky progress of the trailing cord attached to the fetch-knife. He didn't understand humans. Much of their behavior made little sense. But the way the two woman circled each other looked decidedly catlike.

Blood smell meant no bluffs in this face off. Cats postured, hissed, warned with growl, raised fur and claw in display. The loser scatted away, carrying only humiliation without visible wounds.

Not so humans. Ian wrestled other men in contests of mostly bluster and no blood. He always won—before this woman with the knife hurt him. A low growl bubbled at that thought.

The leather strap from the knife swayed, tantalizing, tempting Byron, daring him to make a move. Stalk. Attack. Capture. Maybe fetch the blade back to Ian so quiet in his bloody box to do…something. Humans made things happen he couldn't understand. He desperately wanted Ian to let him to cheek-rub his bristly face until all was well.

The dog emerged from the destroyed booth. Byron hissed, stiffened, crouched with caution, then watched the dog's equally surprising antics.

The dog sniffed scattered objects and chose one that resembled a smaller version of the fetch-knife. His jaws crushed the handle, and it crinkled in his mouth—impressive teeth! Then the dog shook his head as though throttling a squirrel. Loud ferocious growls spilled from his throat.

Byron shrank into the ground, flattening himself. But the black dog only had eyes for the humans. He leaped between them, brandishing the toy sword in his mouth.

The older woman paused, and a guffaw covered up the dog's noise. "The mutt wants to fight me? With that toy sword?"

Byron heard pain in her voice. Small tremors shivered her hands holding the fetch-knife. She pulled back her arm. Slashed the blade at the dog...

"No! Shadow, back." The taller woman screamed the words. She flailed at the attacker with the flimsy shield.

Shadow leaped away. Snarls and growls increased each time he dodged close, shaking the toy in his mouth. He paw-danced this way and that, keeping the attacker's attention on him.

She again slashed at the dog—

He yelped. His toy sword spun away.

Byron revved himself up to pounce, eyes following the swinging cord. It jittered and danced in the woman's shaking hand.

Chapter Sixty-Three: September

D on't hurt my dog!" September swung the toy shield at Robin's head.

The deadly blade caught the plastic again, this time splitting it.

Gillette flung the debris away.

Shadow leaped closer. He tried get within bite-range.

The knife flashed down, aimed at the dog…

The huge gray cat launched his own attack, springing up and out, forepaws spread, and claws extended. He grappled the dangling string, bit it, claws tangling. He hung, swinging in midair from the leather strap. Clawed his way up to the woman's gripping hand. Growls and snarls sang a duet with the black dog's canine curses.

Gillette grasped the haft of the knife with both hands. She twirled around, trying to shake loose the snarling, biting cat.

The cat gripped harder, tenacious despite scary activity. His fur stood off his back, and foreshortened tail poofed to twice its usual dimensions.

Shadow dodged beneath the descending blade. He sank teeth into the woman's tucked up skirt, pulling it free, tripping her. She landed hard on her back, knife still gripped in one hand. Shadow played tug with the clothing. The cat continued to drag and growl at the knife strap, constraining her attack.

Before Robin could yank the knife away from the cat, September rushed forward. She stomped on Robin's wrist, pinning the knife-hand to the ground, then grabbed the weapon and tossed it away.

The cat raced after it and crouched over his recovered prize.

Shadow barked, tail a semaphore of joy in the hot night air.

September straddled the killer's chest. She punched Robin in the jaw as hard as she could. "*That's* for hurting Willie." Another punch. "And *that's* for Alana." Another. "*That's* for threatening my dog! And for *all* the *others* you *tortured*." She wanted to keep beating Robin but forced herself to stop. "Tell me who. Who put you up to this, this *test?* Tell me!"

"Police! Move away. Now!"

September froze. Festival security had arrived. Finally.

"Okay, Officer, I'm standing up. See, I've got nothing in my hands." She held both aloft as she climbed off the prone woman. "I can explain—"

"No, stay down. Kneel. Hands behind your head. Don't move." September took in the man's neon security bib. His unfamiliar face. The gun leveled at her chest. *Not part of Heartland PD. Freelance hired by the festival…unknown training.*

She knelt, hands obediently clasped behind her neck, giving him no excuse to shoot.

With a roar, Gillette lunged upright, grasping the ludicrous toy sword Shadow had abandoned. September recoiled, rolling away.

Bullets peppered the ground, following September. Not Robin. The guard's gun spat, creating divots in the grass.

The bagpipe drone of the helicopter jerked attention aloft. Pierce, at last...to her rescue? Or...

Shadow barked. The cat screamed and sped away. Robin, face twisted with hate, and white from blood loss, swung the toy in a wide arc.

The toy would look real to Pierce from the sky...

September dove, tackling Robin. She needed her alive, needed answers. Shadow yelped and leaped to cover September's form.

More bullets from the rent-a-cop.

"Stop! We give up!" Beneath her, Robin lay still, passed out or dying. September felt the rise and fall of the woman's chest. September craned her neck around to see the man.

He stood with a grin on his face, walking closer to take careful aim. At her.

She pointed. "Shadow, *KA-POW!*"

He leaped, paw-punching the man square in the chest.

As he fell, his gun spat again, catching him in one arm. He rolled, gasping, onto his back. As she watched a bloody blossom bloomed in the center of his neon smock.

Pierce's helicopter zoomed out of sight.

Additional police, this time many September recognized, swarmed the area.

At nine o'clock the following morning, still bloody and bruised, stitches sore, and rancid with sweat, September strode into the Grand Chisholm Hotel lobby, Shadow by her side. A quiet word with Captain Gregory had resulted in a ride with one of Heartland's finest. She waved off reception staff, ignored the concierge offering assistance. "I know the way."

Down the hall a group of men gathered behind the cloudy glass of the conference room. "That's a private meeting."

She recognized the valet who parked her car the day before. She rounded on him. "Who paid you? Did you do it, or someone else? Sabotaged my bo staff?" His eyes grew wide, expression a confession. He put up both hands in surrender at her appearance and expression.

"Open the door." She gestured to the locked conference door. "I'm the owner of this dump. I'll deal with you later, don't argue. I'm not in the mood."

"But miss…"

"Open. The. Friggin' door!"

Shadow barked, his own fur still caked with dust. He favored one paw, but she'd checked him for cuts and although bruised, Shadow had evaded serious injury. Her arms ached where the witch's knife had scored her flesh. The stitches, still fresh and swollen, throbbed.

The valet jumbled the keycard from his belt and waved it at the door. The lock clicked open.

A dozen men, most in three-piece suits, swiveled to see her enter. At one end of the table, stood Jack. He flushed. Across the table from him, Pierce leaned against the wall with arms casually crossed and a half-smile on his face. Bare arms fully displayed the detailed feathered wing covering one shoulder and arm. Gabriel Pierce: archangel or devil?

The rest of the movers-and-shakers of the Family rolled back in their chairs, some with mouths gaping and brows furrowed, and some with fists clenched.

Before anyone could speak, September danced forward and leaped atop the table. Shadow mirrored the action, guarding her flank. She carried the deadly ceremonial Celtic blade that had saved the lives of Ethel and Willie, but nearly ended others.

With one hard motion, she threw it. The razor-sharp end speared the tabletop, and the blade quivered in place.

"I am Sorokin Glass. We need to talk."

Much later, Shadow leaned against September as they rode up the elevator. His tummy rumbled. He wondered if the magic doors would open to the restaurant. Thought of the chicken he'd eaten so long ago made him drool.

But instead, the elevator revealed the hallway to their room. Where they'd played the *show-me* game. Shadow loved games, but hoped they'd wait a while.

His paws ached. Dirt clung to his claws. Fur tugged and itched where dried blood crusted his skin. He yawned. A bowl of treats waited inside. He'd like a taste of the banana, wouldn't that be fine? Then a snuggle and a nap with September. His tail waved at the thought.

As they walked toward the room, he caught a familiar scent. Shadow whined.

"What is it, baby dog? Somebody there?" Her hand

tightened on the big knife she carried. Her scent shifted, September's nerves and worry shouting *danger!*

Shadow wanted to keep her all to himself. To snuggle with her, keep the bad dreams away. Listen to her worries, even if he didn't understand all the words.

But sometimes dogs couldn't help. People needed other people to listen.

So he leaned against her again and wagged his tail. Nosed the hand with the knife until she relaxed, understanding he'd keep her safe. That was his job, to never leave his person. Because some things only a good dog could do.

She waved her hand with the plastic card, and the door clicked open. "Shadow, *check-it-out.*" September waited for him to leap ahead, and make sure the whole room stayed safe.

Except he already knew the room must be safe. Because of the man waiting there. The man who cared about September almost as much as Shadow. He and the man wanted the same thing. To take care of her, keep her safe. To love her.

"Combs! How did you...I wanted to... We need to talk."

Combs sat with his leg propped up on the sofa, an empty place beside him. "Time enough later." He opened his arms wide, beckoning.

With a sob, September dropped the big knife and ran to his embrace.

Shadow hesitated and yawned again. Turned his eyes away. The way a polite dog should. Uncertain...

The man looked up. His eyebrows raised.

Shadow offered a low wag. Slicked back his ears, asking permission. *Please?*

Smiling, Combs shifted on the big sofa. "Shadow, c'mon good boy. There's room for everyone."

With joy and relief, Shadow bounded across the room. He jumped onto the furniture to snuggle with his people, muddy paws and all.

Nobody complained.

Chapter Sixty-Four: September, Two Weeks Later

September checked out the bay window, making sure Melinda was following the rules. The girl wore a bright green bikini—with a filmy cover-up to satisfy her dad—and sat on the pier, keeping an eye on Willie, who floated on a ludicrous inflated unicorn. Part of the renovation of Cat's Cradle included water safety measures. The floating buoy rope, more a suggestion than a barrier, kept the kids from daring too much. At least, while grown-ups watched.

She rejoined the small group. Combs, no longer confined to a wheelchair, had propped his fancy cane by his end of the sofa. Aunt Ethel and Teddy sat in chairs on either end of the small room. Teddy scowled and took off his glasses to polish them. Ethel sat with arms crossed, and brows knit.

Glaringly absent, at least to September, were Jackson

Glass and Gabriel Pierce. Time would tell how those relationships progressed. They'd made plenty of excuses. Said they learned too late about the *test* set up by the Family. When Jack discovered security team infiltration at the festival, he notified Pierce, who, unable to verify which security to trust, neutralized all he could find. She suspected he'd taken out the last one from the copter. So far, Heartland PD hadn't found the mysterious sniper who saved her life. Right now, she couldn't trust either man.

Over the past two weeks, she and Combs had argued, shared not a few angry words, and shed many tears. They mourned the future they'd planned and conceded—reluctantly—on specific issues. September hoped she wouldn't lose any of her chosen family over the decision.

As if he'd read her thoughts, Shadow whined and leaned against her leg as she sat next to Combs. "I'm okay, baby dog."

Combs reached for her hand, squeezed it, and raised his eyebrows in a question.

She nodded. "You first."

He shrugged, cracked his knuckles, and turned to Teddy and Ethel. "I've worked my tail off to get out of the wheelchair. The leg's still healing, gaining strength. Those PT folks, they're relentless!" He barked a short laugh.

"You've accomplished so much, sweetheart." Aunt Ethel uncrossed her arms and leaned forward to pat his arm. "Stan would be so proud." She avoided eye contact with September.

September bit her lip. She didn't blame Ethel, or Teddy, for their anger. But maybe the explanation would lead to healing, and eventual forgiveness. And someday, regained trust.

"Captain Gregory has a desk job waiting for me." Combs

squeezed her hand then released her. He drew himself up. "I love working as a detective, but I can't do the job sitting behind a desk."

When Ethel started to protest, he cut her off. "I love you, and I'm proud of all I accomplished as a police officer and detective. Sometimes reality sucks. It'll be years, if ever, for me to get back what I lost." He took a deep breath. "I resigned from the Heartland PD three days ago."

"No!" Aunt Ethel wrung her hands. "Oh honey…"

Again, September felt the heat of accusation in Teddy and Ethel when they exchanged a potent glance. "It's my fault. I'm sorry."

"No, it's not. Nobody chooses their parents." Combs grabbed her hand again.

Teddy leaned forward. "How long have you known?" His white eyebrows wrinkled like caterpillars and his gravelly voice couldn't hide the hurt. His real question: how long had she lied to them?

"Not long. I literally learned about my heritage the day Combs had his memory breakthrough. In this very room."

They both looked skeptical.

She'd lived in a kind of denial, thinking that hiding the truth would protect them. Instead, she'd put them at even higher risk.

September took a big breath and began. "About two weeks after the wedding, I got a summons to meet here. An attorney from the Family." She explained as succinctly as possible the meeting, and what it meant. "He said I had no choice, that I couldn't refuse the inheritance and all that entails. If I die—"

Teddy's eyebrows shot up.

"—then the inheritance goes to my husband or to our children. Or finally, to my younger brother, Mark." She smiled sadly. "He's disappeared, and I hope he can stay hidden from them. I wouldn't wish this on anyone." She nodded to the window. "Especially not on children." She squeezed Combs's hand again. "I can't ever marry. It puts the people I love at too much risk."

He smiled ruefully. "We'll just have to live in sin."

She punched him.

Aunt Ethel's mouth dropped open. "Oh honey…" Her eyes filled. "You really didn't know?" She turned to Teddy. "She didn't know!"

He adjusted his glasses. "What the heck happened at the festival? Are you in charge of this, this whatchacallit criminal dynasty or not?"

September sighed. "Some of the players questioned my authority. When confronted, they explained it as a *test of my abilities*." Shadow barked when her fist clenched for a moment on his ruff. "Turns out, I'm more of my father's daughter than I like."

Combs nodded. "Y'all remember Officer Teves, on loan last summer to the Heartland PD. She consulted on the trafficking case when several Hawaiian girls were taken. Robin Gillette orchestrated that. Tee alerted me that Gillette was found dead in the area. Actually, Gillette killed Maeve, the fortuneteller, and assumed her identity to set up the ransom exchange."

The police had recovered Maeve's abandoned RV two states over. September asked Jack to find Jared and Alana, arrange for new identities, and ensure they got away safe— with the cash. That poor family deserved a fresh start; she hoped Alana got the therapy she'd need.

Aunt Ethel shuddered. "That horrible woman. Pure evil." She turned to Teddy. "She's in jail now. She also killed the man from the ax throwing. Captain Gregory told me she's holding out for some kind of deal, swapping insider information for leniency. But she'll go away for a long time."

"I'm so sorry you and Willie got caught up in everything." September didn't think she could ever apologize enough. Soft-hearted Willie was still worried about the stray dog that helped them. With the dog's tag he saved, she'd traced the owner to an old man who died. "I'm glad you decided to adopt that poor man's cat."

"Least I could do. Lord Byron saved my life." She sighed. "It's been a long time since I had a cat. He sleeps on top of me, all twenty-two pounds." It wasn't a complaint. "The right furry wonder always seems to show up at the right time."

Teddy smiled, glancing at Meriwether snoozing in the sunny window seat.

September took a breath. Ethel had confirmed some information, and the rest she had surmised. An expert like her uncle—who she didn't trust—or like Teddy, a dear and trusted friend, might learn more. "The Family alerted operatives to coming changes. That sparked a reward offer to get rid of Sorokin Glass." She still couldn't get used to the name. "They wanted the Magpie gone, or at least sidelined, to continue business as usual."

"Wouldn't have happened if you weren't such a bleeding heart." Combs flinched at her look. "Well, it's true. You and Jack shouted about the changes to the rafters."

"What changes?" Aunt Ethel looked from September to Combs, and then Teddy. "Everyone seems to know but me."

Teddy cleared his throat. "Oh thank goodness." He took off his glasses, and rubbed his eyes, maybe wiped away tears. "The online persona Jackson Glass created reads like a superhero righting the wrongs of past sins, standing up for the underdog…"

Shadow looked up at the last word and wagged.

"…and offering hope to the hopeless. A cartoon character that just needs a cape and superpowers." He looked between Combs and September. "Recently, you funded major renovations to this house. Added an elevator to replace that rickety stairway. You could have broken a hip climbing that. And you had me install state-of-the-art computers and more. So what's the deal?"

She glanced at Combs, and he nodded encouragement. "Over the past few months, I have lost the family who raised me, discovered both my heritage and the great destruction and damage caused by the Wong organization. Suddenly, I have nearly unlimited resources at my disposal, and a lifetime of atonement."

"Making amends for other's wrongs, that's not on your shoulders, honey." Aunt Ethel leaned forward, reaching out both hands to grasp September's. "You didn't choose this."

"No, I didn't. If not me, then who?" She swallowed hard. "How many victims? I can't make it all go away. But I can stop it going forward. Maybe I can redress some of those wrongs." She squeezed the older woman's hands. "With help, that is."

Ethel pulled her hands away. Turned to Combs. "Jeffrey?"

He cracked knuckles, and September linked her arm through his, adding moral support. "I can't work as a detective anymore, but I can still make a difference. In the private sector."

"I don't know what comes next." September turned to Teddy, entreaty in her voice. "I hope you and Ethel can forgive me. I've brought trouble to everyone. And if y'all need to walk away, keep yourself safe, I understand." Her voice shook. "I know who I am, and I know what I must do. Combs and I"—she dropped one hand to caress Shadow's brow—"and our good dog Shadow, still love you. We still need you. And we hope you'll join us." She took a big breath. "We're creating the Paladin Group. It's time for some joy, for some happiness. And for doing some good."

Teddy glanced at Ethel, then from Combs to September. Meriwether stood up in the window seat, stretched, yawned, and leaped into Teddy's lap.

Shadow stood up, barked, and wagged. His mouth cracked open in a wide doggy grin.

Teddy looked at Ethel, and she shrugged, and nodded. He grinned at September. "Great name. Where do we sign?"

"Yeah, where do we sign up, September?"

She started and turned around. Melinda stood with one arm across Willie's shoulder, both of them dripping on the floor, expressions daring the grown-ups to say no.

"Melinda," Combs began, "when will you stop eavesdropping on grown-up conversations?"

Willie stuck out his chin. "When will grown-ups learn that not keeping us kids in the loop actually puts us in more danger?"

"Yeah. What my brother said." Melinda glared around the room.

Chapter Sixty-Five: Willie, Four Weeks Later

Willie trudged to the mailbox. He had to keep Kinsler on leash to keep the terrier from pulling a Kinsler and going AWOL. That's what September called it. He'd worked on the dog's automatic check in all summer. Offering a high value treat every time Kinsler looked at him helped keep the dog's attention on him. It encouraged Kinsler to check in every so often, hoping to get that liver yummy. And it worked, kinda sorta in a way, when they were in the fenced garden.

But outside of the fence, if a squirrel happened by, forget about the liver. Kinsler wanted squirrel, raw please, and nothing changed his mind. "You got no impulse control." Willie laughed at the words, cuz Dad said the same thing about him.

No fair that he and Melinda got voted down on joining the Paladin Group. After all, he'd helped save Alana, too. And Melinda, she'd done some brave stuff before, and was pretty cool for a girl. When she wasn't trying to boss him.

Dad and September compromised, a little anyway. They agreed to keep him and Melinda in the loop with any Paladin business, but only grown-ups could handle the bad guy stuff. And they got to have cell phones, winner winner chicken dinner! For emergency stuff, just in case.

"You've both got school." That's what Dad always said. What a cop out. He put a hand over his mouth, like he'd said the thought out loud. Dad didn't like him to say that, called it disrespectful.

Teddy Williams spent a lot of his time up at the lake house now they had it all retrofitted with spy stuff. Not really, but some of the computer tools and security measures reminded him of those awesome spy movies. Not stupid stuff like phones in your shoes—he'd seen some funny older-than-dirt reruns. But some rad stuff from the future realm. That's what Mr. Williams called it…future realm. For an old guy, he was pretty rad himself. Lots of rizz.

Before inputting the gate code to open it and check the mailbox, he followed Dad's instructions. Look both ways, also up and down. He remembered the drone attack from the sky and the bomb that hurt everyone. Willie could run pretty fast, but he had Kinsler with him, and it was a good person's responsibility to take care of his dog.

At the thought, Kinsler barked at him, and wagged, almost like he knew. "Ka-pow, Kinsler!" Willie patted his chest, and the dog leaped up to chest-punch him. "Good dog!" Willie planned to teach him a bunch more commands. To be ready, just in case. Even though they weren't official members of Paladin, you had to be ready to step up.

The usual junk stuffed the mailbox, plus a package. Cool beans, a present for him! Willie checked for a return address, but didn't see anything. The label looked written in red crayon.

Maybe Dad ordered a surprise to make up for…well, for whatever. Dad couldn't play catch too good at the moment cuz of his bum leg. And he spent lots of time doing research and planning with September, even though they couldn't get married. He didn't think that mattered. Love didn't depend on a piece of paper. When Melinda said that, Dad made a face. But Willie agreed.

Willie took care to watch the gate latch close. He stuck the several junk mail envelopes under one arm and shook the big box as they walked back to the house. Nothing rattled. He hurried, anxious to get it open.

Back inside, he released Kinsler and set the mail on the kitchen island. September hadn't got home from training with her self-defense coach. She said for his birthday she'd give him some lessons, too. "Ka-pow," he whispered, and imagined delivering a kick to a bad guy.

"Any good mail?" Dad paused from clacking computer keys in the next room.

"Lots of junk." Willie retrieved a knife from the chopping block to cut open the box seal. "I got a box."

"A package? From who?" He heard Dad struggle to stand.

"Hey, don't get up. Maybe September ordered me something?" He got the top slit open. "I can bring it there…"

"Wait! Willie, don't open a strange package."

He'd already carried the box into the office. "Chill, Dad. I was careful." Well, not really, and Willie kicked himself he'd pulled a Kinsler—SQUIRREL! —and hadn't thought some crazy-eight guy might send a nasty in the mail. "I already cut it open. Sorry."

Grimacing, Combs motioned for him to set the open box on the piano bench, across from the computer desk. "We talked about this. Stand back. No, back in the kitchen."

"Should we call Lia?" She had a bomb detecting dog, but it'd take her a while to get here.

"Too late for that." He grabbed up a long-handled jointed grab stick that had a mirror on the end. Carefully, he extended the tool to look inside the package. "Lots of tissue paper. And a...I think it's a stuffed animal." He looked relieved. "Maybe September ordered you a gift for opening night. Maybe there's a card."

Willie grinned. They'd had a preview performance last night, and everything went great. He loved his puppy part. "That's sure nice of her."

Dad knocked the box onto the floor and the toy spilled out. "A kangaroo?"

Not a puppy? Or even a dog or cat? Why would September buy him a stuffed kangaroo with a pink bandanna... Willie's eyes widened. He grabbed up the toy.

It still had grass stains from the Celtic Festival. No baby Joey in the pouch. Instead, something stuck out of the tummy. Willie pulled out the picture.

Alana, smiling—he'd never seen her smile—and snuggling a small dazzling white dog with darker ears; so clean, Willie almost didn't recognize Noah. The dog clutched the baby kangaroo toy. On the back she'd scrawled a brief note.

"What is that? What's it say?"

"*You and Noah saved me from a flood of badness. Thank you forevermore.*"

Dad shook his head, puzzled. "I don't understand. What does that mean?"

Willie smiled and tucked the picture back in the kangaroo. "I think it means *happily ever after.*"

FACT, FICTION, & ACKNOWLEDGMENTS

Thank you for reading PLAY OR PAY, and I hope you enjoyed this eighth book in the September & Shadow thriller series. Thank you, too, for coming along with me on the adventure. There never would have been *Thrillers With Bite* without you, dear reader, adopting these books. (Can you hear my purrs and woofs of delight?)

After publishing 35+ nonfiction pet books, research fuels my curiosity. While in fiction I get to make up *crappiocca*, as September would say, much of my inspiration comes from news stories, past and present—the weirder, the better. For me, and I hope for you, the story becomes more engaging when built not on "what if" but "it happened." So in each book, I like to include a Cliff's Notes version of what's real and what's made up.

As with the other books in the series, much of PLAY

OR PAY arises from science, especially dog and cat behavior and learning theory, and the benefits of service dogs. By definition, thrillers include murder and mayhem, but as an animal advocate professional, I make a conscious choice to not show a pet's death in any of my books. All bets are off with the human characters, though.

This story took September and Shadow—and me—in unexpected but logical directions. After the last book, I knew they'd have very different ways of dealing with future adventures—my, how September and Shadow have grown since the beginning! Now the pair, and their friends, have wide open possibilities to explore. Thanks for coming along for the ride.

I rely on a vast number of veterinarians, behaviorists, consultants, trainers, pet-centric writers and readers, and rescue organizations that share their incredible resources and support to make my stories as believable as possible. Find out more information at IAABC.org, Dogwriters.org and CatWriters.com.

FACT: The *show me* game is real, created by trainer Kayce Cover as a vocabulary exercise to be used with a variety of animals, and which my own dog loves to play. See https://synalia.com

FICTION: Pet viewpoint chapters are pure speculation, although I would love to read dog and cat minds. However, I make every attempt to base animal characters' motivations and actions on canine and feline body language, scent discrimination, and the science behind the human-animal bond.

FACT: The weight and dimensions of the ransom money is true. The reality of lugging 55+ pounds of paper money around the fair created a puzzle to figure out how to manage. For fun, check out this page:

https://propmoney.info/prop-currency-dimensions.html

FACT: Bo fighting (a type of stick or staff fighting) has been around for centuries, called by many names. The technique not only offers terrific self-defense options, but a staff also looks less threatening but can, in fact, be lethal. It requires no ammunition or licensing. Here's a terrific overview of some of the staff forms September practiced: https://blackbeltwiki.com/bo-staff-techniques

FACT: September's self-defense techniques are real. You can, in fact, escape from a belt throttling your neck. Here's a how-to video.
https://www.youtube.com/watch?v=Ok6MVNeibAs

She also escapes zip ties…really? Yes, and again, here's a video: https://www.youtube.com/watch?v=IY1cI6shatc

Finally, Gabriel Pierce "puts to sleep" several security people at the festival, in under 10 seconds. None are the worse for wear. This choke hold can be dangerous and of course should never be used for evil…but here's the demo: https://www.youtube.com/watch?v=kKpGVV8Njvo

FICTION: September uses her bo staff to block the ax—and the oak staff shatters apart. That's fiction. In reality, a well-made staff with healthy grain takes a lot of abuse and, unless defective, an ax couldn't cut it with a single blow. For purposes of the story, I wanted this to happen, though, so fudged a bit and alluded to the possibility sabotage damaged the staff. Look at this "strength test" of various kinds of bo staffs, paying particular attention to the commends afterward: https://www.youtube.com/watch?v=DPY10JX2fXA

FACT: Yes, many dogs (and some cats) become terrified of loud noises like fireworks or thunderstorms. More pets go missing over July 4th holiday than the rest of the year, so Noah running away sadly has a basis in fact. If you have a noise-phobic pet, check these tips to help and start working with your furry wonders in advance: https://amyshojai.com/pets-fireworks-thunder-fear/

FICTION: While Dallas has many gorgeous highly rated hotels, I made up the "Grand Chisholm Hotel." As far as I know, this fictional hotel is the only one run by a criminal family.

FACT: Willie's theatrical show, STRAYS THE MUSICAL is a real theater production, co-written and produced by Amy Shojai and Frank Steele. The original production featured a cast of 33 ranging in age from five years old to over 70. Yes, it's available for licensing and production (often used as a fund raiser for rescue organizations). To see pictures, hear music, and watch the trailer here: shojai.com/books/strays-the-musical-script

FACT: Both September and Shadow comment in the story about Pierce's polite, dog-considerate behavior when he doesn't stick out his hand to force a sniff introduction. Many of us grew up with this advice—hold out your hand to strange dogs to sniff—and today we know better. Bouncy confident dogs may not mind. But cautious canines, especially those confined on a leash, could react with a bite when startled or they feel unable to escape. Dogs can smell you just fine from a distance and don't need contact. Today, dog experts recommend avoiding this and allowing dogs to approach and sniff if they want. Let your hands hang loose on each side, avoid direct eye contact (can feel threatening) and only pet on the side of the dog's neck or chest if he asks for your touch. Think how startling an unexpected pat from behind on top of your head or back could make you jump out of your skin, after all!

FACT: Just as humans can suffer from post-traumatic stress disorders (PTSD), so can service dogs like Shadow.

Military and police dogs, those trained for helping after disasters, as well as family pets who experience natural disasters like tornadoes or car accidents, can develop symptoms. Learn more here:

https://www.webmd.com/pets/dogs-emotional-problems

FACT: Real-life pets inspired some of the animal characters in PLAY OR PAY. I've held a "Name That Dog/Name That Cat" contest for each of the novels in the series. For this most recent contest I limited nominations to my newsletter subscribers (join the list if you'd like to nominate your dog for a future book!).

I narrowed the nominations down to ten cat finalists and thirteen dog finalists. In the story, I planned for one cat hero winner and one dog hero. See pictures of the winners here.

Congratulations to **Carol Viescas** for nominating the winning longhaired gray 22-pound leash trained cat, **Lord Byron**! He received almost 78% of the votes, totaling 1494. Wow!

"His previous owner had a massive stroke and could no longer take care of him. We were warned he liked to sneak out of doors and after a couple of attempts, we decided to leash train him so he could go outside supervised. His previous owner obviously was a literature lover, hence his name. He is a love bug and purr box and loves attention. If you lie down all 22 pounds will sit on your chest. Lord Byron talks – a lot. He tells you when he wants attention. He tells you when he's grumpy because he's not getting his way. He tells you when he wants outside. He has an unusual tail. It is short and ends with a few inches at an abrupt right angle. Something must have happened to him before his original owner James adopted him."

Congratulations to **Gail Stambaugh** for the winning dog, a lovely rescue boy named **Noah.** He received 59% of the votes, totaling 2873 votes. Wow!

"My dog's name is Noah. During Covid, I had to put my dog Sunshine down and needed a friend and companion because my husband recently passed away. I went to the Humane Society, where he chose me. Noah is a Shishon (Shih tzu and Bichon). He is white, cream, black, and grey. His favorite toys consist of just about anything he can get his paws on. Whenever he sees anyone, he has to run over to them and say hello and give them love."

THANK YOU to everyone who took part in the contest and to all the winners. I think they all deserve treats. Maybe even catnip and bacon!

FICTION: It's unlikely (but possible) that the kangaroo toy still retained enough of Alana's scent to allow Shadow to track her. After all, the toy fell in the water, then stored with her scented clothes in a small, sealed backpack for many months. That helps the scent last. Learn more about how long scent lasts and police dogs detect it in this interesting article from the FBI: https://ourdogssavelives.org/wp-content/uploads/2012/02/Human-Scent-in-Criminal-Investigations-FBI.pdf

FACT: The Dallas Police Academy is real. Lia goes through the Basic Training Academy for 40 weeks of training with a total of 1400 hours of instruction. After the training academy, new officers are assigned to one of the seven Patrol Divisions for 24 weeks of field training under the tutelage of experienced Field Training Officers (FTOs).

FICTION & FACT: For the purposes of the story, I fudged a bit on the typical Celtic Festival. For the past several years, I've attended the annual event here in North Texas (thank you to Hannah Horsley for some insight into the inner workings!). This event inspired much of the setting of this story. In fact, the ceremonial blade described in the book I own, after purchasing from a vendor at the most recent event. Also, the very moving Lord's Prayer was sung in the Choctaw language. The Choctaw Nation donated funds to help the Irish people during the Irish Potato Famine in 1847, and that deep bond continues to this day. Read more about this connection here: Choctaw and Irish History (choctawnation.com)

However, because of the heat, usually the North Texas Celtic Festival takes place in the spring during cooler weather. I moved the timeline to early August to fit the story, which coincides with Lughnasa. And it makes the heat almost an evil accomplice in the plot. Also, using the festival as a ransom exchange location is of course pure fiction.

FACT: Human trafficking, sadly, remains a fact in Texas and many other places. See more: https://www.dallasobserver.com/news/dallas-looks-to-continue-cracking-down-on-human-trafficking-18330143

FACT: A sword-fighting dog? Well… sorta kinda in a way! Shadow taking up the toy sword to distract Robin was inspired by this dog doing exactly that: https://www.youtube.com/watch?v=v2sOUQqPugM

Willie putting Kinsler's behavior on command—KA-POW!—also works very well. Don't you love it when kids learn fun stuff and put it to use? Maybe Willie will become a hero in his own right.

Many dogs like Shadow adore playing tug-o-war games, and Shadow learned the right way to play. Yes, you can include this fun game with your dog, but make sure you both follow the rules to stay out of trouble. As with anything, safety means understanding why dogs love it and how to channel the natural impulse appropriately. My colleague Trish McMillan wrote a brilliant explanation of the concept and how to play safely here: https://tinyurl.com/yhm3857p

FACT: Cats can learn to fetch, recognize different words, and react positively to a variety of commands and even "speak" on cue. While this work of fiction stretches the boundaries a bit, Lord Byron the cat acts and reacts behaviorally in a feline-specific way.

FACT: This book would not have happened without an incredible support team of friends, family and accomplished colleagues. Special thanks to my editor, Nicola Aquino of Spit & Polish Editing, and first readers Kristi Brashier, Carol Shenold, Frank Steele, BJ Thompson, and Andrea Neal for your eagle eyes, spot-on comments and unflagging encouragement and support. Youse guyz rock!

I continue to be indebted to the International Thriller Writers organization, which launched my fiction career by welcoming me into the Debut Authors Program. Wow, just look, now I have eight books in a series! The authors, readers and industry mavens who make up this organization are some of the most generous and supportive people I have ever met. Long live the bunny slippers with teeth (and the rhinestone #1-Bitch Pin).

Finally, I am grateful to all the cats and dogs I've met over the years who have shared my heart and often my pillow. Shadow-Pup and Karma-Kat, and the new Trinity-Kitten inspire me daily. And the pets who live on in my heart continue to bring happy memories.

I never would have been a reader and now a writer if not for my fantastic parents Phil and Mary Monteith, who instilled in me a love of the written word, and never looked askance when my stuffed animals and invisible wolf friend told fantastical stories. And of course, my deepest thanks to my husband Mahmoud, who continues to support my writing passion, even when he doesn't always understand it.

I love hearing from you! Please drop me a line at my blog https://AmyShojai.com or my website https://shojai.com and now my new Amy's Book Store where you can subscribe to my PET PEEVES newsletter, purchase discounted books (and maybe win some pet books!). Follow me on twitter @amyshojai and like me on Facebook: http://www.facebook.com/amyshojai.cabc.

ABOUT THE AUTHOR

Amy Shojai is a certified animal behavior consultant, and the award-winning author of more than 35 bestselling pet books that cover furry babies to old fogies, first aid to natural healing, and behavior/training to Chicken Soupicity. She has been featured as an expert in hundreds of print venues including The Wall Street Journal, New York Times, Reader's Digest, and Family Circle, as well as television networks such as CNN, Fox News, and Animal Planet's DOGS 101 and CATS 101. Amy brings her unique pet-centric viewpoint to public appearances. She is also a playwright and co-author of STRAYS, THE MUSICAL and the author of the critically acclaimed THRILLERS WITH BITE pet-centric thriller series. Stay up to date with new books and appearances by visiting Shojai.com to subscribe to Amy's Pets Peeves newsletter.

Made in the USA
Coppell, TX
13 November 2024

40142106R00184